1/6/15

How I Wonder What You Are

Jane Lovering

Book 4 in the Yorkshire Romances

Where heroes are like chocolate – irresistible!

Published 2015 by Choc Lit Limited
Penrose House, Crawley Drive, Camberley, Surrey GU15 2AB, UK
www.choc-lit.com

ISBN 978-1-78189-191-9

Printed and bound by CPI Group (UK) Ltd, Croydon, CR0 4YY

To everyone who's ever been scared.
You are stronger than you know.

Acknowledgements

With thanks to the physics department, particularly Robbie, the cutest Irish astrophysicist I've ever met – mind you, the sample range isn't huge ... The North York Moors – for being there for me. Well, actually, just being there, I think I was optional. My family for bearing with me, my friends for ... well ... bearing with me. To Tasting panel readers: Emma, Jo, Vanessa, Sonya, Betty, Sarah D, Stephanie, Sarah E, Louise and Liz for not thinking heroes have to be all bulgy and thewy, and TMMQ for unbunging the toilet. Oh, the glamour ...

Prologue

High above the moors, sliding on the updraught from a thousand central heating boiler vents, came the lights. Blue to the front, a tight grouping, twisting and rotating around a core of blazing white, then winding down into a tail of reds and ambers. Soundless and slow they came, their small illuminations making the dark even darker; the stars a phantom imitation of their pinprick brilliances. Ponderous, yet weightless, they hung for a moment over the isolated village of Riverdale, dipped once, low over the hills like a salute, and then swung away towards the coast.

But in that short, windblown minute while they'd passed things had changed, and down below, lives would never be the same again.

Chapter One

The man lay naked, unconscious and, inevitably I suppose given the temperature, slightly blue. I knew he was unconscious because anyone in possession of their faculties would at least have flinched, given the way the northerly wind was making his skin pucker into goose pimples the size of marbles. Yep, definitely unconscious, as his ribs were moving. Definitely naked. And *most* definitely a man.

Oh boy.

I nudged Stan a little closer, keeping my hands firm on his reins to control his approach and ensure he didn't step on anything sensitive. Under the saddle I could feel him advancing warily, as though naked men were well known among the equine community for their tendency to leap up and shout 'Boo!'

'Hello? Can you hear me?'

There was no reply. In fact there was no sound from anywhere except the high, distant song of the skylarks and some faint wind-carried voices from the village of Riverdale tucked like a pimple into the cleavage of the valley below.

I poked Stan with my heels and he inched his nose a little further forward without moving his feet, obeying the spirit of my demand but not the actuality and making it feel as though I was riding a slowly elongating rubber band.

I admitted defeat, dismounted and crept closer over the heather, dragging Stan behind me, although his resentment travelled through his bridle and into my hands.

'Hello? Are you all right?' I asked, advancing, then muttering to myself, 'yeah, Moll, of course he's all right. He's out for the count on the Yorkshire Moors with no pants on. That's a really cracking definition of all right, isn't it?'

The man continued to lie immobile. His arms were outflung, as if to welcome the chilly wind currently nudging around the dark, sparse hair which smudged across his chest and flickered into a line down over his stomach. His long legs were similarly decorated with dark hair, bony bare feet pointed to the sky and, as I moved further in, I could see his head cushioned on a patch of heather, with eyes closed and more dark hair tangled around the bush's roots. He looked oddly comfortable spreadeagled over the greening whin and bracken, as though he'd been planted there as some kind of pagan symbol.

Closer examination told me that his face was thin, covered in at least a couple of days worth of stubble and that he had long eyelashes which feathered along the edge of his eye sockets. His ribs were prominent as though he hadn't eaten a square meal in a while, and a quick glance further down told me that even with the shrinking effects of the March cold he was quite nicely proportioned.

I did the whole 'basic first aid' check and there didn't seem to be anything broken, ruptured or electrocuted, so I took off my fleecy jacket and draped it over him. After a few seconds tugging I managed to get it to cover most of the major areas of immediate concern, while Stan took the opportunity to graze a large circle around me, soup-plate-sized hooves missing treading on either me or the naked man by not very much. One of his feet caught in some fabric half-hidden in the ankle-high undergrowth and I leaned over to disentangle him, only to find that what he'd got wrapped around his fetlock was a leather jacket.

A moment on my hands and knees and I managed to locate some black jeans, a pair of Lycra underpants, which I handled with extreme care, and a baggy grey T-shirt which, if it belonged to the unconscious man, must have only fitted him around the neck.

Stan circled again at the end of his reins and rolled his eyes at the prone figure. The wind tugged his stubby grey mane and twisted his tail into figures of eight. I could feel it drilling through my ears and worming its way under my shirt, the temperature this far up on the moors was probably only in single figures. If it was cold to me, then how much colder must it be for the poor guy lying on the ground? My fingers twitched instinctively towards a mobile phone. Even after eighteen months I still hadn't quite lost the instinct to use one whenever the going got tough, although the signal this far up on the moors was so erratic that a Ouija board would be more use than an Orange contract. I made a decision.

'Okay, Stan, you're not going to like this very much.' I shortened the reins to reel him closer. 'But we can't leave the poor guy to freeze and I can't carry him down.'

I got a truncated prance in response. Stan was bred to be dourly hardy, not to be highly strung and his attempts at temperament were merely token affairs. Which was just as well, because the next half an hour would have tested the patience of a pit pony, as I shoved, poked, dragged and ultimately wedged the man onto the saddle.

He half-woke at one point, for which I was incredibly grateful; despite the fact he looked like a skeleton that had been working out lately, he was heavy and difficult to manoeuvre and I'd had no luck with trying to persuade Stan to lie down like a camel. I tried to keep my fleece between the man's skin and my hands, using it a bit like a tea towel to handle a hot baking tray, telling myself I was doing it to keep him warm, rather than to prevent myself touching him because handling this much naked flesh made me a little squeamish. The man's eyes flickered once, he murmured something that sounded like 'you ape', which I thought was a bit ungrateful, then flailed his arms around a bit and I

4

managed to use his random twitches to help get a purchase on the saddle. I had to drape him over it rather than sit him up, and he lay across Stan's wide back like a load of damp washing, lapsing back into unconsciousness with his head dangling to one stirrup and one hip hooked around the pommel.

I folded his clothes and tried to tuck them underneath him in strategic spots in an attempt to prevent chafing, but I feared that some parts were going to get off Stan with a lot less skin than they'd got on with. The leather jacket I put on myself, the wind was attacking with the fury of an enraged cutlery drawer and I reckoned that naked bloke was really *not* in any position to complain about my wearing his coat, not when he'd got my fleece protecting what little of his modesty was left far better than the chilly leather would have done.

So, with me tentatively grasping one hairy male ankle to prevent a sudden head-first dismount off the far side, holding Stan's reins in the other hand and with my shoulder level with a set of buttocks cautiously draped in my bright red fleece, we made our careful way down the bridle path that I had taken up the hill earlier that morning.

Stan was peppered with little patches of sweat that foamed along his neckline and around his girth, but it was nothing to how hot I was getting, imagining the robust responses I would receive if anyone from the village saw me arriving home with a naked man slung across my horse. I mentally practised my 'insouciant wave' all the way down – or would it be better to adopt a strictly 'eyes front' saunter, as though this sort of thing happened to me all the time, such a bore, yes, yet *another* naked bloke, yawn yawn …

In the event the village streets were empty, swept free of people by the chill wind and early hour. We reached my garden gate without major mishap and I stood baffled by logistics for a moment. Take the man off and leave him on the ground while I dealt with Stan, or leave Stan tied to the flimsy garden gate while I tried to drag the man inside, like the results of an overkeen Stone Age marriage proposal?

I was saved by Caro slowing her Landrover to drive past the notoriously unskittish Stan and stalling the engine at the sight of my dilemma.

'Good grief, Molly, what on earth have you been up to?' She wound down the window and stared, then had to climb out for a closer look. 'It's a man. And … is he naked?'

'I found him up on the moors.'

Caro's eyebrows went up and down in a sort of ripple effect. 'Most women just pick the flowers,' she said faintly. 'Who is he?'

'I have no idea. I thought it was more important to stop him dying of hypothermia than to interview him. Particularly with him being unconscious and everything.'

Stan jogged at the end of his reins and there was an embarrassing noise of bare flesh sliding over the damp leather of the saddle. 'Could you hold on to Stan while I get him down?'

Caro took the reins and Stan instantly began to behave impeccably. Caro was his technical owner and she stood no nonsense from her horses. In the meantime, and with some shoving help from Caro, I dragged my passenger off and down onto the three blades of grass and a dandelion which formed my so-called lawn.

'Now what?'

I looked up at Caro. 'I'm going to get him inside.'

Caro slowly shook her cropped head. 'You could just leave him there. People would think you'd got another gnome. An extremely anatomically correct one.' She frowned thoughtfully. 'I'm sure I recognise him, you know.'

'*What*?'

'There's something familiar about him ...'

'It had better be his face you are referring to, Caroline Edwards, or you are going to have *such* a lot of explaining to do.'

She clicked her fingers. 'I know. He's that bloke who's been camping out in the empty house at the end of the village, up near the main road. You know, old Mr Patterdale's place. I've seen him wandering in and out a couple of times when I've been riding by.'

'I thought you said it was a tramp, squatting.'

'Oh, yeah, and this is so clearly a multi-billionaire with his own yacht and a Swiss bank account.' She looked down at the hairy acres of skin lying at my feet. 'Take him round there. Leave him on his own lawn.'

'I can't leave him, he might swallow his tongue or something. Anyway, I ought to get him to hospital. He's unconscious, Caro. Something must have happened to him up there.'

Stan shifted and the pair of underpants which I'd squeezed between naked guy's torso and the saddle, fell off and landed at Caro's feet.

She sniffed. 'I'll take Stan and put him away for you. You've clearly got your hands full,' she said, giving a sidelong glance at the collapsed figure now decorating my front garden. 'But I think you're bonkers, of course.'

'Thanks.'

'For thinking you're bonkers?'

'For looking after Stan. He's a bit hot, walking down off the hills with a body on board, he might need cooling off.'

Caro gave me another arch look. 'Yeah, Moll. Right now Stan is the least of my worries. I know I told you that you should go out and find yourself a man, but I rather hoped you'd find one that was actually, you know, *upright.*'

'I didn't exactly go looking. He can't help being

unconscious anyway.' I bent down and got my arms under the man's armpits.

'But you could have found yourself a man with money. Or at least loose change.' She glanced down. ''Cos if this guy has any cash, I really *don't* want to think about where he might be keeping it.' Caro was still standing by the gate, watching my efforts at naked man dragging with an element of scorn on her face. 'Talking of which, mind out for his arse, it's dragging along the concrete there.'

'Thank you so much,' I puffed, inching the body another few feet towards my front door, 'for your kind attention.'

'Just saying. After having done a few miles bent over that saddle he's going to have some interesting chafing. You don't want to add to it with cement-burn.' She was leaning against Stan now, nodding slowly as though giving me marks out of ten.

I adjusted the red fleece which kept inching down his midsection. For some reason I didn't want the complete nature of his nakedness exposed to my friend. She'd probably insist on going off for a tape measure. 'It'll be okay once I get him inside.'

'If you're sure.'

I bent my head to redouble my pulling efforts and heard the gentle scuffle and clop as she turned Stan round and began to lead him across the road to the stable yard where he lived, when he wasn't terrorising local dogs.

'I'm sorry about this,' I apologised to the prostrate figure I was jerkily tugging by the arms up the three steps to the door. 'Call it a panic response. Actually you'll probably call it friction burns, but you're not exactly in a position to complain right now.'

Another lengthy yank and we'd reached the top of the steps. The door handle dropped under my elbow pressure, I never bothered locking it because burglary around here was almost unheard of. The Neighbourhood Watch was made up entirely of very attentive little old ladies who would have pestered any burglar to death by calling around mid break-in to ask him impertinent personal questions. Besides, not locking doors meant that I didn't have to worry about losing my keys somewhere in the forty square miles of moorland, whilst trying to force Stan into something approaching a canter.

I half-fell over the threshold with the top half of my burden. The lower half jammed briefly on the draught proofing but, with the added advantage of less friction once we'd hit the lino of the hall, I managed to slide the entire length of him, with an indescribable amount of noise, as far as the bottom of the stairs before I collapsed, panting against the banisters.

'This,' I gasped, 'is not as much fun as it's going to sound when I come to tell it.' I put my hands on my thighs and tried to get my breath back. 'Although it does score highly on the "guess what happened to me today" scale.'

There was no answer from my recumbent visitor. He just lay spreadeagled along the black and white plastic floor, like a fallen Greek statue, only one with better detailing and, well, rather more lifelike proportions. He wasn't that tall, several inches off six feet at a guess, and well-muscled, like someone who's cared about how they look. But his arms and legs were spidery, his hip bones jutted up like a couple of kerbstones and the individual bones of his fingers showed under his skin where his hands curled in upon themselves, as though he was preparing to punch someone as soon as he came round. If he'd looked after his appearance once, it had been a while ago.

Caro was right, he did look rough.

I waited until my heart rate had steadied and then, using an undignified combination of pull and shove, got him through the narrow doorway into my living room, where at least he was lying on carpet.

I dashed upstairs, pulled the duvet from the spare bed and tore down again, using the duvet to replace the red fleece, which really wasn't cutting it in the covering up man bits stakes and kept giving me interesting glimpses of what lay beneath, like an impromptu burlesque show.

Trying to remember everything I'd ever learned about hypothermia, I rolled the bloke up in the duvet so that his head protruded from one end like the contents of a tube of toothpaste and tucked the lower end around his feet, then leaned back on my heels to appreciate my handiwork.

His eyes were open and he was watching me.

Chapter Two

Phinn came round slowly to realise that he'd been better off unconscious. Everything hurt. Something inside his head was jerking and twitching, his eyes burned and his body was in more pain than he could ever remember having suffered before in his life.

'Ow. Ow. No, really, ow,' he muttered, prising his eyelids apart. 'Why do my elbows hurt?'

A brief moment of lucidity showed him that there was a woman crouching down next to him. At least, it seemed to be a woman, his sight was too blurred for anything more than bare outlines to register. 'Where am I? Actually, never mind *where*, can we start with *who* and work our way out from there?'

The figure next to him stood up. 'I was hoping you could help me with that,' she said. 'I mean, I know *where* you are, you're on my living room floor. In Riverdale.'

A vague memory knocked politely at the inside of Phinn's skull but he was too bemused to take any notice. 'Oh, yeah. Riverdale. Always think it sounded a bit *Lord of the Rings*.'

'So, you can remember *Lord of the Rings*, but not your own name?' Now the voice, which had sounded rather pleasant before, had overtones, undertones and just general tones of sardonic disbelief. 'Can you remember what you were doing up on the moors without your clothes on? Or does something have to come with a literary fantasy reference in order for your memory to kick in?'

'Without my ...?' A quick, agonising wriggle so he could peer down his torso showed him that she was quite accurate. Under this, whatever it was that he was wrapped in like something that has just had the sarcophagus lifted off it, he was stark naked. 'Why haven't I got any clothes on?'

'Again, waiting for help on that one.'

The woman moved closer and now he'd stopped his eyeballs from rotating in opposite directions he could get a better look at her. She seemed to be wearing a pair of yellow leggings and a dark top, and had the most untidy hair he'd ever managed to partially focus on. 'Ow,' he said again, less experimentally. 'If I ask why everything hurts, are you going to refer me to your previous answer?'

'Well.' She crouched down and now he could see that she had a smudge of something on her nose, a face that inclined towards the interesting end of the attractiveness spectrum, and a pair of really rather lovely blue eyes – eyes that currently held an expression of shiftiness. 'It might be because I had to bring you down off the moor on my horse. Not exactly *my* horse, I sort of borrow him on a permanent basis because nobody else wants anything to do with him on account of him eating anything that's not nailed down. Actually, now I come to think of it, sometimes he even eats things that *are* nailed down.'

'I see.' Phinn tried to move again and found that he could lift his head about twelve degrees before the agony cut in. 'I don't like horses much but on this occasion I'm prepared to let that go.'

'And then I had to drag you over concrete to get you inside.'

'Ah.'

'And I think I might have banged your head on the lino in the hall. I'm really sorry, but I didn't know what else to do. I didn't want to leave you out there, what with the no clothes on thing and it's really chilly today and so …' She raised apologetic hands. 'I hope I didn't do you any damage.'

'Okay. Well, nothing seems to be broken. Except for some skin.'

'You did get a bit scuffed.'

'But, on the whole, I think it's better than dying of the cold, so thank you. Whoever you are.'

'Oh. My name's Molly.'

'Then, thank you, Molly.' Phinn lay quietly for a few seconds more. 'Do you think I could have some trousers or something? I'm feeling a bit ... Swiss roll.'

There was a blur of dark hair as Molly vanished from sight for a moment and then came back carrying a pair of black jeans and a leather jacket. 'Are these yours? I found them near where you were lying, or at least Stan did, so I brought them with you.' She shook the clothes and a pair of underpants fell to the floor to be ignored with a degree of assumed dignity.

Somewhere behind his eyes Phinn could feel a tiny blacksmith getting the day started. 'I think ... they look familiar.'

'Good. Because I'm not sure that I have anything that would fit you. Can you sit up?'

Cautiously Phinn lifted his head another few degrees, and then laid it back down on the carpet, breathing carefully. 'Not right at this moment, no, I'm afraid not.'

'Then maybe you should stay there and not worry about your clothes for a bit. You do look very pale.'

'Yeah. I feel a bit ... ow.' Phinn rolled so that he lay on his side and could look around him without having to move his head. 'Have I got a wallet?'

Molly shook the jacket. 'Why, do you think you were robbed? I wondered if you'd been knocked out but you don't seem to have a head injury or anything. I checked you over before I put you on the horse.'

'Great. Thanks. I feel so much better knowing that a

woman has been checking me out while I've been lying there naked and unconscious. Gives me a real sense of being in control.'

'I said I checked you over, not out. I wanted to make sure nothing was broken before I moved you.'

'Oh. Right. 'Course.' Phinn closed his eyes but the swimmy feeling continued inside his head. 'So, where are we on the wallet question?'

'Hang on.' There were noises of energetic clothing agitation and a heavy thump. 'Yes. It was in your jacket pocket, and there's a set of keys. So at least you weren't robbed.'

'Right. Am I carrying ID?'

'Caro ... that's my friend, Caroline ... she said that she thought she recognised you and that you were ... um, staying in the old house at the end of the village? It's called Howe End, I think. Howe something, anyway.'

Phinn screwed his face up in an effort to remember. There was ... he could remember ... Bristol. An empty flat. Bottles, yes, lots of bottles. And then a sense of cavernous space, the smell of mice and ... *lights*.

'Ah,' he said. 'I still think the wallet might help. I'm getting a name, but the way I feel at the moment it could be coming through from the world of the dead.'

He had to open his eyes again, the spinning feeling inside his head was making him feel sick. The woman with the startling eyes and deranged hair was flipping open a black leather wallet and the sight of it brought everything raging back, cresting through his head like a razor blade tsunami. 'Stop ...' he tried to say, but it was too late. Innocence shattered.

'Your name is—'

'Phinneas Baxter. *Doctor* Phinneas Baxter, PhD. And somewhere in that jacket are my glasses, which will help enormously, so if you don't mind—'

'You knew? All that "I can't remember" was fake?'

'Sorry, you misunderstand. I remember *now*. I wish I didn't, but that's my business. Oh, my glasses, thanks.' He took the narrow black frames from her fingers with a hand that ached in places he wasn't even sure it had and hooked them on carefully. The world came into sudden focus.

'Gosh,' said Molly, now revealed to be a lot neater and cuter than the blurry half-impressions had led him to believe. 'You look different with your glasses on.'

'So do you. You look human for a start. God, I wish my head would stop hurting so I could think properly. This is Riverdale?' His brain felt like a giant game of Connect Four, things slotting into place with an inevitability that made him think he was losing. 'I was staying here … there were …' A tiny voice that he really hoped she couldn't hear was muttering *no, you didn't come here, you were running away and here just happened to be in the way. You didn't aim for Riverdale, you fell at it from a great height. And now you're naked on some woman's floor with a head that feels like a bladder infection. You are such a screw up, Baxter.* 'Could I have a drink of water, please?'

She was wearing jodhpurs. He could see that now, not leggings, for which he was grateful. Jodhpurs had a reassuring air of competence, of practicality. Molly was evidently a woman who got things done, even if one of the things she did was to practically abduct naked strangers by throwing them over her saddle like some kind of reverse romance novel. Her hair was as wayward as it had looked even before he put his glasses on, it flew outwards from her scalp as though some source of static electricity walked with her through the world and formed a dark background to her face – which was pale, although he had to admit that might be because of the aforementioned naked stranger on her floor. And her eyes really were a lovely dark blue. He'd always noticed eyes. It came of wearing glasses. Jealousy, probably. He wished his head would stop hurting.

'Water? Are you sure?' She hovered around on the edge of his vision making him squint out of the corners of his eyes, which didn't help the headache one little bit.

'Unless you've got vodka.' Then another memory lurched up, borne on a tiny bit of acid and he had to swallow hard. 'Water. Yes.'

'I meant, if you've got any kind of head injury you shouldn't have ...' Her voice tailed off. He supposed his expression must have turned scary. He could feel himself doing it, the narrowed eyes and the drawn in mouth that he'd been accused of doing deliberately.

'Molly whatever your surname is. Look. I don't have a head injury. The only injuries I have were inflicted on me by your good self and, yes, I'm not complaining because you probably saved me from an embarrassing case of frostbite at the very least, but please take it as read that if I am capable of asking for a drink of water, that I am going to be fit to drink it and for the love of God, *please let me have some.*'

She didn't answer. Stared at him for a moment until Phinn felt himself starting to sweat. It was a look which said that she had just worked out why he'd been naked and unconscious and was now desperate for water. He could only hope that she'd got nice enough manners not to bring it up ... urgh, not to mention it right now.

'Right,' she said, with the air of one making a decision. 'Water. Yes. Stay there a moment.'

Phinn blinked his eyes hard. 'In order to move I would have to roll myself out of this bedcover and the room is spinning quite fast enough already, thanks.' But she'd already left the room and he could hear the blessed sound of a tap running somewhere out of sight. His throat ached with the need for a cool drink and he could only pray that it would soothe the timpanic activities currently threatening to burst out of his temples and scuttle about on the floor.

She was back. 'Water. You'll have to sit up or you'll drown.'

At least she hasn't brought me one of those kiddie beakers with a spout, Phinn thought. *Or a straw, as if I'm eighty and unable to hold a cup.* Even though he couldn't, he was bound inside his wrapping so tightly that he suspected he was going to come out three stone lighter.

Molly had to move him further into the living room and push him against the sofa so that he could inch himself into a half-sitting position, during which process his glasses fell off twice and a whole new world of hurt opened up to him. 'Ow. Why does my hair hurt?'

'Not guilty on that one.' She held the glass of water up and he shakily tried to bring a hand to bear on it. 'Do you think it might be something to do with drinking yourself into a coma?'

He paused, one hand rejoicing in the coolness of the condensation around the outside of the glass and the other forming a loose fist somewhere out of sight. 'Ah,' he said. 'I was hoping you might not have realised that.'

I left him shakily drinking the rest of the water and popped over the road to check on Stan. Although he did belong to Caro, this was a technicality involving the changing hands of money and in all practical ways Stan was my horse. Or, more accurately, pony. Or, still more accurately, a four-legged dandelion clock impersonator with the temperament of a hall table and about the same amount of enthusiasm. His real name was Aethelstan, but it was either Stan or Aethel, and, whilst riding a horse called Stan was a bit ... basic, it was definitely better than riding something pronounced as 'Ethel'.

'Still got the naked man?' Caro asked without preamble, squeezing past me in the loose-box doorway dragging a filled haynet.

'His name is Phinneas Baxter.' I nudged Stan out of the way and helped Caro tie the net to the ring in the wall. 'He's come round now and there doesn't seem to be much wrong with him.'

Oddly I didn't mention that the reason he'd been unconscious was that he'd had a blood alcohol level of about one-to-one. Okay, it wasn't my business or anything, but it was still strange that I didn't tell Caro. Normally I told Caro everything ... right, no, scratch that, I told her *almost* everything. Everything important anyway, and the fact that my naked visitor had been falling-down-and-passing-out drunk probably wasn't important. Probably.

'Nothing wrong with him, apart from being dragged around the local countryside with his backside to the four winds. Any after-effects on that?' Caro asked.

'Real interest or prurient curiosity?'

Caro fixed me with a steady gaze from her grey eyes. 'Bit of both, really. I've done a bit of naked riding in my time – and if you ever give me that look again, Molly Gilchrist, I shall have to rethink our friendship – and one thing I remember is that the aftermath tends to be ... well, pinchy. And it's not even as if I've got a scrotum,' she added, reasonably enough I suppose.

'He says everything hurts, and his word is good enough for me. I'm not about to start feeling him for lumps and bumps.'

'So when are you dragging him back to his front door?' Caro let Stan step between us to reach at his haynet, and we looked at each other over his withers. 'Or were you thinking of having him stuffed and mounted on your wall?'

'I'll let him start to feel better and then he can go. He

might not be living here, he might just be staying for a night or two, you know, passing through.' Given the amount he must have drunk, I'd take bets on some element of passing through anyway.

'How long since you split up with, what was his name again ...Tim. Eighteen months?' Caro, queen of the non sequitur leaned against the horse, who grunted in a rather unflattering way.

'About that. Why?'

'You split up with a bloke you never talk about, by the way – and I'm just adding that in a spirit of total disclosure – and then a naked man falls into your lap eighteen months later? Maybe it's Heaven's way of telling you it's time to move on with your life.'

'Does the phrase "Fantasy Prone Individual" mean anything, Caro?' I moved round behind Stan, whose ears flickered in response but he didn't stop munching, even as I slid the bolt. 'And there's nothing odd about the fact I don't talk about Tim. Why would I? He's just ...' I shook my head. 'It was just one of those things.'

Yes, the one thing I didn't discuss with Caro. Didn't discuss with anyone. Couldn't. And who was there to talk to anyway? I'd burned my boats, bridges and all other water-crossing methods when Tim and I had ... no, not split up. He was going to be a part of my life for the foreseeable future, but not a part I had to have anything to do with. In fact, he was a part that I would like to remove, slice off like a gangrenous limb. But I couldn't, so the best I could do was to ignore things. Pretend he had just been a blip, a hiccup in my otherwise tranquil life, and get on with things.

'Okay, you don't need to do that face.' Caro joined me and we both shivered together in the needle-prick wind that finagled its way through even the sturdiest outdoor clothing. 'I'm only remarking on the fact that Mystery Guy—'

'His name is Phinneas.'

'Yeah, Mystery Phinneas ... and what kind of name is that anyway? It's practically Biblical ... that this bloke turns up naked in front of you, dead to the world, and he's not exactly ugly is he, but you're prepared to throw him back without even ... you know, Moll, I think there's something wrong with you.'

'*I'm* not the one bringing Heaven and the Bible into things. *That's* wrong. I'm providing a shelter for a poor unfortunate. Like the Good Samaritan,' I added, dragging what little RE I could remember to the fore.

'A poor, naked unfortunate,' Caro mused, rubbing a hand through her hair.

'Are you obsessed with sex or something?'

'Very slowly say to yourself "I haven't had a man for eighteen months". Then come back to me on that.'

It had been longer than eighteen months, of course. Tim had lost interest in me long before ... I'd put it down to a combination of his being older, having a high-pressure job, *stress*. And then he'd put it down to the strain of planning our wedding, the general anxiety of 'taking the next step' as he'd put it. I'd give him 'next step'. In fact, I'd give him a whole staircase and a hearty shove if he ever tried to speak to me again.

'Anyway. You'd better get back and make sure he hasn't run off with your valuables.' Caro turned to head back into her house, which backed on to the yard.

'I haven't got any valuables. Besides, he's only living down the end of the road, I'd just go round and get them back.'

'Whatever. You taking Stan out tomorrow? I'll leave the tack room key under the mat if you are. I'm going to York for some shopping. Do you want me to call in before I go? To check on progress?'

'You mean to see if I've seduced some guy whose name I barely know.'

'Eighteen months. That's all I'll say.' Caro flipped a hand in farewell and headed indoors, leaving me with no alternative to going home and facing a guy marginally less suitable for a quick romp than Piltdown Man.

When I got back he was sitting on the sofa, with his head tipped back and his eyes closed. The duvet had been rearranged around him so that he could move more freely, and left the upper quadrant of his chest bare.

'Are you feeling better yet?'

He jerked. 'Sorry? Oh. Yes. Much better.'

Since he was still as green as an unripe plum I doubted this was the case. 'So, is there anyone you want to call? You know, to let them know where you are? Someone who could come and pick you up?'

Fingers closed over the edge of the duvet and pulled it up to chin height. 'No. Just give me a few moments more and I'll go and … I live at the end of the road, you said? Is it a big house? One I'm going to be able to find with both eyes shut?'

I glanced at him quickly. He'd closed his eyes again but I didn't think it was the after-effects of the alcohol now. There was something else, something that seemed to be pulling at him from the inside, his expression flickered from shame to hurt and back again but without him acknowledging it. Which meant, I guessed, that he'd been dealing with this for some time. This drunken episode might have been nothing new, nothing even remarkable.

'Have you done this before? Woken up somewhere and not known where you were?'

'I do know where I am. Riverdale. And I'm expecting the elves to come calling any minute.' He spoke without opening his eyes, tilting his head to rest it on the back of the sofa again, his hair trailing down over his brow and propping itself over his glasses like a wig. 'Any jokes about my ring will have to wait until I feel human again.'

'Mr Baxter, look —'

'Doctor.'

'Sorry?'

'Doctor Baxter. That's what the PhD is for. I'm a doctor. Astro-bloody-physics.' His voice was oddly bitter but with a resigned edge to it. I wished he'd sit up and let me see his face properly, it was extremely hard to read his meanings when, even crouched down in front of him, all I could see was the tip of his chin and a lot of wayward hair.

'All right, Doctor Baxter then.'

'Thank you. I worked hard for that. Wouldn't want it to go to waste, would I?'

Now his eyes flickered open and I got the full expression. Wished I hadn't, it was the look of a man who has been trampled on by fate, and staggered to his feet against all odds only to be run over by the train of destiny.

'Phinneas Baxter, PhfuckingD. Thank you, world.' A pinch of colour rose in his cheeks and the downtrodden expression was replaced by a flare of anger. 'Sorry, Molly. Feeling a bit … yeah. Sorry.'

There was a pause. I could hear him breathing, an uneven restless sound as though he was about to get up and run. Then, to my surprise, a hand extended from the duvet bundle and touched my shoulder. 'Look. I'm really grateful that you saved me from a putative frozen embarrassment, even if that was at the expense of a good deal of agonising discomfort, but you don't need to worry about me any further. I'll just … recover and be on my way.'

He had gorgeous eyes. Whether it was because the puffiness of alcohol had receded or because his glasses magnified his pupils at this close range, I noticed them for the first time. Almost black, and highlighted with shadows.

'No, you're right. You're none of my business, I just happened to be in the right place at the right time to save you. You can stay here as long as it takes to get your metaphorical breath back and then …' I shrugged. 'It's fine.'

A sudden smile dashed behind his eyes. It didn't touch his lips or raise his cheeks but it lifted his expression out of the desolate category for a moment. 'Cheers. I'm getting a kind of *Wuthering Heights* vibe, so I guess I ought to be able to find my way back home. I'll just follow the consumptive coughing.'

'It's an old farmhouse. I think Mr Patterdale sold off the land when the last of his sons moved out, but he kept the house on. Do you know why you're there?'

A sudden, dismissive shake of the head and then a stretch that made the duvet slide a little lower. 'This is a nice room. Lots of books.'

'Yes. They're research. I work for a walking magazine, that's a magazine about walking, not a magazine that moves about a lot. It's called *Miles to Go* and we review equipment and maps, all kinds of gear like that. I'm in charge of the Outerwear section and I also write articles based around the North York Moors.'

'Nice.'

A conversational slump ensued.

'Doctor Baxter?'

'Phinn.'

'Phinn, then. I don't mean to sound rude but do you mind if I get on with some work? I was out on Stan today getting some material for an article on bridleways for the summer edition and … they need it by tomorrow. Six months lead time, and all that.'

'Of course. I'm sorry I've held you up.' He spoke a little stiffly. 'I would have arranged to collapse a little further down the dale if I'd known.'

'I didn't mean—'

'No. I know you didn't.' His mouth twisted as he bit his lip. 'Look, just ignore me. I mean completely. Take no notice of anything I say or do, in fact, pretend I'm not even here. I feel as if I'm only half in the world as it is, so you'll be doing me a favour. Work, write, whatever, I'm only sorry that I can't help you with anything practical. Astrophysics and horses – not really any point of compatibility there, I'm afraid.'

'I suppose not.' I waited another minute in case he was going to follow up but he didn't. He sighed and slid a little further down on the sofa until the duvet reached his nose. 'I'll just … get on then.'

Moving as slowly as was compatible with trying to give the impression that I cared a damn about his opinions, I collected my things together and set myself up at my usual workstation on the end of the big dining table that occupied the major part of my single living room. I'd already started on the article, which was about access for horses across National Park land. Several bridleways had been reported as being closed off recently with concrete blocks and barbed wire and I'd been following up and taking pictures for the past couple of months. So it wasn't as if I had masses to do, but I did want something to take me away from the necessity of making conversation with Doctor Phinn Baxter.

As I uploaded some of the photographs to go with the article I found my eyes occasionally drifting over to where he sat. It looked as if he'd fallen asleep, his head had settled at an odd angle against one shoulder and his hands lay relaxed on the portion of duvet where I would guess his lap was. Every so often he would twitch as though his body was preparing for flight while he slept, his head would jerk up and his eyes would open but he didn't seem to be aware of his surroundings when it happened, as though he was dreaming about being awake.

He looked sad. All right, I knew nothing about the man, wanted to know even less – he was just a stranger who'd needed me for a division of time and now only needed a place to sit quietly and let his brain regain control of his functions – but he had a kind of sad aura about him. There was a lack of eagerness to smile, as if he'd forgotten how to, a haunted look about the eyes when it seemed that his mind whispered things to him that he'd rather not acknowledge. It all added up to a man in the throes of despair, or at least a deep misery not occasioned by everyday disappointments or setbacks.

Plus the fact that his wallet was full of antidepressants. That gave me a bit of a clue too.

Chapter Three

Phinn kept his eyes shut. He knew she was looking at him from time to time because the rattle of the keyboard would stop and she'd move her chair a fraction against the bare wooden boards of the floor so that she had a view of him unobscured by her screen. He was playing dead, he knew. For the same reason as possums did probably. Was it possums? His brain swam through the brandies and broke surface, treading vodka, while he tried to bring his thought processes online. Yes, possums. Pretending to be dead to avoid predators. Or, in this case, questions.

Why he was scared of questions from ... what was her name again? Polly ... no, Molly ... yes. Molly put the kettle on. No, that was the other one, Polly. This was Molly. A softer name, a floppy rag doll of a name. She didn't seem floppy though. Was more stern. A bit schoolmistressy, but that was probably because she didn't speak to many people. Working for a magazine, sending in the articles, living in this rural backwater with a friend she spoke about as if it was her only one. So. Maybe a bit shy? That might account for the awkwardness of their conversation – oh, wait. The awkwardness might be because she'd seen him naked and he was unable to string together a sentence that wasn't curling at the edges with bitterness or just plain alcohol-induced confusion. Yeah. The situation was awkward.

Still. Another half-hour, say an hour tops. Then he'd be feeling steadier, get dressed, get out, get his bearings, make his way back to where he'd been staying; sleeping on bare stone floors wrapped in inadequate sleeping bags. Waiting.

His half-sleeping brain sucked him back through time until he almost believed he was in his own flat in

Bristol, crashed out on the futon after another argument. Another desperate attempt to explain himself, to justify his existence. Another sleepless few hours spent waiting to see if it would be all right in the morning, his fears flicked off and forgotten, his emotions dismissed. He twitched, his muscles attempting to put him back on his feet, send him back into the fray, and he was suddenly awake again to the knowledge that this was not where he should be. But then, where was? Everything was gone, everything.

The lights were the only constant now. The lights and the permanent headaches, the hangovers which padded along at the back of his brain like faithful hounds awaiting their unleashing. There was nothing else.

I read through the article once again, checked that the pictures were in the right format, and mailed the whole thing off to Mike, editor of *Miles to Go*. The article had come together just right, the pictures taken from Stan's ample back earlier in the week showed the moors in their spring colours and, although my words had a bit of a condemnatory tone regarding farmers who blocked rights of way, the pictures would please the Tourist Board, so it all cancelled itself out in the end. Deprived of any further activity that would distract me, I pushed my chair away from the table and stood up, stretching out my back.

'I'd better go and turn Stan out into the paddock.'

He didn't move or acknowledge my words although I had a feeling that he was pretending to be asleep again. The rhythm of his breathing was nowhere near steady enough to be that of someone sleeping. Well, that was fine by me.

I squinted another look at him as I pulled my jacket on. He was what Caro would call 'cute', but I didn't know if I'd go that far. He did have good bones, most of which were visible under the tightly stretched skin and unruly hair, but he certainly looked like someone who either doesn't care or doesn't do anything to maintain good looks, what with the stubble and the shadowed eyes. I found myself wondering what he'd look like if he relaxed, had a few good nights' sleep and put on a bit of weight. Nice, I should think. Pretty, in a rock-star kind of way, perhaps.

My jacket settled over my shoulders bringing the smell of wet horse and damp blankets to my nose and I gave an inward sigh. How or what Phinn Baxter might be was none of my business. I had about as much interest in men as I had in … well, astrophysics, and I wanted it to stay that way. After Tim, who hadn't so much hurt me as killed me stone dead and then jumped on my corpse, it was going to take mankind to evolve into a whole new species before I seriously looked at a bloke again in any way other than the practical.

I tried to close the front door quietly in case Phinn really was asleep, but it stuck and I had to drag it closed over the lino, with a squealing noise like a rabbit in deep distress. I listened from the garden side, if the noise had woken him then he might call to find out where I'd gone, but there was nothing, so I shoved my hands deep in my pockets and went to rug up and turn Stan out for the rest of the day. Exercised, fed and let out, one less thing for me to feel guilty about.

When I returned to the house, Phinn wasn't on the sofa. The duvet was folded up and draped over the cushions and his clothes were gone.

I stopped, frozen in the act of taking off my coat, feeling ridiculous at missing someone who'd only been in my life for a couple of hours. He had woken up, felt better and remembered where he was supposed to be, that was all. Recovered and headed out. Wasn't that what I'd wanted him to do? It wasn't as if I'd offered to cook him lunch or put him up overnight until he felt well enough … Woah.

Was that what I'd been going to do? In the back of my mind, had that intent been working away? And if it had, then why?

I felt sorry for him, of course I did. No one drinks themselves into a stupor and then tears off all their clothes on a chilly March morning on a whim. Although he walked and talked coherently, he'd had the air of a man who's hanging on to sanity by the tips of his fingers, which wasn't really the sort of thing I needed right now. What I needed was what I'd come here to find: quiet, peacefulness. A horse to plonk around on without the attendant excitement of occasionally being hauled off into the next county at speed.

Calm. That was what my life was beginning to be, a little oasis of peace after the tumultuous events of the previous year. Untrammelled, if that word meant what I thought it did. And the last thing I needed in all this lovely serenity was some bloke with issues making me feel like I had to do something. Even if the bloke in question did look like a science pin-up.

No. The events of today would seem like a dream in a few weeks' time. Doctor Phinneas Baxter would have moved on from his squatting impermanence in the deserted and largely derelict farmhouse. I would have regained my feeling that this tiny village hidden away in the depths of the moors was the only secure spot in a frightening world, and I'd be able to roll my eyes at Caro if she ever wondered in my hearing about 'what happened to that naked guy you found that time'. It had been a little blip in my semi-hermetic existence.

But, as I found when I folded my laptop and went to carry it upstairs, the blip had left his wallet behind.

I arrived in Caro's huge kitchen carrying the wallet and a bottle of wine just as she came in from evening stables. It was cold and getting dark outside, but her Aga was warm and there were cats and dogs all over the flagstoned floor in total contrast to my slightly sterile cottage.

'I need your advice.'

Without preamble I opened the bottle and poured two glasses.

'Okay.' Caro washed her hands, shoved a cat off a chair and sat down. 'What about?'

'Naked guy.'

'Right.' She rested her elbows on the pine tabletop and scrubbed her hands through her hair. 'So, where've you left him?'

'I don't know.' I explained about my leaving Phinn asleep on the sofa and his being gone when I got back. Caro listened quietly. It was one of the things that had drawn me immediately to this crop-headed woman when I'd blown into Riverdale in a state of near breakdown a year and a half ago. I'd come in search of somewhere to hide out and lick my wounds, a place where no one would ever think to come looking, and I'd met Caro in the pub, when sheer luck, and the busiest night I'd ever known the place to have, had squeezed me between a darts match and the kindest woman in the world. She'd asked if she could share my table and then drawn me into a conversation, gently teasing out of me some basic story to explain my bleak expression and my red-rimmed eyes.

With no outward display of sympathy or anything other than practicality she'd offered me the lease on the little cottage opposite her house without even asking for the usual month's rent up front or bonds or any kind of references. In return all I had to do was help her out with the horses whenever the usual bevy of teenage girls that mucked out and rode exercise were elsewhere, and she'd never once asked me anything about my past. I'd volunteered the occasional piece of information. She knew for example that I'd come from London, that my relationship had ended badly and that if anyone asked, I didn't live here. But she accepted everything I said with a quiet placidity that belied her tendency for efficiency and hard work. She wasn't religious, didn't believe in great acts of generosity – she was just, plain and simply, *kind*. And Caro, as they said, got things done.

'Okay. You've got nothing to feel guilty about, Moll, you know that, don't you?' Caro raised her glass to me.

I wouldn't say that, I thought, but I knew what she meant.

'It's not that. It's that I don't know if he recovered and went or whether he went because he knew I didn't really want him there. And I don't like the idea of him dragging himself out because he thought he had to.'

Caro twisted her mouth. 'Did you say anything to make him think you wanted him to go?'

'No.' I had wanted him to go but not like that, not without warning.

'You can't second-guess his reasons then. He went, leave it at that.' She refilled her glass.

Behind the windows the shadows lengthened, pointed at the light. The air was chilly despite the Aga's best efforts.

'I know. He probably just felt that he was outstaying his welcome and went back to where he's living. But he left this behind.' I dropped the wallet onto the table. It landed with a thump and several cards slid out.

'Oh, I see. Well, take it back then. It's not like he's a million miles away, is it? Up to the end of the road, turn left and up the drive.'

'I thought I might wait until tomorrow morning.' I smoothed my fingers over the leather casing, it felt lumpy with content. 'It's a bit dark now.'

Caro let out an explosive chuckle. 'Molly Gilchrist! You are not going to tell me that you're scared, are you? What of, exactly? A bloke you've already seen in the altogether, and who might be desperately in need of his wallet? Or the ghost of Mr Patterdale?'

'I don't … there isn't a ghost, is there?'

Caro shrugged. 'Who knows? That place is old, sixteenth century or something, there's bound to be things hanging round, spirits of ill-used serving girls, that sort of thing. You know Riverdale, we're like … I dunno, a magnet for the weird.'

'Well, thanks a lot for that.' I pulled a face at her. 'Oh, talking of weird, though—'

'Don't tell me, he's got two willies.' She toasted me with her glass.

'Shut *up* about him for a moment, will you? This has nothing to do with the vanishing naked guy. This is about me. Last night I was looking out of the window and I saw these … *lights*. In the sky, I mean, not in the village – I might be a bit mental but I think even I would know if I was looking at house lights. These were … twinkly. Colourful.' *Disturbing*.

Caro shrugged again. 'Could be anything. Chinese lanterns, lasers if they were having a disco in Pickering – do people still say "disco"? Or maybe …' she drew her eyebrows down and hunched her shoulders, curling the fingers of the hand not holding her glass into witches' claws, '… maybe you saw the Alice Lights.'

I sighed. 'I know I'm going to regret asking this but what are the Alice Lights?' I felt a lot better now that I'd put the subject out into the open. There had been something otherworldly and ethereal about those pinpricks of illumination in the sky, but now Caro had possession of the facts they'd lost the unearthly aura they'd had in my head. Caro was so 'down to earth' that she was practically magma.

'Nothing. Stupid stuff that my dad used to make up. I remember him saying something about lights in the sky being the Alice Lights.' She swigged another mouthful of the wine with a healthy disregard for early morning starts. 'Like I said, this place is all ghouls shrieking and headless women walking and strange black shadows that move when you're not looking at them.' She wiggled her eyebrows. Especially round at Mr Patterdale's old place.'

'Right, that does it.' I put my glass down heavily. 'I'll go round there tomorrow. When it's light. And the sun is shining. I'll be the one carrying a fully-loaded crucifix, two Bibles and a shotgun. He can manage without his wallet until then. After all, what's he going to use it for? The shop's closed until the morning and I really don't think he'll be doing any Internet shopping, not with our wretched broadband connection out here.'

'Not even sure Howe End has electricity.' Caro got up and peered in a cupboard, returning with crisps. 'Mr Patterdale was a bit old school.'

'Having no electricity isn't "old school", it's practically workhouse!'

Caro tore open the crisp bag and stared at the wallet that was lying innocently on the table. 'Have you looked inside?' She poked it with a forefinger. 'To check that he isn't a multimillionaire?'

'I looked when he asked me to. When he couldn't remember his name.'

She made a face. 'Oh. *That* kind of unconsciousness. You sure you don't want me to come with you to give it back?'

'I'm only going to shove it through the letterbox. I'm not going to enter a debate.'

'So, what's he got in here?' Before I could stop her Caro

had picked up the wallet and tipped its contents onto the table. 'Blimey. She's a bit tasty.'

In a transparent section at the front was a photo of a woman lying in a deckchair, wearing an enormous sun hat and a bikini. She was slim and pretty, head turned towards the photographer to show a wide, appealing grin.

'He's obviously got an eye for the girls. Funny, could have sworn he was far too cute to be straight.' She flicked through the things that had fallen out. 'Pretty girlfriend, plenty of credit cards, one bank card, a driver's licence ... and half a packet of Prozac.'

'I don't think we should be going through his things, Caro.'

'Why not? He must have found out that he's lost it by now, and known exactly where it was, if he asked you to check it out. Hasn't been back to pick it up, has he? He'll have to take his chances that we're not a couple of international Internet fraudsters hell bent on squeezing his cards until they squeak.' She held up a platinum American Express card. 'Mind you,' she said thoughtfully, 'the feed bill is due, and China could do with a new set of shoes all round.'

I snatched the card from her fingers. 'Stop it. I'll take it back tomorrow.'

'Good. And if the whoo-whoos come to get you, I'll be in York.' She let me tuck all the receipts, cards and pills back into the wallet. 'In York, no one can hear you scream.'

'No ghosts,' I said firmly, after all I had to walk back across the road in the dark to get home. 'I don't believe in anything that I can't personally poke in the eye.'

'Well, it's time you did some kind of poking.' Caro divided the last of the bottle between our two glasses, erring slightly in favour of her own. 'Even I get more success than you do, and I'm nearly ninety and completely without any favourable features at all.'

'Liar.' Caro was thirty-eight, with a boyish figure and a laugh that could stun pigs. 'I hope you're not suggesting that I start making eyes at a tramp squatting in a deserted house with no mod cons.'

'An *attractive* tramp, though. And he's a doctor.' She flicked the wallet.

'No thanks.'

Caro's eyes were suddenly serious. 'It's not good for you, Moll, being hidden away here. I mean, I know you want to be hidden but ... eighteen months? Don't you think you've let long enough go by now? Isn't it time you stopped locking yourself away here and got out and found yourself a real job? Met some real people?'

'I'm going home. Before you persuade me to sit here all night and I end up taking Stan out tomorrow with a hangover from hell.'

Caro waved me towards the door. As I left, her cry of 'You can run, but you can't hide!' followed me out and across the narrow potholed road that separated Caro's old farmhouse from the row of cottages where I lived.

But she was wrong. I could both run and hide. And I had.

Chapter Four

Phinn woke slowly, not so much to a world of hurt, more a universe of agony. His back ached and his body felt as though a field of virulent nettles had risen up against him. Everything stung, throbbed or twinged. He let out a sigh and lay back on the inflatable air bed, which had lost a considerable amount of inflation during the night and now formed a kind of plastic skin between him and the floorboards.

A knife blade of sunlight had inserted itself between the ragged curtains and the illumination it provided let him see the dust lying thickly on the window, the cobwebs that adorned the ceiling like grubby tinsel and the mouse droppings that condimented the floor and over which he'd tiptoed reluctantly on his way to bed. Hell. He sighed, and even that hurt.

He'd been hoping that the whole Riverdale thing had been a dream, that he'd wake up back in the flat in Bristol with the king-size bed, the carpets and the clutter. To think he'd once wanted minimalism, bare space, that he and Suze had fought many of their lesser squabbles over her inability to stop collecting and his unbending desire for clear floors.

Suze. Even the memory of the name squeezed his heart. Less now than it had; time – as everyone repeatedly told him – was a healer. But he'd discovered that it was an inept nurse, sticking plasters over wounds that ripped open anew without warning, leaving him bleeding all his hope for a future into the dark.

With another sigh that made his ribs click, Phinn rolled over, reluctantly climbed out from underneath the duvet, and began to get dressed, sniffing as he went. Damp.

Definitely damp. The house seemed to suck the moisture from the air and deposit it straight into any fabric that he'd brought with him. His jeans smelled mildewed after minutes on any floor and all his T-shirts were turning mottled. But better than the flat as he remembered it, would *always* remember it, with the silence and the half-packed suitcases.

Yawning and scratching idly at his chest, he made his way down the creaky staircase and into the kitchen, where he'd left the primus and a loaf of bread, if it wasn't already growing a lawn of mould, feeling the need for coffee writhing through him. Coffee. Proof that intelligent life existed on this planet. Licking his lips he reached a hand to the corner cupboard and jumped several feet into the air when the kettle was pushed into his hand.

'What the—'

'Keep your PhD on, you four-eyed twat,' the blonde-haired visitation said, leaning back against the unlit iron range. 'What, didn't you think I might come looking for you? Shove the kettle on, some of us have been up all night with inadequate GPS trying to find this place.'

With the feeling that he was moving through a dream, Phinn lit the primus and complied.

Cautiously, I turned off the main village street and into the driveway of Howe End. The marks of tractor wheels had bitten deeply into the mud and half-hearted gravel, churning it into an almost impassable Somme of high-sided ruts and stagnant pools and my jodhpur boots only came up to my ankles. I tiptoed over the highest peaks, trying to avoid breaking the surface crust and being plunged into depths of generational frog-hatcheries.

I'd never been here before. Never needed to. Howe End had been the home of Mr Patterdale, a semi-reclusive old farmer who'd somehow managed to persuade the truculent owners of the village shop to deliver his groceries and had only occasionally been seen from a distance, pottering around his sizeable garden. He'd waved to me once when I'd cantered by on the ridge that overlooked the house, but since I'd been rather afraid that I was trespassing and that he was simply waving to warn me off his land, I'd not waved back and felt rather bad when I'd found out that he'd died the following week.

The house was impressive, if your tastes ran to the shambling Gothic, but in this early spring sunshine, with the mellow walls and creeper-adorned frontage, it looked attractively *Homes & Gardens*-ish. A few windows held remnants of curtains, wisping across dark spaces like coy eyelashes as I crept under cover of some overgrown blackcurrant bushes towards the front door.

A blackbird's panicked flight made me jump and I fled the final yards to the door. The area where I would have expected normal domesticity, such as a washing line or outdoor furniture, was crowded with just-leafed elder which meant that I couldn't see the front door until I was almost at it, and then found that it was contained within a deep porch, edged with stone seating like a church coffin-gate. I entered the forbidding gloom and bent to grope for the letterbox, wallet held out ready to push through as soon as I found it.

I'd just located the hinge end and was fumbling for the flap when the door opened and I was staring at the knees of someone wearing jeans.

'It appears to be a hunched woman offering us money,' the jeans-wearer called back over his shoulder. 'Yorkshire is clearly far more friendly than I'd thought.'

'Shut up, Link.' Phinn Baxter's voice travelled from somewhere close by, and I straightened with as much dignity as I could manage.

'I've come to return your wallet.'

Link, a chunky man with hair so blond that it made him look prematurely grey, stood back and waved an arm in invitation. 'The master will see you now.' He bowed as I passed him and then winked and whispered, 'Nice arse.'

'I've ... I'm here to bring this.' I advanced into the deeper gloom of the house, holding out the wallet as though to ward off a financially motivated supernatural attack. 'You left it yesterday.' I was ignoring the arse comment as hard as I could, but had become very conscious that Link was following right behind me as I walked in.

Phinn was standing in an enormous room where the floor was made up of huge slabs like gravestones and the low ceiling bore beams covered with hooks. It was dark after the brightness of outside and I could only make out his outline, although my nose was compensating for my diminished sight by giving me the whole olfactory experience of mouldy dust with just a hint of territorial tomcat and a top note of sour milk.

I blinked a couple of times and his shape gradually resolved to reveal that he was leaning against the wall with his arms folded. He was taller than he'd looked horizontally, and more austere; dressed all in black that made him look as though he'd draped himself in shadows. I stopped, and said without thinking, 'You look really different with your clothes on.'

Behind me Link snorted like Stan.

'Right. Yeah, thanks a lot.' Phinn pushed off the wall and came over. 'And thanks for the wallet. I'd forgotten about that.'

There was an impasse during which I could hear Link stifling laughter. 'Right. I'll be off then,' I said, performing a tricky turn so as not to walk slap into his chest. 'I'll just ... yes. Right.'

'Oh for God's sake, Baxter, you can't let her leave

without at least offering coffee.' Link moved over to where a tiny camping stove was supporting an old-fashioned kettle. 'Come on, man, you've got a woman in here! Stage one of your plan to prevent an overdeveloped right arm and cellophane bedsheets!' He pulled a set of mugs from a cupboard. 'Although, if she's already seen you starkers, I reckon you've got up as far as stage five, with a possible option on stages six through to nine.'

'Ignore him,' Phinn said with a sigh, taking the wallet from me and pushing it straight into his back pocket. 'God knows, I try to.' The light from the little window was reflecting on his glasses so I couldn't see his eyes, but there seemed to be a touch of humour in his voice.

'But I'm like a movie zombie.' Link poured water, which looked to be hot rather than boiling, into mugs and passed me one. 'I just won't lie down and die. There's no milk, by the way, it went off. Rather like Baxter.' He shot a meaningful glance at Phinn, who was back to leaning against the wall again.

'Look, Link—'

I wrinkled my nose. 'How come you can't believe in a place called Riverdale, which happens to be a dale with a river in it, and yet you've got a friend called Link?'

'Pure bad luck on my part.' Phinn sipped at his coffee, grimaced and put the mug down on a stone slab.

'There is a long and interesting history to my name.' Link took the final mug and began drinking from it without any kind of acknowledgement of the awfulness of its contents. 'And one day I shall explain it to you.'

'It's a character in a video game.'

'Shut up, man, I'm trying to build a sense of allure and mystery. All right, maybe it's not *that* long and interesting but I'm trying to engage in social chit-chat here, people, come on, help me out. Don't you two ever talk?'

'We only met yesterday.' I sipped my coffee. It was lukewarm and bitter, rather like the reception I'd got from Phinn.

'Wow. And you've got his clothes off already? That is impressive.' Link toasted me with his mug.

'It wasn't like that.' Phinn came to my conversational rescue. 'Molly found me up on the moors. I was ... ah, I'd ... had a bit of an episode.'

Link's mouth twisted. 'What the hell is it with you? Are you determined to screw up every single thing you touch right now?'

'I wanted ... look, never mind, this isn't the time and place for this discussion.' Phinn rolled his eyes in my direction, clearly trying to indicate that he didn't want to talk with me in the room. Which was fine, because with the way these two were squaring up to each other, I didn't want to be in the room either.

'I'd better go. You've obviously got things to talk about.' I put my mug down, its ceramic clatter as it hit the stone work surface echoed into the chilly silence. 'It was nice to meet you both.'

I got as far as the dimly lit entrance, and was trying to find the door handle, when Phinn caught up with me.

'I'm sorry,' he said. 'I've behaved badly. I *continue* to behave badly, and having the bloody conscience-fairy there turn up unexpectedly hasn't helped.' He scrubbed a hand through his hair. 'It was kind of you to bring my wallet back. Thank you.'

''S all right,' I muttered, desperate to be gone.

'And I'm sorry I left yesterday without saying thanks.' This time he smiled. 'That really *was* badly behaved of me, and I can't even blame Link. You were very kind to go to all that trouble for a guy who could have been – well, anyone.'

'Are you really an astrophysicist?'

The change of conversational direction seemed to baffle him. 'What?' A frown made his glasses slide forward down his nose until he poked them back. 'Yes. Why? Do you want to know what my thesis was?'

'You don't look like a scientist, that's all.'

'He's got a *Doctor Who* T-shirt!' came a voice from the kitchen. 'And he quotes *Monty Python*.'

Phinn gave me a sudden grin. The shadows under his eyes disappeared. 'I can't keep apologising, can I? Yes, I'm an astrophysicist. If you ever find yourself short of someone to do a little deep space research, well, you know where I am.' He opened the front door, being able to locate the knob in the deep gloom. 'Thanks again, Molly.'

'And UFOs! Did he tell you about the UFOs?' Link called and the smile fell away from Phinn's face.

'Goodbye,' he said briefly as though he'd already lost any interest he might have had in me, and the door closed with a swing and a slam that told me he'd gone back inside before I'd even reached the end of the porch.

Chapter Five

I took Stan out onto the moors to try to clear my head. The day was bright and the wind had dropped, giving us a tiny foretaste of what summer might have to offer, always supposing we had a summer since the weather this far north showed a distressing tendency to drop us straight from chilly spring into damp autumn. Stan plodded along, happily undisturbed by my attempts to chivvy him into a canter and I soon stopped trying to ride seriously and let my thoughts wander.

I'd have to do something soon. My savings were being eaten at a remarkable rate by the necessities of rent, bills and food; they'd probably only float me for another couple of months and then ... something would have to change.

I loved working for Mike, writing for the magazine, but he couldn't afford to pay me much more than the basic freelancer's rate. I'd been trying to knock out a few articles for other magazines, even a couple of short stories, but my lack of confidence was clearly showing, everyone had turned me down. They may have given me more consideration if I'd sent them my CV, but that would mean putting my head above the parapet, maybe drawing the attention of people that I'd rather not see – hell, stop being so mealy-mouthed Molly, it might draw *Tim's* attention.

So there was my choice. Pull myself together, flaunt my past experience and stand a chance of making a living or keep my head down and starve. No, not starve, Caro would never see that happen. She'd already offered to let me move into her place, work in the stables in return for my keep if I had to give up the cottage, and a tiny part of me was tempted.

But another part of me wasn't. The part that knew the whole of my life in Riverdale was only temporary. The part of me that was driven by the ambition to write, *seriously write*. To unpack facts that so many people would just ignore, to examine, understand. The part of me that had pricked up its ears when I'd heard that Phinn was an astrophysicist, and had surged to the surface when Link had thrown in his comment about the UFOs.

The lights. Maybe he had seen them too.

Stan stumbled and I almost rolled off over his head. Even given his total lack of temperament of any kind, this inattentive riding could be dangerous, so I pulled myself together and shortened up the reins. I forced him into an energetic trot until we'd circled the dale and were moving along the ridge overlooking Howe End, where, to Stan's relief, I let him mooch back into his customary amble and then drew him to a standstill.

Below us the farmhouse stood bathed in full sunlight. Although the front was screened from my view by the undergrowth that had concealed my approach that morning, the back of the house faced onto an open paddock, currently grazed by half a dozen sheep which had broken through the hedge from the next-door field. In this open space I could see two men standing.

Their figures were indistinct at this distance but, since one was dark and the other fair, I would have taken any bets that it was Phinn and the mysteriously-named Link. A vanishing puff of grey showed that one of them was smoking a cigarette and they were facing each other, seemingly in serious debate. I strained my ears but couldn't hear more than tones, changes in volume or the odd, staccato laugh.

I let Stan lower his head to the grass and watched the men. Tall and skinny, short and slightly chubby, it looked like the number 10 having a falling out. There was clearly an argument going on, the cigarette trail came and went, accompanying upraised arms and the voices came more distinctly for a moment before descending down the register again. After a moment the shorter figure moved a few paces back and the streak of dark, which was obviously Phinn, disappeared into the house, punctuated a moment later by the bullet-like sound of a slammed door.

Link stayed put for a minute. The smoke died away, I saw the bright flare of a lighter, and then Phinn was back. Smoke was replaced, voices raised again, then fell to a mutter, the figures moved closer together for a moment as though confidences were being exchanged and I saw Link reach out, whether the gesture ended in a blow or comfort I couldn't be sure. Beneath me Stan moved and I had to gather the reins to turn him back around, and by the time I had him facing the right way again, the two men were gone. Back inside the house? Or had they walked around the outside and gone elsewhere? The sheep moved, jerkily, through the overgrown gardens, occupying the silence that had fallen, and I wondered what the men had been arguing about.

'Well ... *sort of* spying, I suppose,' I said, laying the table. 'But they were out in the open, anyone could have seen them.' I opened the oven and took out a stew, carefully manhandling it to the table wrapped in an overlarge tea towel. 'I just happened to be passing.'

Caro screwed up her face. 'Yeah, anyone that happened to be on an old track that no one uses, whilst they were in a private garden – course you were spying.' She plonked a jacket potato onto her plate and helped herself to a ladleful of the steaming stew. 'This smells great, by the way. What is it, chicken? Mmm, tarragon in there too.'

'I found a clump sprouting in the garden.'

Caro went still. 'Oh. Yes. Dad was a great gardener, I'd

forgotten. Herb patch, everything. Funny how things like that slip your mind, isn't it?'

The cottage had belonged to Caro's father, who had died two years before. She'd refitted the place, intending to use it as a summer let, and then I'd come along.

'Hey. He'd be glad it wasn't going to waste, I'll bet,' I said.

'Yes. Yes, he would.' The sadness crowded onto her face, drawing her mouth down. 'Still miss the old bugger, y'know. Lived in the village all his life. He'd have been able to tell you about the ghosts at Howe End. Born storyteller, he was. Every night he'd sit on the end of my bed and come out with some tale of a traveller lost in the fog or the mysterious noises from a deserted barn and then my mum would come up and slap him silly for scaring me so much I couldn't sleep. He wrote a book once, my dad, about the folk tales of Riverdale, still got it around somewhere.' Her eyes misted for a second, then she shook her head. 'Ah, probably better off where he is now. At least he'll be warm.'

Briskly she sorted out her cutlery and cut a long swathe of butter to put on her potato. 'So? What were they arguing about? And who was naked this time?'

'Both dressed, I think.' I gave her a quick rundown of the lack of events at Howe End. 'Don't you think we're a bit weird getting so caught up in what really isn't any of our business, Caro?'

'Mmmmf.' Her mouth full, Caro waved a knife at me. 'Firstly, it *is*, kind of, our business, being as how you pulled him down off Blackly Moor without a stitch on, and secondly, is there *really* anything on television these days?'

'Clearly not.'

We ate silently for a bit, Caro obviously relishing a meal she hadn't had to cook herself and me thinking.

'You're very quiet, Molly. Falling into daydreams about

the gorgeous young men at Howe End? Because if you want any advice in that direction, you know I'll be only too pleased to help you out, don't you?'

'I'm intrigued, that's all. What the hell is a doctor of astrophysics doing squatting in a derelict farmhouse and having arguments with a bloke who has turned up out of nowhere?'

'Mmmm.' Caro chewed for a moment. 'Particularly when said astrophysicist looks like an underwear model. Lovers' tiff?'

'Don't think so.'

'Okay then. Why are you so intrigued by him?'

I waved a piece of chicken. 'Just as I was leaving his friend, Link, said something about UFOs, something that made Phinn twitchy. He'd been quite nice to me up till then, but he nearly shut the door on my head he was so keen to get rid of me as soon as UFOs were mentioned. *That* is intriguing.'

'If you say so.' Caro helped herself to seconds of the stew. 'This is really very good, Moll. Where did you learn to cook like this? London?'

'Yeah, Tim sent me on a residential cordon bleu course when we got engaged. Think he was sick of eating burned boiled eggs to be honest and wanted to be able to have dinner parties where the guests didn't have to play "guess the meat".' I sighed. 'So there were some good things to come out of that relationship, like an edible chicken stew, for example.' *Or maybe he'd wanted to get me out of the way.* The realisation was new and made me grit my teeth against the current forkful of chicken. *Bastard.*

'You don't talk about him much. Does it still hurt? I mean, you broke up suddenly, it must have been hard, bad enough for you to run all the way to Yorkshire without knowing anyone here and bad enough for you not to want anyone to find out where you're living.' Caro dropped her eyes to her plate, almost as though she felt ashamed of probing so much. This was the most she'd ever asked me about the relationship.

'It was … there's nothing to say. We were engaged, we fell out. I came up here because he'd never think to look for me anywhere this far from a Waitrose.' I tried to keep my tone breezy enough to prevent any more questions, but Caro was clearly on a roll.

'So it *was* bad. Otherwise you'd at least have let him know where you were, in case he wanted to come grovelling back on bended knee with four hundred red roses and the entire diamond output of one large South African mine.'

I tried to imagine Tim grovelling, and failed. 'It wasn't that kind of relationship,' I said.

Caro gave a hollow laugh. 'Believe me, sweetie, at base they're *all* that kind of relationship.' She dug deep into her potato. 'So, what was he like then, your Tim, if he wasn't the kind of man to beg you to come back to him?'

Despite myself I smiled. 'Clever. Funny.'

'Older?'

I flinched. 'Oh, yes. Twenty years older.'

'Weren't they all though? Any bloke you've ever mentioned, you've given the impression that he had one foot in a cheap Ferrari and the other one in the grave.' Caro chewed at me.

'Have I? I suppose … well, yes, men my age never really appealed to me.'

Caro grinned. 'Figures. Your mum brought you up on her own, didn't she? So, there you go, father-figure complex.'

I swallowed a lump of something that made me start to cough and choke and it took Caro five minutes of patting, slapping and a half-hearted attempt at the Heimlich manoeuvre before I could speak again, and I managed to restart the conversation on less inflammatory topics.

Chapter Six

The nights were the worst, Phinn mused, tipping the dregs of the bottle down his throat, feeling the burn numbing into acceptance. Nights were shitty when you were on your own. He bent his knees up until he could rest his elbows on them and scooted along the floor until his back rested against the bare plastered wall behind him.

The house was quiet. Link must have taken off again. Or found himself a room to sleep in, bloody place was big enough. Phinn tipped the bottle again but it was definitely empty this time and the mouth of it clattered against his teeth.

'Bugger.'

He climbed to his feet using the wall as a support and stood there for a second, breathing heavily. He'd taken his glasses off so the room was all rounded edges and tucked in corners, with the alcohol making things a fizz and blur of shadows and he swayed for a second, fighting the urge to walk out.

Here is where it happens. Here is where the answer is.

Phinn Baxter hated himself. But he figured that was all right because he hated pretty much everyone else too, and huge chunks of the planet with small exceptions. Scarborough. Scarborough was nice, his parents had taken him there on holiday once. Mauritius. And that girl with the blue eyes, Polly … no, Molly. Molly put the kettle on. She was nice too. Nice. Was that all he could say these days, that some things were nice?

He whirled away from the wall and stomped over to the low-ledged window sunk into the stonework like a deep-set eye. He crouched down and leaned his arms against the sill looking out over the blackness of the moors behind the house. Nice. When once things had been magical, stupendous, astounding, breathtaking, now they all blended, swirled and sank into the greyness of 'nice'.

He rested his forehead against the glass. Cool. Outside the window, the March wind whipped through the branches of the elder trees, flapped the bushes like a careless hand but left the distant hump of dark moorland untouched. He imagined the wind passing over its hunched surface like a caress, stroking the timeless contours like a lover and then cursed himself for his rising erection; useless, unwanted.

The sudden bang of the door made him jump and turn awkwardly back into the room.

'Oy, Bax mate, what you doing in here?' Link came in and stared at him, head on one side. 'As if I didn't know.'

'I'm … nothing. Leave me alone.' Phinn's mouth felt thick, his tongue too wide. ''M thinking.'

'Yeah, I can see that.' With a sigh Link subsided onto the reinflated air bed, which gave a farty groan and lost another few pounds per square inch. 'Bax, look, I thought we had this out this afternoon. Drink solves nothing. You've already found that anti-Ds solve nothing. Have you forgotten everything I've taught you these past few months, young Padawan?'

'Knock off the *Star Wars* refs, Link. Astrophysicist, not freak.'

Link shook his head. 'So. One screwed up relationship and you take to the bottle like vodka's going to save you? You really think drinking yourself stupid is the answer to anything?'

'I am not,' enunciated Phinn carefully, 'an alcoholic.'

'I know that. If you were, you wouldn't get pissed. Not on half a bottle of voddy, anyhow.'

Phinn could feel Link's stare through the darkness. 'I

don't know what else to do,' he said finally. He could feel the alcohol draining from him, its effects slowly falling away to leave his brain heavy and his heart solidified in his chest. 'Everything ... everything hurts.'

'That's how you know you're alive, Bax.' Link stood up, ostentatiously brushing himself down. 'You just need something to live for, that's all.'

'I've got something.' Phinn's voice sounded wrong, even to his own ears. Sounded sulky, self-justifying. 'I'm working here, Link. Research.'

'Research.' The disbelief in Link's voice was so strong it should have burned like acid through the air.

'Yes.'

'Into ...?' Link waved a hand. 'Deaths from boredom? Rising incest rates? The fact that everyone living in the countryside has evolved an inability to digest Starbucks coffee?'

'I'm going to write a book.'

'Oh, yeah? And what might this mythical "book" be about? Because there's not a lot of quantum theory going on in rural Yorkshire, as far as I know. Not a lot of dark matter being investigated, unless it's the locals poking shit with sticks.'

'Actually there's a dark matter lab at Boulby mine. Went there on a trip when I was taking my A levels.'

'Aged about eight.' Link sounded sour. 'Come on, you're a sodding genius, we both know that. And you've decided the best way to use all that brainpower is to hole yourself away in this ... this ... *swamp* and write a book? You could be, I dunno, curing cancer or developing stardrive or something and you're here, drinking yourself into a fog every night. If you've knocked off taking the anti-Ds, replacing them with the fun juice isn't exactly cleaning up your act, you know. At least the pills just made you boring, alcohol makes you slur *and* boring. Suppose I should be grateful though, I don't have to listen to it if it all comes out "fnnfffnnnn". I can just nod and smile.'

Phinn turned back to the window again. 'I've taken leave. Giving myself twelve months to write a book and after that ...' He rested his forearms on the ledge again and gazed deep into the night. 'After that I'll go do something worthy, all right? Cut me some slack here, Link, it was a bad time, and I never asked you to come looking for me.'

'Yeah, I know that but—'

'So why *are* you still here? You've found me, you've seen I'm alive. What more is there? Are you waiting to see whether I've finally learned to juggle?'

'Hey, don't flatter yourself. I'm not just here for you. I'm lying low for a bit. Woman trouble, you know the kinda thing, and this place is on the map as "here be dragons", so no bunny boiler's going to come looking for me round here. It's like compassionate leave.'

Phinn glared at him. 'From what? You haven't got a job to take leave from!'

'Hey, millionaires need compassion too. It's not my fault I've got a trust fund, is it? I'm taking leave from women. No more women for me.' He looked down at his watch. 'Right, now that's over, where are the women?'

Something caught Phinn's eye and he twisted his head to look sideways, where the shoulder of moor slumped down, curving into the dale. A light. A bright speck, almost like a star but brighter, moving. Moving *fast*. 'Where's the camera?'

'There's one on my phone if you—'

'No, the video camera. We'll need it, and the Canon with the 50mm lens. It's over there in that box. Come on, hurry.'

There was a knot in his stomach, that tight, wound feeling as though he was somehow connected to the light in the sky by an invisible thread and it was tugging at him, pulling him out into the darkness to follow it.

His ankle wrenched as he missed his footing but the alcohol prevented any pain messages getting to his brain. Rationally, he knew that he was tearing his hands on bracken as he used its tough stems to haul himself up the hill behind the house. His nails split and his boots slid on the peaty soil but he didn't care, wasn't even aware of the pain, keeping his eyes on that spot high in the sky where the lights were merging now. Dancing, swooping, then breaking off and moving away as he dragged the camera from its box and tried to focus.

'Get the video on them, Link!' he shouted. 'Try to get the house in, for scale! They must be bloody enormous!'

Beautiful. So serene and lovely, riding the air like messages from deep space. He found he was lowering the camera to watch as the lights separated, whirled once more then formed into stately constellations before waltzing decorously away behind the curve of the moorland. The knot in his stomach had moved to his throat, his eyes stung with tears and he had to fight the urge to lie down on that heather covered mound and sob like a child, although whether with relief that they'd returned or disappointment that they'd left again, he couldn't have said.

'Come *on*, Baxter,' he whispered to himself, using the newly felt pain from broken nails and bleeding palms to pull himself together. 'Objective. You are objective. You are a scientific observer not a teenage girl. So for goodness sake, *don't cry.*'

'Bax?' Link's voice floated up to him from somewhere down in the field below. 'Where've you gone, man?'

'Here. Hang on.' With an effort Phinn swung himself around, noticing that the track where he stood was broken and torn with hoofmarks, and that the churned peat had covered his jeans to the knee with crumbly smears. 'Coming.'

He threw himself back down the path of bashed bracken that he'd ripped on his way up. 'Did you see them? Did you get film? It's incredible, just …' He arrived between two stunted rowan trees which delineated the edge of the Howe End property, bursting from between them and making Link jump, '… incredible,' he repeated, trailing off as he noticed the way Link stood, camera trailing from his hand, the 'standby' light not even winking in readiness. 'Link?'

Link sighed, flicking a hand through his hair, then letting it drop, heavily. 'Bax,' he said, and Phinn wondered about his tone. It was wary, almost scared. 'You need help, man.'

'What?' Phinn could sense what was coming. 'What do you mean? Link?'

A slow, steady, appraising look. 'What is it? 'Cos I've never even seen you smoke the regular; which doesn't leave much. Tabs? You dropping the acid like a sixties boy? Because the way you hauled ass out here I was expecting, I dunno, some kind of *Battlestar Galactica* moment, and then we're here and …' An expressive hand and a backwards tilted head indicated that the universe had let him down in some fundamental way. 'Nothing. Nowt, as they say round here.'

Phinn felt his flesh creep closer to his bones. 'But – the lights, Link …'

A slow headshake. 'Sorry. You're tripping, man. Something in that voddy, I reckon, something that shouldn't have been there, that or someone's cut your coffee with mushrooms. You want to watch yourself, Bax, because if you carry on like this there won't be a job for you to go back to when you've written your great masterpiece. Sod the Uni research programme, you'll be lucky to get in as night security at CERN.'

The chilly breeze that came at me through the thrown-open window scoured my skin and whipped the curtains into dog-tail flapping until I struggled the catch into its hole and shut the night out. I sat back down on the edge of my bed with my eyes aching.

My legs were shaking. Two nights ago I'd hardly believed my eyes when I'd seen them swooping and looping above the high moor, leaping like so many prismatic fairies. But today I couldn't put it down to a vivid dream or a sleepy-eyed mistake. I was wide awake and vibrating with curiosity as to what they might be. Low flying planes? But those would have droned their way through the skies like a squadron of wasps at an open-air doughnut eating competition.

These lights had moved silently and surely been far too agile to be any kind of aircraft. Party lanterns? But the way they'd grouped together and then wheeled in patterns, kaleidoscopic breaking and reforming of colours, it had looked far too purposeful to have been simply windborne candles beneath paper globes.

What *were* they? The mysterious Alice Lights that Caro had mentioned?

I drew the curtains, leaving a thin slice of night visible at the window, just in case they should come back and climbed into bed. As usual, the village was completely quiet. A dog barked somewhere down the road and my next-door-but-one neighbours returned from a late-night shopping trip in their car with the squealing fan belt, but apart from that there was no sound.

I hunched under the duvet and pined for London for a moment. Not just the noise … in fact, not the noise at all … but the solidity of knowing who I was and what I was doing with my life. My neat little flat, where the sun sloped in through the windows early in the morning rather than being blocked until breakfast at this time of year by that claustrophobic threat of bog and fell which lay surrounding the village like a sleeping dragon around its hoard. Tim, coming to pick me up in his snappy Aston Martin, making me feel like a Bond girl as we headed out of town to country pubs and chalk downs. The lunches, the awards dinners, the ...

... *UFOs.*

The initials snapped into my head almost as if they'd been said aloud. I fumbled for the light switch and sat up. UFOs. That's it. Not that I subscribed to the little green men theory, of course – why would anything fly halfway around the galaxy for the fun and stimulation of anally probing humans? No. But these things, these lights in the sky, they had to be *something.*

I got out of bed again and peered out of the window. It was past midnight, almost everyone in the village was in bed, although a dim glow at Caro's bedroom window told me she was awake and reading. A few houses further down a bright pink glimmer showed that a Barbie-princess had her nightlight fully activated. Nothing moved. Not so much as a cat prowling through shrubbery broke the darkness, although somewhere distant an owl hooted and was answered.

The strange lights in the sky were gone completely. But surely if they *were* UFOs there would be something, some residual oddness, wouldn't there? Not this manifest normality of bedside lamps and hunting birds; an atmospheric change or some kind of meteorological abnormality – rains of fish, perhaps?

And then, as though the possibility of oddness drew him to mind, I thought of Phinn Baxter. He had something to do with UFOs. Was it coincidence him turning up here when these lights were appearing overhead? Or was it pure fluke, just an accident that he'd arrived in the village now?

I snuck back under the covers where it was warm and tucked my feet up under the hem of my pyjama trousers to thaw them out, turning the whole thing over in my head. Maybe I was overreacting. Maybe the lights were something normal, something so everyday that anyone who did see them simply brushed the sighting off. I'd heard of UFO sightings being put down to marsh gas and, well, it was certainly marshy up on the high moor that the lights had appeared over.

Marsh gas. Yes. Even though I only had the sketchiest idea of what that was, it was comforting to think that what I had seen had some normal explanation, and I snuggled back into the pillows and turned the lamp off, only to switch it back on when another thought struck me.

Maybe he wasn't here because of the lights – *maybe they were here because of him.*

Chapter Seven

I prepared carefully for my visit to Howe End. Bacon, check. Some fresh eggs – only slightly stolen from Caro's bantams – check. A packet of shortbread biscuits that had languished at the back of my cupboard since Christmas but, hell, never mind, these were men weren't they, and since when did men worry about things like 'best before dates' when they lived in a house that looked one step away from typhoid-central.

I brushed my hair and put on a pair of black jeans. Even with my romantic track record and current aversion to anything with a penis, I still felt I owed it to my ego to appear presentable in the face of Phinn and Link's above-standard looks. After a last mirror consultation, which reassured me that I still had my face on the front of my head, I pulled on my boots and headed along the street towards the farm.

Riverdale village ran along both banks of the River Dove. It lay several miles from the nearest town, on an outflung arm of no-through road that cut into the moors then looped back onto the main A road. Narrow, one house wide on either side, and crowded together at the end nearest me, where the continuous run of what had been farm workers' cottages were crammed together. The majority of the village was hemmed in, corralled at one end by the sheer rise of moorland and at the other by the medieval bridge that spanned the occasionally vicious river.

Between bridge and moor lay a half acre of village green, more grey at this time of year. It housed the maypole, which rose from the grass mound like a huge, priapic excrescence with a weathercock on the top, a metal fox which swung with a rusty, grating noise to indicate wind direction. Beyond the bridge the houses spaced out more, were larger and more expensive and finally petered out altogether, leaving a stretch of fields between them and Howe End. The houses were all similar in style, if not in design, silver-grey brickwork presenting a stolid front to the world and eaves straight out of the gingerbread school of architecture; central front door and small windows all the better to keep out the wicked east wind.

Howe End broke that mould by being made of red brick and set at a different angle to the rest of the buildings, as though trying to sidle through the village. It meant walking almost all the way around before I reached the door, moving beneath the elder and blackcurrant bushes whose branches hung with moisture and newly emerging leaves and where the air smelled of crushed greenery with a faint whiff of muck-spreader.

In the absence of a knocker I pounded with a fist on the door. I heard the echoes dying away and wondered why anyone would choose to squat out here. There must be empty flats in York, or some old warehouse somewhere, and anyway, wasn't squatting desperately out of fashion these days?

In the absence of any reply, I stepped out of the porch and shouted up at the front of the house. 'Phinn! Link!'

There was a sound above me and I looked up to see a window open squeakily slowly and a tousled dark head emerge. 'What is it?'

'It's me, Molly.'

'Yeah, that's why I didn't ask "who are you?". I can see it's you.'

I stood further away from the porch so I could see him properly. He was leaning out of the window with both arms on the sill, hair careering around his face in the breeze and another day's worth of stubble on his chin. It was annoying that he could look so good and so rough both at the same time. 'I wanted to ask you something.'

'All right.' He showed no sign of movement other than to settle himself more comfortably against the window frame and to try ineffectively to swipe his hair from his eyes. 'Go on.'

'Can I come in?' I jiggled my carrier bag. 'I brought you some breakfast. Bacon and eggs?'

'Mmmm. Bribery. I think I like it. Kick the door hard, it's not locked, it just sticks.' And the head vanished back inside the room to the squealing sound of the window being refastened.

By the time I'd kicked and forced my way into the kitchen Phinn was coming through the other door, yawning and bedraggled in jogging bottoms and fleece top. 'What time is it, anyway?' He stretched, the top rode up to reveal a couple of inches of flat stomach with a sketching of hair covering it, and I suddenly became very interested in the contents of my bag.

'About ten.'

'Early call then?' He wasn't wearing his glasses, and I suddenly noticed his eyes, very black and slightly amused.

'Phinn, this is farming territory. Around here ten is nearly lunchtime. Anyway here's the eggs and bacon, I'm no good with naked flames, so you'd better do the primus thing.'

He raised an eyebrow but lit the primus and hauled around in a few cupboards until he found a frying pan. It looked a bit sooty and we both stared at it for a moment.

'Anything you've not caught as a result of sleeping on the floor in this place is probably something you're immune to by now, so I say go for it,' I said and laid the bacon in a single layer over the base of the pan.

He rested both arms behind him on the worktop. 'Okay. Bacon is cooking, therefore now is a good time.'

'Good for what?' I wiped both hands down my jeans and left smears of bacon fat on both thighs.

'You said you had something you wanted to ask me?' There was something arresting in the way he tipped his head to one side and looked out at me from under the resulting flap of hair. 'Or was that a false pretence to get into my house? Because, you know, bacon on its own would have been enough.'

'I wanted … last night … the lights …'

It was as far as I got. Phinn's face went very still as though he was inwardly processing information, then his eyes flickered and went to my face, scanning it slowly.

'You saw them?' He almost exhaled the words.

'Yes, I was looking over …' But I got no further before Phinn dragged me against him and hugged me so close that I could tell he wasn't wearing underwear beneath those joggers and that his arms were surprisingly strong.

'Thank you.' He spoke almost into my ear. 'Thank you, Molly, you amazing woman.'

My nose was squashed into his chest bone and there was an almost obscene amount of bobbing about going on around my navel but I stood still and let myself be hugged. It was rather nice, even given that he smelled of dusty damp linen and I could see from the wrists that protruded from his sleeves that his arms were covered in goose pimples, not at all like being hugged by Tim had been. Phinn was taller, skinnier, it was like being embraced by a plank of wood covered in knotted ropes. But still oddly pleasant.

'Does this mean you did see them?' I managed to get enough air between us to ask. 'Or am I just generally amazing?'

'Oh, I think yes to both.' He raised his head so that he no longer spoke directly into my skin and the tiny, impatient little hairs that had spiked along the back of my neck relaxed. 'Above the moor over there, yes?' One arm let me go and pointed towards the high peak. 'Although, if there were two incidents, I might have to go for a lie down.'

Trying not to make an issue out of it, I slid a slow step back. 'About midnight. A load of tiny lights, moving through the sky. Like ... like they were checking us out and then heading over to the coast.'

'And the coast is ...?' He let me go, unresisting.

'East of here. That way.' I pointed now.

He nodded slowly, pushing both hands up to snatch his hair out of his eyes. 'That's what I saw too, but Link couldn't see anything.' His expression was distracted. 'And you said "again". The lights came again. When did they come before?'

'A couple of days ago ... the night before I found you up on the moor.'

'Yesssss!' He jumped and punched the air and the front of his jogging bottoms bounced around as though he'd got a couple of water-filled balloons down there. 'Oh, Molly, this is fantastic!'

'But why couldn't Link see them? They were – well, not clear as day, but pretty clear. And you couldn't mistake them for stars or anything, they were moving.'

'I don't know.' He was back to pushing his hair around again, rubbing the back of one hand over his cheek as though gauging the stubble depth. 'I don't know, Molly, but I sure as hell want to find out.'

A sudden crackle from the direction of the primus made us both leap across the kitchen to rescue the charring bacon. While Phinn piled it onto plates, I fried four of the bantam eggs, tipping the lot on top of the bacon. Two rather tinny looking forks came from a drawer and we perched ourselves on the worktop to eat.

'Where's Link? Isn't he going to want some of this?' I spoke with my mouth full and gestured with my fork.

Phinn gave a one-shouldered shrug and carried on shovelling egg and bacon down like a starving waif, saying nothing. His hair fell over his face and hid his expression.

'You've not killed him and buried him out in the paddock, have you?' That got me a half-smile.

'Apparently he's hiding out here from some woman. Silly sod's probably got himself engaged to another reality TV star and he's trying to lie low until it all blows over. He's done that before.' Phinn looked around at the bleak kitchen. 'Although this is lying so low that it's practically subterranean. But we had a bit of an argument last night. When he couldn't see the lights, he accused me of ... I dunno ... doing drugs, I guess, simplest explanation.'

I thought back to our first meeting, his shaky grasp of reality, his near transparency. 'I'm assuming you're not.'

He raised his head and looked at me, a stern, direct look. 'Reality got a bit harsh for me and my doctor prescribed me antidepressants. I stopped those, and started drinking more than was good, but that does not make me some kind of substance abuser, Molly. All I'm doing is blunting the edges, making it easier to sleep. Definitely not shooting junk or smoking crack, all right?'

'You don't need to justify yourself to me, Phinn.'

Another direct look, which was quickly dropped back to the rapidly clearing plate of bacon. 'I know.' He scraped the last of the egg onto his fork, licked it, and dropped the plate into the sink. 'Okay, so. Lights. Tell me what you know.'

I gave him a brief rundown of my experience so far with the lights in the sky. 'I asked Caro and she just muttered something about Alice Lights, which sounds like some folk story. I did try asking the people in the shop but ... well, they're a bit odd and they tried to sell me a packet of cream crackers. So no one else in the village seems to have noticed anything. Except you?'

I let the question hang in the air between us for a second. Phinn was staring over my head out of the kitchen window. Marks against the walls showed where blinds had once hung but, like the furniture, they were now nothing but shapes of brighter paintwork and scraped woodwork. Eventually he dragged his eyes from wherever they were focused and back into the room to meet mine.

'That day you found me ...'

'I was riding up there because I wanted to see if there was any trace or in case they'd left anything behind. Nearly wet myself when I found you, I thought you might have been ...' I let my words trail off – he could tell what I meant. I could see it in his face.

'You thought I might have been some alien invader that they'd left behind?' A hollow kind of laugh. 'That's quite funny, y'know, Molly. Because that's why I went up there. I mean, okay, I was blasted out of my skull, but I knew what I was doing. I wanted ...' Now it was his turn to tail off, a gentle blush creeping up his pale skin, tinting his cheekbones with the first signs of healthy colour I'd seen on his face.

'You wanted them to take you.' The sudden realisation made my heart hurt. *He'd wanted to be abducted.* 'So why did you take off your clothes?'

A sudden spreading of long, curled fingers along the granite top, a digital shrug. 'Thought they might ... that it might persuade them to pick me up. I was very drunk, after all.'

My insides squeezed and I touched his hand. 'I'm sorry,' I said. 'Whatever happened to you to make you like this, it must have been dreadful for you to want to leave the planet.'

A slow headshake which made his hair brush against the collar of his fleece with a soft sweeping sound. 'A usual story. Wife left me, I didn't handle it well.'

Now I could see the faint tracery around his finger where a wedding ring had once seated itself against his flesh. 'I'm sorry.'

His fingers slid out from under mine and clenched back into pockets. 'Yeah, well. It happens. I just wasn't expecting it, that's all.'

I slid myself a little further away along the stone worktop and pursed my lips. 'Would it have been any better if you had?'

A sigh. 'Maybe. I don't know.' His voice was quiet. Almost dangerous. A light year from the man who'd hugged me in relief. 'Suddenly another planet looked like a good bet.'

'Wow. Little green men, all that probing?'

A flash of smile, not aimed at me. More as though he was smiling at the memory of a memory. 'If there is anything out there, it's more likely to be a super advanced kind of pure intelligence than some bipedal life form with a fascination for shoving bits of metal up unguarded orifices.'

'So you don't believe in UFOs.' I felt suddenly betrayed. All his effusiveness when he knew I'd seen the lights too, and it turned out that he didn't believe in them any more than, say, Link.

'Molly, I don't even believe in humans right now.' Phinn glanced at me and seemed to see something in my face, my disappointment perhaps. 'Hey, UFOs aren't called that any more either, it's UAP now. Unidentified Aerial Phenomena, which, for the record, definitely exist. The term covers everything from earthlights to meteorological abnormalities – anything in the sky that can't be easily recognised.'

Ah. It hadn't been a comment on my gentleness the other night, then. He'd been saying 'UAP', not 'you ape'.

'Is that what our lights are? UAPs?'

He chewed the side of a finger. 'Do you know what they were?'

'No.'

'Neither do I. Think that makes them UAPs and brings them right up under my area of interest.'

A sudden smatter of rain struck the window and made us both jump. 'I suppose I ought to get back,' I said, surprised at my own reluctance. Howe End was cold and draughty, and we were sitting on a freezing granite slab because of the lack of furniture. Phinn wasn't exactly Mister Chatty, and yet I was dragging my feet over leaving. I must have been more relieved than I thought to finally be able to discuss those mysterious lights.

'Okay.' Phinn hopped off the worktop. 'Thanks for the bacon and eggs.'

'If I see the lights again, should I ...?'

'Get pictures. An ordinary camera will do, but try and get something in the foreground so we can make an assessment of scale.' He was moving around the kitchen, distracted, looking for something. 'Or a video recording, if you've got the technology, but put a timer on-screen, just a clock would be fine.'

'Why?' I slithered rather gracelessly onto the flagstones of the floor and the cold immediately bit through my boots to my toes.

'Because we're going to be accused of faking it,' his tone was matter-of-fact. 'Harder to fake if the pictures are sequential. Ah, there they are.' He hooked his glasses out of the dark corner and pushed them on, instantly gaining a layer of insulation against the world. His eyes still had a slightly haunted expression but it was milder and more quizzical than it had been when they'd been darkly naked.

'But I wouldn't fake pictures, that would be stupid. Why say I saw lights if I didn't?'

Phinn leaned against the hideous iron range and looked me up and down. 'Innocence. I so rarely see it, sometimes I don't recognise it when I do.' Then his gaze travelled down to his own feet. 'Bugger, this floor is cold. I need some clothes on.' And without another word he walked out of the room and I heard his bare feet stepping slowly up the wooden staircase that led from the hallway to the first floor.

I stood awkwardly for a few seconds, then slipped out through the still partially open front door and breathed deeply of the rainy air outside.

Phinn watched her go. From his room above the porch he had a pretty good view all along the side of the house, so he saw her stop and turn and frown up at the gable end, almost as though she could see him poised there in the dusty darkness. But then she shrugged and her slight figure was swallowed by the shadows behind the overgrowth of elder. He blew out a breath that made the cobwebs swing and shoved his hands into his pockets.

There was an emotion moving around in the back of his brain, he didn't know what it was, didn't even know if it had a name, but it was burning its way through enough synapses to make him suspect that his eyes might be glowing. *She's seen the lights.*

The untidy woman with the reckless hair had shared something he thought was his own madness. When she'd described her experience, he'd had the unnerving feeling that they were the only two people in the world who had understood some fundamental truth; that magic had happened, the world had changed just a little, and they were the only ones who'd seen.

He blew out again and an irritated spider rotated in its web, spinning its way up and down a single thread like a machine running on liquid silver. *She saw them too.* He found his mouth pulling itself into a grin, an expression so unaccustomed on his face that his cheeks literally ached with the effort. *Whatever else you might be, Baxter, you aren't a nutjob. Or, if you are, then she's one too and at least you'll have company in that padded room.*

'What are you smirking about to yourself in the dark, Bax?' Link's voice made him jump. The grin fell away, leaving what he feared to be a surprised grimace. 'Your psychiatric ward called, they want their straitjacket back. Did Molly come by? I noticed two plates in the sink down there, so either you had a visitor or you are beginning to externalise your inner geek to a dangerous degree.'

'Thought you'd gone back to your collection of Pot Noodles and alphabeticised joints-through-the-ages.'

'Bax, you underestimate my capacity for self-punishment.' Link came over to the window and leaned against the wall next to him. 'I got the bus into Pickering. Well, I say a bus, it's more like a trolley powered by a large dog and run by Hobbits, but, hey, it got me into the town.'

There was a moment's silence which contained the ghost of a conversation in which Link apologised for calling Phinn a junkie and Phinn, in his turn, apologised for getting so shitty about it. 'Why the bus? You've got a perfectly good, if rather ostentatiously over-priced car, haven't you?'

Link gave a sideways nod, acknowledging the overt fact, as well as the unspoken apology. 'Yeah, with a petrol tank the size of a fifty pence piece. She's sitting in the red, and I didn't want to get out there and find that the nearest petrol station is in Doncaster. Thought I'd suss things out on the ridiculously expensive public transport first – hell's teeth, Bax, you could run a Bugatti for the price of those bus tickets!'

'I remember Pickering. Nice little place, got a castle, yes?'

'Oh yeah, I was forgetting you used to hang here when you were … I was going to say "a kid" but you were never really a kid, were you? Just smaller then. Yep, still got the castle, I guess eight hundred years of history doesn't go down easy. I bought some food. Oh, and there was this camping shop, so I bought some torches, proper sleeping bags, stuff like that. They didn't have any solution to the shower problem though.' Link wrinkled his nose. 'And, I hate to say this my friend, but you are beginning to smell a bit ripe.'

'Molly saw the lights.'

'Sorry?'

Phinn turned to face his friend. 'Last night. Molly saw them too.'

Link put his hands up. 'Oh, hey, man, you didn't ... you know, *persuade* her, did you? Don't forget that I've seen you in action. One flutter of those eyelashes and the girls will say they saw Bigfoot and ET getting down and heavy.'

Phinn simply raised an eyebrow and waited.

'Okay, so there were lights. *Invisible* lights that mysteriously only you and the hot chick down the road could see. I don't know how you did it, and I hope she's not a serious screw-up, but ...' and Link slapped Phinn on the shoulder, '... gotta hand it to you, man. Way to get the girls.'

Phinn opened his mouth to reply but Link was already walking out of the room, heading for the staircase. 'If you're determined to keep playing the Hermit of Nowheresville, then at least we can do it in a bit of style.' Link continued talking, Phinn suspected so as not to give him a conversational opportunity. 'I got some *very* funny looks bringing this lot back, but then there was a guy on the bus holding two chickens, so I guess they kind of do funny looks by default around here.'

Phinn gave up. Even stretching his memory back as far as it would go he couldn't remember a time when he and Link hadn't been friends and it looked as though it was going to take more than a nervous breakdown and a lack of mod cons to shake him off. 'Yeah, all right,' he said wearily. 'How the hell did he get two chickens on the bus anyway?'

'One under each arm.' Link passed him a box. 'Dynamo torches. Get winding.'

Chapter Eight

I scanned the subject matter of my bookshelves in search of inspiration. 'Walks around the moors – done it. The old lime workings – done those; the wildlife of North Yorkshire – done the bits of it that stood still long enough. Bugger it, there *must* be something I haven't written about already.'

Most of the books had belonged to Caro's late father, but the rest were mine, dragged with me from London in the back of my old Micra, whose wheels had almost grooved the tarmac all the way, weighted down as it was with my possessions and my heart. I hadn't even known where I was headed, I'd just pointed the car at the first motorway I'd found and kept driving until darkness forced me off the road and I'd found myself in Riverdale. A September evening, with the dusk lying thick and heavy in the dale, the air sodden with the smell of old leaves and peaty water and no sound but that of the river scouring its way towards a distant sea.

I'd parked up, walked into the pub and almost instantly fallen into conversation and then friendship with Caro. A cottage, a horse and a sort-of job writing articles for Mike had all followed, and I'd never questioned any of it, apart from the pathetic level of income.

I felt, I had to admit to myself, a little bit like one of those bugs trapped in amber. Fossilised in beauty, fixed in a setting so unbreakably lovely that it made my heart ache to look at sometimes. But still trapped.

The phone rang and I glanced over at the caller display with the usual pang that caught me in the back of the throat. Mike. I picked up.

'Just callin' to ask if you've settled on an article yet?'

Mike's 'Norf Lundun' accent was completely assumed because he was from Weybridge and had been to Oxford University. I think he did it to 'put people at their ease', which really only worked if you were at ease in the company of cockney wide-boys and the cast of *EastEnders*, but still made me momentarily homesick. He was a bright and eager magazine publisher who also ran a shop for extreme sports enthusiasts, survival courses in the wildernesses of Hampstead Heath and had a long-suffering wife and three, equally hyperactive, children.

He'd expressed disbelief when I'd first mooted the idea of writing 'outdoor' articles for him but, thankfully, hadn't asked questions and had bought said articles regularly and without fuss. 'Only I'm 'avin' a bit of a crisis 'ere, love.'

'What sort of crisis?' I felt my heart start to sink. Times were hard, I knew that, and the circulation for *Miles to Go* wasn't exactly stratospheric. Was Mike about to fold the magazine? I held my breath.

'Advertisers mostly. Bastards, all of 'em. Also, Derry's bust 'is leg, laid up in 'ospital in traction, so 'e won't be turnin' anythin' in for a bit. Any chance you could come up with a real cracker for me, love? Fill a bit of space? I could get some other freelancers to chip in, but I knows your work and you never gives me much to do, edit-wise. Well, I suppose you wouldn't would you, you bein' an award-winner an' all.'

And then I felt it, the stabbing pain somewhere underneath my heart. The agony of knowing that there was so much more than this, this column in a magazine no one read, this tiny cottage in a village no one had heard of. This tiny life. It had once been so much bigger, reached so high that I thought I could touch the stars.

'There's always UFOs,' I said, hopefully. 'Very popular. And I've got some first-hand experience.'

A pause and I heard Mike sucking his teeth. 'Got any pictures?'

'Well, no, not as yet, but—'

'Y'see love, what it is, the *Fortean Times* 'ave all that guff sewn up. Not really our brief, see.'

'Oh.' I let my eyes roam the shelves again. 'I don't suppose we cover busty blondes being saved by dinner-jacketed heroes either, do we?' Caro's father had had a very seventies blockbuster approach to literature, it seemed.

'Not this month, no. Unless it happens up Snowdon.'

'Hm. Usual six month lead time?'

'Yep.'

'Something autumnal, then.'

I heard him sigh. I was keeping him talking and he knew it. 'You got anything, Moll?'

Then suddenly I saw it. A plain, off-white spine, slightly bent, with simple lettering. *Traditional tales of Riverdale – old stories from an ageless village* by Jack Edwards.

'Folk tales,' I said, my voice rising in excitement. 'Traditions and ghost stories and old legends and stuff like that. It'll be Halloween for this edition, won't it?'

'Hey, yeah. Sounds good.'

'I can write up a lot of stuff from this village and the surrounding moors. North Yorkshire is awash with spooks and smugglers, all kinds of stories.'

'Bloodcurdling?'

I crossed my fingers. 'Oh, yes. Lots of gore and mystery.'

'Well, all right then. Can you make it a double for me, Moll? Take up some of Derry's slack? I'll get some stock photos in, all dark and moody shots, 'it the 'Alloween thing running.'

I heard him smile and I relaxed a bit. 'Are you sure you don't want UFOs? Very trendy right now, very "happening".'

'Nah, you're off base with that one, babe. Get a draft off to me soon as you can, will ya?'

With my eyes still fixed on the warped spine of the book at the top of the bookshelf nearest to the window, I agreed and hung up. Then I walked the length of the room, not daring to move my eyes in case the book evaporated. I banged my shins on a stool and hardly noticed.

'Now that,' I said, reaching up on tiptoe to pull the book towards me, 'is what I call a close one. How long has that *been* there?'

It wasn't completely surprising that I'd not noticed it before. It was a smaller than average book and had got pushed between a dog-eared *Jaws* and an Ian Fleming novel with a missing cover that *still* managed to give the impression of being full of over-endowed women being patronised by over-endowed men. The spine of Jack's book was only visible because of the angle of the sun, which had illuminated the recess in which it lay.

'It's like one of those murder-mystery things that are solved with a clue that can only be seen at midsummer, when the sun shines on a certain brick.'

I clearly had also got a touch of seventies blockbuster.

I tipped the book into my hand and took it over to the table to read. I'd just pushed back the cover when there was a cursory single-knuckle rap at the back door and Caro came in. 'Hey, it's a nice day, wondered if you and Stan fancied an outing?'

'Look.' I held the book up, cover first. 'I found it on the shelf.'

'Gosh. Dad's book.' Caro sat and gently took the book from me. 'I knew I'd seen a copy over here once, but I didn't think it survived the redecoration. Wow.' She turned it over and ran a finger over the name printed on the cover. 'He had them privately done. Sold a few in local bookshops but ... I thought they were all lost.' Her eyes were swimmy and she was biting her lower lip. 'This must have been his copy.'

Caro was lost in a world of memory, tracing the letters on the cover with the tip of a well-worn finger. 'Mum died when I was very young so it was only me and Dad. He bought me my first pony and supported me while I was doing my BHSI qualification to teach people to ride. And then, when I'd just qualified, he made Moor Farm over to me and bought this place for himself to live in. All done just for me.' Her voice firmed up and she looked at me. 'I wish you'd known him, Moll, he was a lovely man.' She flipped some pages. 'An incorrigible old bugger, of course, but still a lovely man.'

'Can I keep this for a while?' I indicated the book. 'I've just told Mike I'm going to write about folk tales, and this is my entire source material.'

She grinned. 'Course. Just give the old sod a credit, would you? It'll probably be the biggest exposure this book's ever had, he was hardly in the J K Rowling league as a writer. Anyhow, you up for a ride? I want to find out what you were up to raiding the banty coop at stupid o clock this morning, and don't think I didn't see you heading out to the old Haunted Homestead down the road there, swinging your carrier like Shirley Temple.'

I realised suddenly that I didn't want to tell Caro about the lights. She'd pretty much taken the piss last time I'd mentioned them, all that 'ghoulies and ghosties' stuff, and I didn't want her practicality brought to bear on this. There was something about the way those points of colour had swung about the night sky that had been unbearably intimate somehow. As if they'd been meant for me, and me alone. Although where that left Phinn Baxter I wasn't quite sure.

'I took them some bacon and eggs. Thought it would be

a neighbourly thing to do, and you are always complaining that you've got too many eggs now the hens are in lay.'

'Sure, yes, I don't mind, obviously.' Caro raised her eyebrows. 'So, you and that scientist banging yet?'

'*What?* No, of course we're not! Caro! For the record, in fact, he is so rude that he walked out on me in the middle of a conversation this morning. So I don't even think a gentle tapping is in order, let alone ... what you said.'

'I saw that other bloke heading in there this morning. Looked to have got off the bus.' Caro held the door open for me. 'You coming, or what? Only Stan's chewing his way through another rug in that stable, so it's either get him out for a hack or give him a crossword to do.'

'Link?'

'Dunno what his name is, but he looked far too cute to be allowed on public transport.' Caro waited for me to grab my hat from the rack, force my feet into my jodhpur boots and find my jacket. 'I wouldn't mind throwing him over my saddle and riding off into the sunset. Except you've cornered the market in that sort of thing, haven't you?'

I gave her A Look as I pulled the door closed behind me. 'Once, Caro. Once. And absolutely never again.'

'If you say so. I wonder if he can ride?' She gave me a lusty wink. 'In every sense of the word.'

'You two would get on like a house on fire,' I said. 'You both appear to have taken your approach to life from *Smutty Jokes for Twelve-Year-Olds*.'

'Nothing wrong with a bit of smut.' Caro did the wink again. 'You know me, a place for everything and everything in its place. Hur hur.'

I gave a deep sigh and led the way across the road to the yard, where I saw Stan's head appear over a loose-box door, shreds of expensive New Zealand rug hanging from between his teeth like enormous strands of dental floss.

Chapter Nine

Phinn sat on the floor in the dusty square of sunlight and chewed his pen. His hand ached after only half a page of notes and he absently wondered if anyone had invented the wind-up laptop yet as he stared at the broad stripe of sky visible through the low window. The earlier breeze had built to near gale-force level and the trees he could see etched against the skyline were flexing and arching like a set of skeletal bodybuilders. Occasional leaves left over from autumn flicked past on an upward trajectory as though trying to get back to the ancestral home.

He sucked the pen again. A half-page of notes had turned into a line drawing of Howe End with the position of the lights marked as inky blips on the paper, even though this wasn't supposed to be a book about UAPs but a serious polemic on the subject of cuts in funding for the deep space projects and in particular his own research programme on plasma fields.

A sudden sharp thwacking sound made him start and the pen scribbled across the sketch of the house, joining the light blips together to make a puzzle picture of something that looked like an irritated hornet. 'What the hell is that?'

'Branch.' Link spoke from his corner where he was glumly fiddling with his mobile in an attempt to get a signal. 'What were you thinking, poltergeist? Man, not even evil spirits would hang around this place.'

The noise came again. To Phinn it sounded more like the knocking sound that he made on his desk when he had to give a lecture and the students were too busy chatting or ogling each other to listen. A sort of rapping for attention. 'Sounds like it's coming from the roof.'

Link looked up. 'Probably the place finally falling apart then. Hell's teeth, that's not even a normal gale going on out there, that's like a tornado. We're gonna find ourselves in Oz.'

'I'm sure the roof is sound.' Now Phinn looked up too. 'Guess it could be slates coming loose.' He tucked his leather jacket closely around him, poked his glasses more firmly onto his nose and stood up. 'I'm going to investigate.'

'How up are you on yellow brick roads?' Link watched him head for the door. 'I'll watch from in here. I see you go up on that big cloud thing, then I'll call 999, okay?'

'Shut up,' Phinn said cheerfully and fought the wind for control of the door. 'I just want to check. This place is mine, remember, in all its mousy glory, so I ought to take care of it.'

'Yeah. Why couldn't your uncle have owned the Dorchester?' Link's voice followed him out, where it was snatched away by the power of the wind and torn to shreds on the brickwork.

Phinn grimaced. The fact of his uncle leaving him the semi-derelict farm had been ignorable while he'd been in Bristol. Suze had never wanted to come up here, even a weekend visit to the wonderful city of York hadn't changed her mind. She'd wanted him to sell. Preferably to some town-types who wanted a weekend cottage that they'd pay London prices for, though he'd told her that even Londoners wouldn't want somewhere where the water came from a spring underground and the electricity didn't come at all. That was beyond picturesque and into privation.

A bad-tempered squall caught him under his jacket and flipped him out across the yard, running to keep up with his own clothes as the wind dragged him. He managed to catch hold of one of the rampant elder bushes and turn himself around to face the house, which brought the wind full into his eyes and ears and it began forcing itself up his nose like artificial respiration.

There was no visible damage to the house and Phinn sighed with relief. It would have been like watching a favourite aunt injure herself with a steak knife, he thought, and then wondered at the emotion, at the attachment he'd started to feel for Howe End. It had become more than simply somewhere to run, a convenient place to hide and lick his wounds; it was beginning to wrap itself around him like … like … Phinn groped for a suitable simile as the wind snuck inside his clothes and attempted an act of gross indecency. Like a blanket. Like an old, holey blanket which smelled of rodent-nests and mushrooms and yet enfolded you in its damp wool and kept the bad things away.

Yeah, those bad things. They had a way of coming after you that not even a snuggly blanket barrier could work against. He shuddered and refused to let the memories come, deciding instead to do a circuit of the house to make sure that the noise hadn't come from something on the far side.

He strode into the wind, using its force to drive the memories out as he concentrated on battling his way through the elder, gooseberry and blackcurrant undergrowth to reach the far gable end. Where the garden was at its most neglected, the grass grew untrimmed even by the sheep and the ground looked suspiciously boggy.

From this angle the chimney concealed the roof. A swirl of plastic from a feed sack had caught in a gutter and waved a cheery blue greeting as Phinn tried to squint past the myriad of pots and stack that obscured his view. Finally he opted for backing up towards the far hedge, keeping his eyes on the roofline for any anomalous sag or slippage as he went.

The ground grew soft beneath his boots. Water seeped through the leather and he cursed himself for not wearing the wellies that Link had found tucked in the understairs cupboard, muttered imprecations at the woodlice and silverfish that had occupied said boots and put him off ever pushing his toes into them. Right now he'd have squashed any numbers of invertebrates to prevent this seeping wetness ...

The ground swayed. Against all laws of physics it moved, slid and then disappeared from beneath him, giving him an adrenaline-filled moment of blank wonderment before the earth parted and shot him straight down into a blackness so stench-laden that he spent one brief second contemplating all his sins and wishing he'd been a better person.

Then his whole body was wet. He was bobbing around in something too thick to be called water, thank God, too shallow to recall those drowning dreams that sometimes drove him to insomnia. Under one foot something unknown squished, releasing a further burst of stink into the miasma. Above him he could see the hole he'd fallen through, but around him all was dark. Dark and deep, although if he stretched both feet down he could touch a solid base, but since this would have meant submerging his mouth, he continued to bob.

'Help!' He couldn't swim through it, it sucked at him like treacle. 'LINK!' And, oh my God, the smell. Like a thousand drains had waited for this moment. 'Link, if you're up there ...!'

'All right, all right.' Above the noise of the wind he heard Link's grumbling approach. 'Where are you? One minute you're there, then you'd sodded off.'

'I didn't "sod off". I fell.'

'Wow. Great echo you've got going.' Link's face became visible in the circle of sky above Phinn's head, with his hair whipped into a blond halo by the wind. 'Hey, man, I don't think you're in Kansas any more.'

'No. I'm in ... what *am* I in? A tank of some kind? God, don't tell me Uncle Peter built himself a nuclear bunker, that would be too weird.'

'Nah, mate, you're in the septic tank.' Link disappeared briefly. 'Yeah, top's cracked all off round here. All overgrown. The rain must have been getting in, keeping it all nice and moist for you ...' A sudden cackle and snort of laughter floated down. 'Don't think I've ever seen you so deep in the shit before.'

'Very funny.' Phinn raised an experimental hand. 'Can you pull me out?'

'Can, but not going to. Hang on while I get some rope or something.' And Link's voice grew distant. 'Don't go anywhere, will you?' More laughter, which Phinn thought was, quite frankly, in very bad taste.

By the time he'd been hauled panting onto the relatively clean grass bank by a near-hysterical Link, who'd stopped laughing and started wheezing so funny did he find it, Phinn had almost regained his own sense of humour. Only almost, because it was slowly dawning on him that he'd ruined his leather jacket and that nothing he was currently wearing would ever touch his skin again.

'Shit, man ...' Link started, and then tailed off again as he tried to force air into his lungs. 'You have got to clean up your act. You smell like ... like you fell into a shit pit.'

Phinn glumly contemplated the options. Lying in the river or lying in the bath both involved arctic-temperature water and he was already shivering, big blobs of unknown substances dropping from him with every shudder. Boiling a kettle took forever, and it was going to need more than a couple of kettles-full to wash this lot off. Something peeled away and fell from his hair. 'You could hose me down.'

Link shook his head. 'It is going to take more than that to get the smell off. Couple of bottles of Chanel Number Five in a bucket, I reckon.' He walked around Phinn, carefully not touching him. 'Oh, now that is disgusting.'

'Also cold.'

'You need about ten gallons of hot water and four bars of soap.'

'What you are describing there, Link, is a bath. Thank you for further drawing my attention to the fact that we don't have one.' Phinn's teeth had begun to chatter. 'All right, so I'm going to die smelling like a toilet brush. Fantastic. And I've had this jacket for fifteen years, it's practically vintage.'

'Man, you've had *all* your clothes for fifteen years. That's not vintage, that's lazy.' Link frowned and then suddenly grinned. 'Molly. Molly must have a shower or a bath or something. She smells terrific. Well, under the smell of horse she does. Let's go round there, I'm sure she won't mind.'

'Oh, no. No, Link, I can't. Not after last time. She must already think that I'm a complete weirdo. Turning up on her doorstep covered in ... ordure is not really the look I'm after this time round.'

But Link had vanished into the house. He reappeared moments later carrying a bath towel and a plastic bag. 'So, you're after staggering her with your charm next time, are you?'

Phinn looked down at himself. 'Well, I was, yes.'

'Does that mean that you've got a bit of a thing for Miss Blue-Eyes? Oh, come on man, you're not a saint! After Suze, yeah, I can understand you being a bit off women but you've got to get back in the saddle sometime. And Molly doesn't look the type to hurt for hurt's sake, does she?'

They were walking now. Phinn had lost the will to protest. 'I dunno, Link. When she came round earlier, it was weird, we were talking, then I said I had to get some clothes on and she just buggered off.'

'Hang on, back up man. You had to get dressed mid-conversation? What the hell kind of chat were you *having*?'

'I'd just got up. Fleecy PJs.'

'Oh.' Link seemed to relax a little. 'Right. So you went up to get dressed and she …?'

'She just went.'

'Right. She did know that you were only going to get dressed? You didn't do your "wandering off mid-sentence" thing again? 'Cos that always confuses the hell out of girls, you know, they don't like waiting half an hour for the follow-up.' Link looked as though he was going to nudge him conspiratorially, but then the smell got the better of him. 'Trust me, Bax. Immediate resolution, I've told you before.'

'Well …' Phinn stopped and thought. 'I suppose …'

Link gave a little snort of frustration. 'Jeez, man! Here I am giving you the benefit of my many years of experience with the fairer sex, emphasis on the "sex" there, and you're still doing the whole Sheldon Cooper thing. I despair of you, I really do.'

They walked on in silence for a bit. Luckily the village street was mostly deserted, although two women chatting outside the shop turned to watch them go by and a small terrier followed them the whole length of the village with its tail at a wary angle. Phinn knew he was leaving a trail of slime and lumps but he couldn't bring himself to care.

'Okay. In you go.' Link looked as if he was about to shove Phinn through the gate but pulled back at the last minute and made 'shooing' gestures with both hands. 'I'll be back later, much, much later. When you've had the chance to get Molly to scrub your back.'

'Shut up.' Phinn squelched a sad step forward. 'Or I'll drip on you.'

'Look on the plus side, you didn't lose your glasses. This is for your clothes.' Link passed the carrier bag at arm's length. 'And this is so you don't soil her no-doubt co-ordinated bathware.' Between fingertips he handed Phinn the towel. 'And for God's sake, strip before you go up the stairs or you'll make her whole house stink. Now go.'

Phinn went. He watched Link's back disappear back up the road towards the shop again, making sure that he'd properly gone before he tapped gently on the door. 'Molly, it's Phinn Baxter. Could I come in please?'

Although the wind had dropped since his immersion, what was left of it was cold enough to strip the flesh off a cooked turkey. Phinn felt himself shrinking inside his clothes, trying to keep the worst of it out by wrapping his arms around himself, pulling his sodden jacket closer. 'Molly?'

No answer. Phinn looked up at the cottage. Its weather-greyed woodwork and polished windows looked back. There was no sign of movement or life. Maybe she was upstairs. Or out in the tousled strip of garden at the back, which still had the old pigsty and wash house. Or perhaps she'd gone out for the day and he would stand here until he died of hypothermia or embarrassment.

'Molly?' He put a finger on the door handle and to his amazement the door swung inwards. Surely this meant she was inside somewhere, she wouldn't have gone off and left it unlocked, would she?

'Molly, it's Phinn, are you up there?' Conscious of the nature of his seeping ooze he laid the carrier bag on the hallway lino and stood on it. 'Oh, please be in.'

Still no answer and Phinn made an executive decision. She'd come to his rescue before, she was a nice woman, she wouldn't expect him to stand around like this. If she'd been here she would have invited him in, shown him to the bathroom and let him get on with the clean up, wouldn't she? So he'd take all that as read and sort himself out. He'd clean the bathroom and come back later to apologise for letting himself in … yes. It would be fine. Obviously.

He stripped off his outer clothes before even setting foot on the stairs. Boots, socks and jeans joined his jacket and shirt in a pile behind the front door and, wearing just his underpants, he headed up the stairs keeping one hand cupped under his chin to catch the wayward splashes from his hair. He found the bathroom after a false start that showed him Molly's bedroom was colour coordinated and mercifully lacking in cuddly toys, glad to note that the bathroom was carpeted in practical sisal with a softer mat over the top, which he carefully folded up and tucked behind the toilet. No shower, but a nice, deep roll-top bath which looked like an antique. Room painted nautical blue with seaside pictures dotted around, a single towel, flannel and toothbrush ornamenting the side of the scalloped sink and looking rather lonely, he thought to himself as he put the plug into the bath and began running water.

He didn't care if it was even hot. Lukewarm would have done. But there was a gush of steam and wonderful heat and as the bath began to fill he found a large bottle of sandalwood bath soak on top of the cabinet, tipped half of it into the bath, removed his underpants, which stuck painfully where they'd started to dry and solidify, and climbed into the water.

It felt fantastic against his skin. He'd not encountered hot water for nearly a fortnight, since he'd finally decided he had to run, to leave Bristol and the memories, the sadness and the university with its minor political struggles in which he was supposed to take an interest. Leaving the flat had been a wrench. He'd lived there for ten years, alone, then with an intermittent collection of girlfriends and then, finally, with Suze.

He closed his eyes and ducked his head under the scalding water to escape thinking about her, letting the bubbles prickle into his ears and his hair stream out behind him. All he could hear now was the clanging metallic noise of the tap running and the echoing sound of the water and the white-noise nature of it blocked out everything else. That was what he wanted. Everything to stop, but the background buzz of life; no more thoughts, imaginings or fears encroaching, zigzagging through his head like contrails made by particularly nasty aircraft.

He stuck his nose above the waterline but kept his head submerged. Yes. This was what he wanted. *Peace*.

I was slightly surprised to find a heap of disgusting old clothes dumped just inside my front door, but not completely put out. My washing had disappeared from the line in the earlier gales and I supposed that a neighbour had found these in the garden and thought that they must be the lost items. Although – I held up a slimy garment that looked as though it might once have been a coat but now, phew, smelled as though a pig might have worn it – why they imagined I'd wear these boggled my imagination.

I kicked them outside onto the step with the tip of my toe, and it was only then that I heard the sound of trickling coming from upstairs. 'Oh, not again!' I ran into the kitchen where only six weeks ago a burst pipe had flooded the entire room and ruined the contents of all my lower cupboards, but at least that was dry. So …

I tracked the sound. Definitely upstairs.

As I climbed, I wondered how a pipe could have burst when the temperatures had been above freezing for a whole week now. Dodgy plumbing? But Caro had had the whole place professionally redone, unless the man who'd fixed my last disaster hadn't sorted it properly. I was working up a nice case of ire against cowboy plumbers as I flung the bathroom door open and scanned for the source of the noise.

There was a nose in my bath and, at the other end, a pair

of feet poked above the waterline, otherwise the surface consisted only of an extreme amount of my best bath foam, smooth and unbroken like a snowscape.

Burglars? *Clean* burglars?

I dashed into my bedroom and fetched the doorstop. All right, it was a corduroy cat, but it was filled with sand and extremely heavy, plus it had a long tail, which acted as a draught excluder when the door was closed. I carried it by the tail to give myself a decent swing-arc, tiptoed back into the bathroom and stood behind the bath.

'Who the hell are you and why are you in my house?'

Then I dropped the half-empty bottle of bubble bath right on top of the supine figure. It lurched up out of the water like Venus rising from the sea, only with much worse language.

'Ow! Bloody hell, where did that come from!'

I swung the corduroy cat.

Of course, by now I'd realised who it was, but been too late to stop my instinctive reaction, so I was already plunging forward to stop the cat connecting with his head, as he reared up from the soap and grabbed my arms. Unbalanced I tipped forward, dropped the cat into the bath and fell after it on top of the naked, lathered and slightly smelly form of Phinn Baxter.

Who unexpectedly started to laugh.

It was the first time I'd heard him really laugh. He sat there with water streaming down, his hair plastered to his head and with the weight of me nearly forcing him back under the water and he laughed. Unselfconsciously, head back, laughing as though this was the funniest thing that had ever happened to him. After a moment, during which a lot of things crashed about in my head looking for pole position, I started to laugh too, although my laughter was a bit more suppressed because all my clothes were uncomfortable and my face was pressed into the side of the bath.

'I'm sorry,' he said eventually. 'It's just ... how the hell did I *think* this was going to end up? *Of course* you were always going to catch me in your bath – it's like some kind of weird script being played out. Don't you think?'

'Mmmmfff,' I said, my nose squashed against the enamel. I wriggled back a bit, down the length of his body and knelt up in the foam. 'So, why *are* you in my bath?'

While he told me the story of his falling in the septic tank – which explained the general indefinable but very much present smell – I clambered ungracefully off his naked body, out of the bath and into my dressing gown which was hanging on the back of the door.

'It's like a conspiracy of circumstance,' he said at last, sitting up with his knees protruding from the foam like a couple of clam shells. 'I am *this* close to starting to believe in destiny. And being as I am still struggling to believe in string theory, that is pretty amazing.'

I squeezed my hair. It had flopped from its usual take-flight-in-panic style and was lying down to my shoulders. 'Well, anyway.' I just wanted to get out of that bathroom before he stood up. 'I'd better get changed.'

Phinn looked me up and down. Dark, dark eyes. I shivered – not sure how I could explain that, the bathroom was full of steam. 'I don't suppose ...' he started.

'Mmmm?' My voice had gone a bit squeaky. I wasn't sure what he was about to suggest, but even more scarily, I wasn't sure how I was going to react.

'... you've got any clothes I could borrow, have you? I kind of expected Link to come over with a change of gear for me, but he's probably hiding round the back to give me maximum chance for humiliating myself.'

'Oh.' I looked at him sitting there, long dark hair plastered to his head, rivulets of water beading their way down his chest and getting caught in the small strip of hair that ran down the centre. Then I found my eyes travelling to that area of foam that was covering his groin and wondering how much of that mound of bubbles was actually bubble. 'Er. I'm sure I've got something.' My cheeks flamed scarlet like a good sunset and to cover the fact, I fled from the bathroom.

We were sitting downstairs drinking tea when Link finally turned up to reclaim his friend. He stood on my doorstep, shifting from foot to foot like a schoolboy.

'Is Bax still there?' He was staring at the pile of festering clothes that were draped over my bootscraper. 'Can he come out to play?'

'Oh, just come in.' I held the door wide and Link came past me with a leer and a small wink.

'Got him out of the bath, have you?'

'No, he did that all by himself.' I indicated the table where Phinn was sitting, hands cupped around a mug, staring into the steam. It was, pretty much, all he'd done since he came downstairs. 'Being an adult, and everything.'

Now Phinn looked up. '*Please* tell me you brought some clothes over for me.' He hunched further forwards. 'Either that or a shovel, so we can bury what's left of my dignity.'

'Oh, man.' Link started to smirk. 'No, no, suits you. Lovely. That lilac is really *you*.'

'It's all I had that would fit,' I said. 'I'm not exactly Topman, am I?' Then I turned to Phinn. 'You only need something to get you down to the other end of the village, you'll be fine.'

Actually, the pale lavender *did* suit Phinn with his dark colouring. He'd tied his wet hair back away from his face and the floppy collar of the jacket made his cheekbones more prominent. Unfortunately the legs of the trousers stopped short of his ankles by a couple of inches and the expanse of bony shin that they revealed, tapering as it did into a pair of moccasin slippers, gave him a 'dressed by mother' look.

'No, I'm sorry. I'm grateful, Molly, of course I am. It's either this or walk down wearing a dressing gown.' He and I exchanged a look. It had been my first option for clothing for him, only when he'd put it on the nylon fabric had proved to be rather skimpy in the crotch region and we'd both, silently and individually, agreed that it wasn't suitable. Hence the lilac trouser suit which I'd bought at a car boot sale for some reason, which now escaped me totally, it being three sizes too large and a colour I would only wear at knifepoint.

Phinn stood up. The trousers sagged, despite the safety pin keeping the waist in, his hips being insufficiently female to keep them up, but disaster was averted by Phinn clamping his hands to his sides to hold them through the pockets of the jacket.

'We off then, mate?' Link tried to keep a straight face. 'I hear it's tranny night in Pickering.'

'It's not busy out there, is it?' Phinn looked anxiously at the window. 'There's not, like, I dunno, a tourist bus just pulled into the village or something?'

'You'll be fine.' I straightened his collar and he gave me a weak smile. 'People round here are very forgiving.'

'And at least you smell better.' Link walked around him sniffing appreciatively. 'Crabtree and Evelyn, if my radar doesn't deceive.'

Phinn turned. 'Thank you, Molly. You've saved my life.'

For one second he was standing very close to me, I could feel the drips from his still-wet hair against my cheek. My eyes were level with the dark swirl of hair that began before the buttons of the jacket and disappeared down onto the torso that the jacket concealed and I had a sudden vision of that chest naked and with water trickling down it.

I stepped back. 'It's all right,' I said. 'I wasn't even here for most of the life-saving part.'

Our eyes met and I was horrified to see his eyebrows lift. It was as if he'd seen my sudden, unreasonable lust and found it amusing. 'I promise not to break in again.' His voice was softer now.

Link cleared his throat. 'What about offering to take this young lady out for a meal tonight, to say thank you properly?' He grinned at me directly and I was glad to switch my attention from that dark gaze. 'I mean, he could offer to cook for you but really? Unless you've got a thing for tinned soup, I'd go with the eating out option.'

'There ... there's the pub,' I found myself stammering. 'They do food. Nice food, not just sandwiches and things.'

'They do *sandwiches*?' Link slapped his forehead. 'Jeez. Enough with the tinned stew stuff already, Bax, mate. Right. You and him, seven o'clock, pub. Okay?'

'Are you sure?' I asked Phinn directly. 'It's very nice, but unnecessary, honestly.'

Phinn and Link exchanged the look this time. Link grinned while Phinn had a slightly shell-shocked expression. Finally he said, 'Yes. Yes, you're right. Dinner. I'll meet you there.'

I watched them walk back towards Howe End. Phinn's trousers flapped in the stiff breeze like a couple of mourning flags, his hands still clamped tightly to his sides so it looked a bit as though a shop window dummy was making its way down the street. Link was clearly talking earnestly, I could see him leaning in now and again to make a point, while Phinn just stalked along, probably desperate to get indoors again before anyone saw him.

And I wondered to myself – how the hell could I fancy a man wearing a mauve ladies' trouser suit. Because, despite myself, I did.

Chapter Ten

Phinn sat behind the table in front of his third Coke and felt the hot, tight sensation of embarrassment close itself around him.

Molly had stood him up. All right, he could live with that. After all it wasn't as if he'd even asked her out himself, she might have said yes just to get Link to shut up and leave them both alone – yep, he knew exactly how *that* went. No, it wasn't the humiliation of having his third party arranged date not turn up, so much the fact that it seemed that the entire pub knew that he was supposed to be meeting Molly and were giving him little matey grins and encouraging smiles every time the door opened and didn't reveal Molly standing there.

'You want another in there?' The barman nodded towards the nearly-empty glass. 'Or are you going on to the hard stuff?'

'No, it's okay. I'll just finish this …' Phinn looked at his watch, unnecessarily because there was a huge clock behind the bar but he wanted to look as though he was an active participant in his own downfall. 'Then I'll get on back.' *Besides, the hard stuff hasn't solved any problems yet.*

'Ah, you can give her another ten minutes. Moll's usually pretty prompt. There must be something keeping her for her to be this late.' The barman polished a glass, seemingly unaware of the discomfort his apparently even knowing the time that they were supposed to meet was causing Phinn.

'Probably one of them horses,' said an old man, raising his pint. 'She's a devil for mucking around with those things.'

There was a general chorus of 'thass reet' and Phinn sunk

his head lower towards his chest in an attempt to become invisible. It wouldn't have been so bad, he thought, if he could have lost himself in alcohol. Blurred the edges a bit, taken the razor blade of awkwardness which he could feel scraping along his nerve-endings and blunted it down to an ignorable ache. He glanced up at the display of bottles behind the barman's shoulder, let his eyes travel over them looking for a favourite; something, anything that would let him slide back into the haze that had sustained him for the past few months.

His fingers tightened around the glass in his hand and the thick brown liquid within it slopped in protest. *No. Come on, Baxter, it's not the answer, you know that. It just makes the question look more interesting.* He took another mouthful of fizz and swallowed it quickly, feeling the last lonely ice cube bump against his teeth. He'd finish this and then he'd go. Perhaps he could pretend that he'd misunderstood the date, that they were supposed to be meeting *tomorrow* night ...

But the cheer that went up when the door swung back to show Molly, a flustered vision in a red dress, stopped that thought dead.

'We thought you wasn't coming!' The barman put a wine glass on the bar and filled it without consultation. 'Your young man theer, he's been proper bothered, you're a bad lass to keep him waiting. Horses, was it?'

'Mmmm.' Molly stepped down into the bar and Phinn could see that she was wearing heels that made her legs look fantastic. Heels, sheer black – oh Lord, were those stockings? – on her legs and a short red dress that showed off her neat figure to perfection. His libido gave a little moan.

When she picked up her glass and came over to the corner where he was sitting, he got a puff of some musky perfume which made him wish that his stomach wasn't so full of coke bubbles. 'Sorry, Phinn. Caro had a breakout. Stan is such a little sod, he managed to unbolt his door and then went round the yard letting the others out. We've been hoiking them out of the hay barn all afternoon and then I had to have a shower and get changed and ... are you all right?'

Phinn's inner cynic, the one that had spent the last year telling him that all women were only after him for one thing and that he'd better figure out what that thing was before he ever touched another one with anything other than a laser-pointer, was struck dumb. 'You look ... legs,' he muttered.

'Not seen you in a frock before, lass,' commented one of the older men. 'Thought you was just having a quick meal, like, and here's you done up like Frank's donkey! Very nice, though.'

'Thank you, Dave.' Molly turned to give the whole pub the full value of the outfit, and curtsied. 'It makes a nice change.' Then she muttered over her shoulder to Phinn, 'For God's sake let's go through to the restaurant, before they start doing my colours.'

She turned back to him and Phinn got another whiff of that smoky scent she was wearing, knocked his glass with his elbow and managed to splatter himself with the remainder of his Coke. He struggled to his feet amid much inner cursing, aware that his decent white shirt now looked as though he'd been sick down himself and followed Molly's rapid steps out of the bar and into a much quieter back room, where a few tables were laid up for dinner.

'Wherever you like, we're not busy.' The barman, now with a cloth over one arm, clearly doubling up as tonight's waiter, waved an arm. 'Over by the window's favourite, not such a draught, and you can't smell the bog house.'

'Thanks.' She slid into her seat, leaving Phinn standing

awkwardly, not sure whether he should have pulled out her chair for her, and whether now was too late. 'Are you sure you're all right, Phinn? You do look quite peculiar. But really, really good. Well, better than you did this morning, anyway.'

He finally felt the tension break as she grinned widely at him and pumped her eyebrows up and down. Just a meal to say thank you. That's all this was. He looked down at his white shirt and black jeans. 'I thought violet might be a bit much for tonight. But I'll let you have it back tomorrow, if you're desperate.'

'No, no, keep it. Actually, no, burn it.' Molly settled herself in her seat and consulted the menu. 'And then bury the ashes.'

They ordered their food and Phinn felt, with something like relief, the creeping return of normality between them. It was lust he'd felt, seeing her there in her tight dress and lovely long legs. That was all. Lust. Hormones. *Look but don't touch, Bax. Like a nice painting, good to look at but it's only pheromones, only biology making your tongue hang out and your cock twitch.*

'I shouldn't be out late tonight, I've got to make a start on reading about the local folklore tomorrow for this article,' she said, her matter-of-fact tone reinforcing the return of his clear head.

'Article?'

And then she was explaining about her column and her editor, Mike, and Phinn felt a faint idea beginning to crystallize around the back of his brain.

'I don't suppose … I know this is a long shot but is there any chance that he might want a column on stars?'

'Stars?' Molly looked taken aback. 'What, like celebrity interviews?'

Phinn sighed. 'Black hole singularities rarely get drunk and fall out of bars.'

The first course arrived, set on the table by a grinning barman, who'd slipped a black coat on over his shirtsleeves and seemed to be attempting to turn into a waiter by degrees.

Molly sipped at her soup. 'I'm not sure. He might, I suppose. Actually, yes, Mike's a bit of a frustrated scientist, he keeps trying to get me to do things about local geology, and I can just about tell a lump of chalk from – actually, the chalk had better be the only thing on the table or I'm lost. Even chalk might be pushing it, science was never my thing at school. And to think Mum spent all those hours trying to get me to learn the periodic table.' She concentrated on her soup very hard for a moment. 'Why did you become an astrophysicist, Phinn?'

Ow. Phinn felt the impact of the personal question in the centre of his chest and buttered a piece of toast to cover his uncertainty. 'I ... my parents ... it all seemed like a good idea at the time.' He layered pâté and a gherkin with immaculate precision on top of the toast but found that his appetite had largely gone. *I could tell her about my mother's expression when I was five and told her I wanted to be a fireman ...*

'You must be really intelligent.' He could see her eyes through the soup steam, blue and innocent, making a simple observation with no intent to flatter him. And suddenly he hated himself yet again.

'Yeah, I'm clever.' He knew his voice sounded bitter and welcomed it. 'A levels at twelve, degree at fourteen. I'm the youngest PhD in Astrophysics that my university ever turned out. And, do you know something, Molly?' He leaned forward across the table, surprised when she leaned too, bringing their heads almost into contact. 'The whole thing is a crock of shit. Being clever, what does it get you? No kind of life at all.'

He waited for her condemnation or her anger. But instead

●

all he got was a sigh. 'Yes. Sometimes it does seem that being pretty and blonde and giggling a lot is the secret road to happiness, doesn't it?' Through that leek-and-potato scented steam, blue eyes met his and it seemed to him that they held an iota of understanding.

'Conforming. Yes.'

'So we are clearly doomed, you and me. Pass the salt please. Barry is one hell of a cook but he can't condiment to save his life – now, what were you saying about asking Mike if you can write an article?'

Phinn slid the salt cellar across the table to give his mind time to unwind this triple-conversational loop. 'Er.' It was no good, every time he tried to let the cynicism out she just cut right through him and caged it away again. 'I just wondered. Cash is a bit tight at the moment.'

'Oh, don't worry, we'll go Dutch.'

'That's not what I meant.' He found he was still leaning in, as though trying to compensate for the rollercoaster twists that the conversation was taking. 'I've taken a year off to write a book, y'see. I've written stuff before and I've done a bit of popular astronomy with some of my students, that's kind of where I'm aiming. Writing something for your magazine, if he'd have me ... it might be good practice.'

'I don't know. Mike tends to hire freelancers who've got a track record. It's not really an amateur kind of production.'

'No, I understand that.' Phinn bit his toast and shrapnel flew from his mouth to land in dusty fall out all over the tabletop. 'I'm not exactly an amateur. I've published papers, research documents, some articles in *New Scientist*. If it helps, you can send your editor a YouTube link of me doing a talk last year; some of my students filmed it.' He gave a kind of modesty-cough. 'Went a bit viral, actually. Well, among what I'm aware is a fairly limited and, now I come to think of it, not all that impressive bunch of dark matter theory undergraduates, anyway. They seem to think it's rather good, it might just convince him that I'm worth taking a chance on.'

And you could take a look at it, see me doing what I do best. Maybe wipe out the impression that you always seem to be getting of me as a complete idiot, and usually a naked idiot at that.

Molly paused with her soup spoon halfway to her lips. 'It's not fantastic money,' she said warily. 'You'd be better paid if you went house to house selling dishcloths.'

'But I'm not qualified to sell dishcloths. I am qualified to write about the sky and stars and plasma fields and brane theories. Which, I realise, might be pushing things for readers of a magazine about walking, but ... do you think he'd give me a shot?'

Phinn realised he was actually being serious about this. If he sold some articles, it might mean that the book he was rather afraid he was going to have to actually write now could be based around them. That he wouldn't have to write a bloody physics handbook for future generations of people like him, he could write something lighter. Maybe even *entertaining*?

'I can ask,' Molly said. 'One of his writers has broken his leg, hence me being promoted up from writing about footpaths and badgers, so he might go for it.' She stopped spooning soup and looked at him, twisting her mouth slightly. 'You're always very serious, Phinn, aren't you?'

No, he wanted to shout. *No! This isn't me! The man you're seeing, the man you're talking to, he's not the real Phinn Baxter, he's an imposter wearing my face. A man who's had all the joy and fun knocked out of him, beaten down by lies and loss. In here somewhere is the real me, can you see me waving?*

Instead he just shrugged.

'Depression isn't something to be ashamed of, you know.' She had her head down, sipping soup again, delivering the statement as unweighted as water. 'It's perfectly okay not to be able to cope with stuff every now and again.' Now she looked up. Met his eye. And he knew, just *knew*, that she had seen a glimmer of the real man underneath the heavy grey shroud he wore, that she could see the shadow behind his eyes that was his old self jumping up and down to try and get her attention. The *him* he'd once been, the man who sometimes managed to rise to the surface and escape for a moment; a laugh, a sentence.

'Your wife must have hurt you very badly.' Molly went on and for one flicker of a second Phinn thought he'd spoken his inner thoughts aloud. Maybe it was time to tell her.

'Molly ...'

But she was standing up now, looking over his shoulder out into the night. 'Phinn,' she said, her voice tight and odd. 'The lights are back. They just went right over the village.'

The weird atmosphere that had enveloped us almost from the time I'd walked into the pub was gone in a second. Phinn was on his feet too, swivelling to look out of the dark window into the night that stretched over the dale. 'Are you sure?'

'Yes.' I fumbled in my bag, dropped a twenty pound note on the table and grabbed my jacket from the back of my chair. 'Come on.'

Phinn looked down. 'Isn't that rather a lot? We only had starters ...'

'I'll pick up the change tomorrow! Come on!'

And almost before I realised it we were running, out of the pub and across the road, defying the honked horns of two cars, weaving our way out into the night. Above our heads the lights swung and flickered, almost as though they were leading us on.

'They're following the river.' I stopped to take off my shoes, the heels made it impossible to run fast enough. 'If we head up this trackway we'll come out onto the old railway line and be able to follow them along that.'

He gave me a quick look but didn't speak, just came along behind me as I led the way between two of the oldest houses in the village, squelching in mud that was a welcome change from the hard tarmac of the road, and burst out onto open moorland. Still above us the lights seemed celebratory, dancing a kaleidoscopic pattern in the sky.

We raced over peat soft as melting butter, running, running, trying to keep the lights in sight. I was sweating under my jacket, feeling my hair sticking to my forehead even as my feet froze on a ground frosted into rucks and puckers. The lights drifted, seemingly wind-blown, tracing the line of the distant river, glowing like burning metal against the velvet night. And then, suddenly, they stopped. Hung as though nailed to the sky.

'Phinn, what *are* they?'

'No idea.' He leaned forward, hands on thighs, trying to catch his breath. 'I'm going through everything I can think of, but nothing fits.' He straightened again and looked at me. The faint moonlight made him look sculpted, it highlighted his bones, shaded the hollows and flattened any emotion out of his face. 'Are you frightened?'

'I don't know.' And I didn't. There was a curious elation which came with the lights, a pounding of pulse and a quickening of blood, but also a feeling of standing on the edge of something. Something which might tip me over at any moment. *Into what, though?*

'Yeah. Weird. That's the feeling I had when I tried to catch them, half terrified and half not.'

'The other day, when you ...'

'... tore off all my clothes and begged to be abducted, yes.' He took half a step forward and, as though triggered by his movement the lights took off again and, with one final swoop like a cheery farewell, dropped down beyond the horizon and were gone, leaving the skies empty except for the distant chilly stars.

'Chinese lanterns?' I tried.

'You think?' He tipped his head back and stared directly upwards. 'Yeah, maybe. Party lanterns that make us feel they're putting on a show just for us. You get that? That feeling that this is all somehow because we're watching?'

My feet hurt and had gone through my tights, leaving me barelegged up to mid calf and the remnants tattering around my knees like frill-edged bloomers. 'I don't know. You're the expert on this aren't you? UFOs?'

'Not expert.' He stopped looking at the sky but, oddly, when he looked at me I could still see stars reflected in his eyes. 'I talk to some groups, take an interest, that's all. It's amazing how much UAPs intersect with my theories of plasma fields – missing time, electrics cutting out, people falling unconscious – all reported side effects of close encounters with UAPs and, coincidentally or not, of contact with massive magnetic forces.'

'I'll bet Stephen Hawking is keeping an eye on you.'

Phinn gave me a quirked-mouth smile. 'He reads over my research, yes.'

'Are you showing off?'

A broader smile now. 'Maybe.'

'All right, clever clogs. What do we do now? Do we file official reports or something? And then sit back and wait for the "Men In Black" to come round?'

Phinn looked back up at the sky. 'It's freezing. I think we go home. Where are your shoes?'

'I'm all right,' I lied. The adrenaline that had resulted from our mad dash up the hill was gone, leaving me chilled and flat and rather in awe of Phinn's self-possession and capability.

He moved closer. 'Are you sure? You look a bit shaky.'

I just shook my head. Tears were pressing behind my eyes, reaction or shock or plain ordinary cold, I didn't know. I did know, however, that I didn't want to cry in front of him. I kept my face immobile in the hope that I could freeze the tears in place.

'All right. Come on then.' He held out a hand, frowning when I hesitated. 'I'm only going to help you walk down, not propose.'

'I can manage,' I said stiffly.

Then Phinn surprised me. 'He must have hurt you very badly,' he said softly, echoing my words to him, was it really only a few minutes ago? 'Oh, don't worry, I'm not going to pry, Molly, but I know there has to be something behind the way you've buried yourself here. I read some of your articles, did you know? Well, I'd hardly offer to write for a magazine I'd never even looked at, would I, and you are *good*, Molly Gilchrist, I can tell that much. But that house, all those things that aren't yours ... you don't look like a woman who'd have seahorse pictures on the bathroom wall. Severed fingers maybe, but not those cutesy little show home prints.'

My arms went rigid down by my sides. 'Bloody hell, I thought you were an astrophysicist not a PI. Have you been going through my things? When you broke in this morning, did you have a quick rummage through my knicker drawer too?'

'I just thought I'd mention it.' Phinn's voice was still soft, but relentless. 'Maybe ... maybe it's something to do with why we can see the lights when Link can't. Perhaps no one else can see them either, maybe it's just us. Did you think of that?'

My throat felt as though it had swallowed a house. 'Yes,' I said, and my voice sounded distorted, spacey.

'Yes?' The breeze moved Phinn's hair, swept it aside like a lover to expose his throat. I couldn't take my eyes away. The cold gnawed my bones but I was only aware of that in a hollow, plastic sort of way.

'That it might be something to do with us. A deserted husband too many drinks in and depressed to the bone ... and a runaway fiancée who can't look her family in the face again. Would that make some alien race come looking for us, Phinn? What the hell are they, from the planet Jeremy Kyle?'

Slowly Phinn took his glasses off. He stared at them, dangling from his fingers, for a second, then polished them on the part of his shirt that didn't have stains down it.

'This has, I think you'll agree, been a completely rubbish evening, hasn't it?' he said, at pretty much the same moment that I realised that my tears had escaped from their stasis and were scalding their way down my cheeks. 'Let's not do it again some time.' Then he held out his hand again. 'Come on. Let us, as Link would say, get the hell outta here.'

This time I took the offered hand. 'I am not pathetic,' I said. Or rather, I sobbed it, sounding about as pathetic as possible without being a kitten in the snow. With an injured paw.

'At this moment, Molly, I think we are both pretty pathetic. C'mon, I'll take you home.' He pulled me forwards for a few strides and then stopped. 'Actually, I have no idea where we are, so you might need to take us home. But I'll help.'

So with me leading the way, sobbing and occasionally snorting and with Phinn holding my hand like a blind man holding the harness of his guide dog, we made our way down off the moor, intercepting my posh shoes at the top of the lane as we went.

'This will be all round the village in the morning.' I gave a half-hysterical laugh. 'The lads in the pub will have it that I was blind drunk and got shagged by some incomer and had to be carried home.'

'Better to be talked about than not talked about,' Phinn said, with a flash of a smile. 'Next thing you know you'll be notorious.' He stopped to let me slip my shoes back on. 'But I don't think you want people to talk about you, do you?'

'If you invent invisibility in your next round of quantum-whatever, then please let me try it out first,' I muttered as we processed down the street, my shoes clopping and sliding on my bare and muddy feet and the remnants of my tights fluttering behind me like leg shadows.

'And yet you let *me* walk around in that horrible trouser suit.' We reached my front door and stopped. I was very aware of his hand still holding mine, of his fingers cupped into my palm. 'Molly ...'

'Thankyouforalovelyeveningmustdashgoodnight,' I blurted out, dropping his hand as if it was made of dog pooh and hurling myself at the door, both shoes slipping from my feet as I went. I landed headlong, barefoot and shivering uncontrollably, shoved the door closed with a trailing leg and lay still on the chilly lino, letting the quiet familiarity of the little cottage wash over me.

Phinn sat for a while in the weedy front garden with her discarded shoes on his lap. Part of him wanted to knock on the door or call through the letterbox, just to let her know she wasn't alone but he didn't think she'd want that. Didn't think, more to the point, that she'd want *him*.

God knew, he didn't even want himself much right now. He glanced down at her pretty red shoes sitting so pertly on his knee and imagined her putting them on earlier that evening. Getting dressed up for a meal out. And now she was the other side of the door, probably, if his own feelings were anything to go by, wondering what the hell had just happened while he sat, only a couple of inches of plywood away from her. Hell, he could probably kick the door in if he put his mind to it. Kick it in and … what? Have the two of them stare at one another, share a couple of embarrassed grins, make his apologies and go? Leaving a flapping front door and not much dignity on either hand?

Oh, sod it. Why does everything have to be so complicated? I like her. She's … yes, cute. Smart. Kind. Nothing like … yeah, nothing like Suze. But. Oh yeah, so many buts.

Suze had bewitched him with her pretty face, her broad ready smile. He'd thought they could make it, hadn't realised that she didn't want to make it, or at least, not with him. That she'd married him for an upwardly mobile lifestyle he had no intention of getting; his mind was the key to dimensions, to M-theory, not to owning a Lamborghini and living in Monaco. Hell, he didn't even *have* a car and had only a notional idea of where Monaco was.

Phinn sighed. It wasn't as if he and Molly were … what was it? She was just someone who had come to his rescue a few times. No obligation. And tonight, the strange atmosphere out there on the moorland after they'd chased the lights, that would be down to the sheer oddness of the situation, the uncertainty of what they were seeing.

The lights. Ah, that's better. Something solid to worry about. Never mind all this angst and high emotion, what about those crazy, semi-invisible lights?

Feeling a little more secure now that he had something

concrete to concern himself with, Phinn stood up, juggling the high heels from hand to hand. Maybe he should leave them on the step? Only, they looked expensive, if it rained they'd be ruined, and the way things were going he'd probably get the blame for that. Only other thing to do was to take them home with him, like a fetishistic Prince Charming, and bring them back tomorrow. Or possibly the next day. Anyway, he'd bring them back as soon as he could be sure of being received without his and Molly's joint humiliation causing some kind of rift in the space-time continuum.

He wondered about saying something, telling her he was off, but then it would mean her finding out that he'd been hanging around outside all this time. Would she think it was gentlemanly or would she, as he thought more probably, think that it was creepy and possibly even stalkerish behaviour?

He was hovering with his hand on the gate when he saw Link bouncing towards him on the balls of his feet, like a man who is very pleased with himself.

'Man, I was coming to look for you,' Link announced in a stage whisper. 'Not *too* hard though, don't worry. I was prepared for you to be doing the earth-moving thing, in which case I was just going to walk on by.' And then he saw the shoes, Phinn's general air of dishevelment and the fact that the front door was closed. 'Oh, what? Why have you got those? Going for the full outfit, are you? Only red with lilac won't work, not even with your colouring.'

Phinn opened his mouth to tell Link about his evening, and then realised that there wasn't one part of it that didn't sound completely off-the-planet weird. Escaped horses, semi-invisible lights in the sky, bare feet, weird atmospheres – it all sounded like the kind of oddness that would make Dali want to go for a long rest. 'I don't suppose you'd consider letting me get totally wasted tonight, would you?'

Link pulled a face and shook his head. 'Can do you a cup of tea though.'

'Oh, all right.' Phinn looked over his shoulder at the firmly closed door. 'Best offer I'm going to get.'

And ignoring Link's raised eyebrows, he climbed over the garden gate and led the way back to Howe End.

Chapter Eleven

The phone woke me up and I answered it without thinking, without checking. 'Hello?'

'I think we need to talk, Molly.' *My mother.* 'There are ... it's important.'

'I don't have anything to say to you.'

'Then maybe you could listen. I've had some news from—'

I slammed the phone down so fast that the handset bounced back out of its cradle and fell onto the floor, where I left it, kneeling myself over to the far side of the bed as though it was a cobra, interrupted mid-strike. My heart was in my throat, swept there on a tide of nausea and bile, but prevented from escaping by my gritted teeth.

'You think I want to talk to you?' I screamed, so loudly that the words cracked. 'You think I ever want to talk to you again?' And then, embarrassingly, I fetched the phone from the floor and beat it with my slipper until the buttons made a strange buzzing sound and the battery fell out. It didn't really help, but it made me feel a bit more proactive about the situation. Then, breathless, I sat back.

Why did she ring? To apologise? To explain? But those aren't things I would ever associate with her, the woman who blithely rattles through life as though performing a series of complicated manoeuvres simultaneously is her natural state of being. Unless ... No. That part of my life is done and over. She can't hurt me any more, can't fail to be there for me any more, can't make me feel like a disappointment any more. She denied me the childhood I wanted and took away from me the life I should have had. Now all I can do to protect myself is stay well away from her.

York. I'd go into York for the day. The city environment would be the perfect antidote to the claustrophobic angst that my life seemed to have fallen into, it would get me away from the phone if it rang again, I could do some shopping and maybe look for a proper job, hell, even shelf-stacking in one of the big supermarkets would pay more than I was bringing in with my articles.

Friendship was all very well but life was expensive; I couldn't expect Caro to keep subsidising my misery and besides, maybe it was time to move my life forward rather than let it keep circling the emotional drain.

And York would be busy. There would be people on the streets. I could lose myself in the crowds and pretend that none of this had ever happened – maybe get to the library and hunt down some local history books, research some folklore … yes. Throw myself into real life and forget that I'd ever seen those lights. *Or taken that phone call.*

My car had been relegated to one of Caro's old hay barns by lack of use and had been subjected to a slight attack of horse during yesterday's mass breakout. One of the wiper blades was askew and there was a small dent in the bonnet where a pony had jumped clear over it to avoid capture but, bless its little Japanese heart, it started first time.

Thankfully Caro was out schooling her mare and, while she raised a hand in greeting as she cantered around an ever decreasing circle, she didn't stop to ask how my date went – perhaps my obviously being alone and lacking radiant vibes prevented her. Perhaps she still felt guilty for making me late. It wasn't just my car that still bore the traces of the escaped herd; Stan had been put out to graze as far from the others as possible, in the equine world's equivalent of a Gulag camp, with only a bad-tempered Shetland for company.

I got into the car, removed the clutch of eggs from the

back seat, cleared the windows and prepared to drive off, only to be brought up short by an incredible rattling sound from somewhere underneath. I got out, peered dubiously into the strawy depths under the car, couldn't see anything. Pulled forward a few inches and the rattling started again.

I got out again and tentatively poked at the exhaust pipe which bore traces of having been barged against at some point by swinging freely from side to side. I couldn't fix it and I couldn't drive to York in a car which sounded as though its insides were making a bid for becoming one with the road. Could I? I got in again and revved the engine, which made smoke billow out from somewhere mysterious, then pulled forward a few more inches.

If I drove carefully, keeping my foot away from the accelerator, the noise wasn't too bad, and the smoke wasn't too noticeable. I made an executive decision – York might be too far away, but Pickering wasn't. Ten miles, only one major hill. It was either that or start digging a tunnel to freedom. I'd fix the car when I got back. Caro would have wire somewhere.

I drove very, very carefully into town. No one turned to look as I passed by, at least as long as I kept the speed under thirty-five miles an hour, and I parked, pulled myself together and headed for the library.

I sat in a comfortable chair with a pile of books on local history, my notepad and a pen. Wrote nothing. Didn't even open a book. Just sat, chin in hand, my blood pressure singing up and down the scale as I tried to work out what the hell I was going to do. That phone call from my mother had rattled me more than I'd admit to myself. A reminder of a past life where money and excitement had ruled; posh cars, designer dresses, dinners at restaurants with names in the paper. A life that was never coming back, a life I never *wanted* back. So, what *did* I want?

Bugger.

I gave my head a little shake, which probably looked odd to the other library patrons. Why should I give up everything I'd worked for? Why should *I* change *my* life, just because ...

Screaming, accusations. A double betrayal, by the two people who should have cared most about me, bringing everything I'd ever thought to the fore. I wasn't worth loving, and they'd proved it. However much I tried, however much I threw myself into life and hoped a man would catch me, in the end I'd always just been on the outside of everything ...

All these thoughts ran through my head while I stared blankly into the middle distance and tapped my pen against my notebook. I was facing towards the half-dozen computers that the library made available for customers, not really registering the comings and goings of the handful of people using them until I became aware that the back of one head was vaguely familiar. It wasn't so much the head itself, more the way it kept tipping back, hair hanging over the back of the chair that was recognisable. I'd seen it only the other day, on my own couch.

'Phinn?' The distraction of the realisation that he was here was so welcome that I almost yelled his name across the book-filled silence.

He spun the chair around so suddenly that he hit both knees on the desk and the monitor rocked alarmingly. 'Molly? What are you doing here?'

'Getting out of Riverdale. Research. Stuff. You?'

'Yes. Although I suspect my "stuff" is somewhat different to yours, unless your eyesight is worse than it appears.' He took his glasses off and blinked those big, black eyes at me. 'Optician. Apparently these are still doing fine.'

'Why would you ... oh.' Only now did I look at his

computer screen, where he'd got the results of a Google search for 'optical illusions night sky'. 'But I saw them too! How could *I* see *your* optical illusions?'

'Well.' He turned back to the screen, typed a few more words and another search result popped up and I read 'Telepathic transmission of crisis images'.

'There's the possibility that we were involved in a hallucinogenic incident where I somehow "sent" you a vision of what I was seeing.'

'Bollocks.'

He nodded slowly. 'Yes, I'd pretty well come to the bollocks conclusion myself.' He pushed the chair back and it wheeled a few squeaky inches away from the table, letting him stretch his legs out. 'But scientific methods, you know.'

'Eliminate the impossible and whatever's left is the answer?'

The glasses went back on. 'Mangling Sherlock Holmes is not scientific methodology, Molly. And everything about ... about what we saw is pretty impossible. Eliminating it isn't leaving me with much.'

A librarian came over. She was young and blonde and pretty and she propped herself between the computer and Phinn in a way that gave her bust maximum exposure. 'Doctor Baxter? Your half-hour is up but we're not busy. I can let you have another half-hour if you'd like.'

Phinn looked from me to her and back again, as if trying to work out how two members of the same species could be so different. 'Hold on a second. Molly, would you like to come and have a coffee?'

I glanced behind me at the unopened books, at my unmarked notepad and unused pen. 'Yes, please.'

'Right. In that case, no thank you. I'll leave the computer for someone else.'

The librarian's face dropped, she shrugged and took

her boobs somewhere else, but for one second I saw Phinn as she must have; tall, dark and with that attractive air that comes when men don't have the faintest idea of how attractive they are. He'd got another leather jacket on today, obviously the septic tank one had been binned, and this one was more biker than SS officer. His jeans were probably the same ones he'd worn last night but he'd got a plain black T-shirt over the top and the 'all in black' look suited him.

'What? Why are you looking at me?' He looked down, checking his fly probably.

'I don't know. You just look different.'

'Probably because I'm not naked, drunk or falling over anything.' He gave me a half-smile and something inside my stomach revolted. 'Let's find that coffee.'

We sat in a steamy little café at the top of the marketplace and blew foam off our cups. Phinn had gone quiet again. He seemed to have the ability to just sit, not speaking, seemingly absorbed in his thoughts as though nothing going on around him could touch him. It was an ability I envied, I thought as I sipped my coffee. I would have loved to have been able to take no notice of my surroundings.

'So, then.' He dunked a small almond biscuit that had come with the coffee.

I took a sip. It felt odd being here rather than being in Riverdale. Somehow Riverdale was like being in a bubble, enclosed by people I knew, even if only by sight, while this was more like Real Life. Having Phinn in it with me gave me a shivery feeling that I couldn't place. 'Mmmm?'

'How many times have you seen them? The lights I mean.' Steam rose from his coffee and for a moment his eyes were obscured. 'Not that there's much else I could be talking about, all our conversations seem to revolve around those bloody things.'

'Two … no, three times. Last night with you, the night

before and … just before I found you up on the moors. Yes, three.'

'Never before?'

I shook my head. Looking at the night sky had hardly been a priority but, even so …

'Odd. I've only seen them three times too.'

'Well, you've not been in Riverdale long, have you?'

He shrugged. 'Not this time, no. But over the years I've spent a long time in the village, what with one thing and another.' He drummed his fingers lightly on the tabletop as though trying to decide something. 'Howe End belonged to my uncle. I used to spend holidays there sometimes when my parents …' His voice drifted for a second, his eyes lost focus and then he closed them briefly. 'I had an odd childhood.'

'You're having a pretty odd adulthood too, I'd say.'

I got a smile for that.

'I was reading that Howe End is haunted,' I said, to draw him away from whatever thoughts were causing that creased look around his eyes. 'I've got this book about local folklore, fascinating stuff.'

'Seriously?' He seemed to welcome the change of subject too. 'Haunted by what?'

'It's not specific. Something that moans in empty rooms, apparently.'

'Yeah, I've got that. Link will just *not* shut up about the lack of furniture. Or the weather, for that matter. He was born with "moan" as a default setting, it's like living with Victor Meldrew. I've had to buy him a futon to sleep on just to keep him quiet.' His eyes were warmer now, watching me with interest.

'He needs a hobby.' I fiddled with my cup. 'Apart from verbal sexual assault.'

'Well, he rides, so I sent him over to your friend. Maybe

an hour galloping around the countryside will cheer him up a bit.' Phinn grinned now. 'Or he might fall off, break his leg and have to go back home to be nursed. Either is good.'

We finished our coffee and I looked at my watch. 'Well, I'd better go. I only parked for two hours and that's pretty much up.'

'Do you know what time the next bus goes back to Riverdale? I got a lift in with Link but he's gone back to ride. Or chat up a horse, wouldn't put it past him. So I said I'd make my own way back.'

We both stood up. 'There's only one bus back, at three.'

'Oh.' Phinn pushed his hands in his pockets. 'What time is it now?'

'Half past twelve.'

'Oh.' A pause. 'I don't suppose ...'

'Yes, I'll give you a lift.' That got me another smile. 'And ... you know ... if you ever want to use a computer ... you can borrow my laptop.'

'No electricity. My uncle never got round to putting it in. Not really one for mod cons was Uncle Peter, hence the septic tank and the spring. Still, if the whole of civilisation founders, at least Howe End will remain untouched.'

'Yeah, untouched by central heating, proper toilets and hot water.'

'Well, there is that.'

We walked down to the car park. 'This might be a bit ... noisy,' I warned, slipping the car into gear and trying to ignore the way people looked up at the sudden onset of a rattling noise accompanied by puffs of smoke. 'I'll do something creative with metal when we get back.'

'Why don't you take it to the garage?'

'Because we don't all have professor-sized bank balances.'

'Then why do you live here, middle of nowhere, where there's no work? Why not move to where you've got family?'

I froze him out, keeping my eyes on the road, on my mirror, my hands on the wheel. 'I don't have family.'

'You're from ... somewhere south. London, Home Counties? Not much of an accent, but enough. There's no family pictures anywhere in your house, you have a caller display on your phone – you've got family all right, you're hiding from them.'

The wheel twitched under my fingers and we nearly hit the kerb. 'How on earth do you reason that one out?'

Phinn sighed and tipped his head back again. It seemed to be something he did when he was thinking. 'If your family had died you'd have pictures. Old ones, but they'd be all over the place. You don't even have anything beside your bed – yeah, okay, I admit it, I *did* poke my head into your room yesterday but only by accident when I was looking for the bathroom. No pictures. You don't want to be reminded of them. Caller display – they're alive but you don't want to take their calls. From the south but no connection to Yorkshire – you're hiding. Am I getting warm?'

I pulled the car over to the side of the road. 'No. What you *are* getting, is out.'

'So I am right.'

I leaned over him to open the passenger door. 'Get out of my car.'

'Molly, you asked how I reasoned it out, so I told you. Besides, I have no idea where I am. Put me up *there*,' he jerked a thumb at the sky, 'and I can navigate my way round any one of three hundred galaxies and counting, but down here ...' a shrug, '... I'm a klutz with no sense of direction and a whole host of social anxieties. Please don't make me ask for directions, I might die.'

Despite myself I laughed. 'You forgot to mention your persistent use of hyperbole.'

'I was hoping you'd take that one as read.'

As the anger ebbed I became aware that I was still leaning over his body with my back pressed into his chest and my arm stretched across his groin. He still smelled slightly of my best sandalwood bath oil overlaid with coffee and the soapy, organic smell of his leather jacket. In the close confines of my Micra it was very noticeable. I couldn't think of anything else to say, or a graceful way of extricating myself, but that problem was sorted for me when a car coming up fast behind us blared a horn at our less-than-ideal parking position and made me jump.

I jerked backwards and my elbow connected firmly with Phinn's crotch which made his legs twitch upwards and a whole host of involuntary swearing broke out while he hunched miserably over his mid-section and I rubbed fervently at my forehead where he'd kneed me in the side of my temple.

'Y'see?' He eventually managed to force out from between gritted teeth. 'You wouldn't want to release me onto the general public, would you?'

'Technically that was me.' I straightened away. 'But still, how do you ever manage to measure stars or whatever it is that you astrophysicists do, without terrible things happening?'

'Stars stay put.' There was a moment of furtive rubbing and he managed to sit up properly again. 'Mostly. Sometimes they go boom but that's not generally my fault. And, up there I can't do them any real damage. It's down here I manage to cock up spectacularly.' There was another layer to his words, an underlying bitterness.

'Is that why your wife left you? Because you cocked up spectacularly?' He deserved it for all the prying and poking he'd done into my life. 'What did you do, fall over a woman while naked and she wouldn't believe it was an accident?'

Phinn went very still. 'I was never unfaithful,' he said quietly. 'Never.'

'So why did she leave you?'

Now the black eyes turned my way and they were full of something, some nameless emotion. 'Technically she didn't leave me. Well, no, she did, but then she came back, and then she died. All it needed was for her to turn into a vampire and rise from the dead and I'd have levelled up.' He closed his eyes. 'Let's go home.'

'Phinn, I'm sorry. I didn't know.' My words sounded thin, so inadequate for what he must be feeling that it was like trying to kiss better an amputation wound. 'I'm really sorry.'

'Yeah.'

I started the car again and we drove back to Riverdale in silence.

Chapter Twelve

Phinn remembered he'd meant to return the shoes as soon as he walked through the door but it was too late, Molly had already driven away and he was hardly going to run after her car brandishing a pair of stiletto heels. She clearly already thought he was only one step away from being dangerously deranged – he didn't want to fall flat on his face in the mud whilst carrying her shoes and remove all doubts.

The shoes sat on the window ledge in what he remembered as the old farm office. In his uncle's day the room had been mostly occupied by an enormous table strewn with papers, the walls covered in calendars and notes from one agricultural agency after another. He'd always been able to tell when Uncle Peter was in there by the fact that the big grey collie took up station outside the door and lay, one baleful eye pressed to the crack, full-length on the hallway flagstones like a mouldy rolled carpet.

Phinn turned slowly around, seeing the ghosts of clutter amid the quiet chilly spaces. One day, maybe, it could be like that again, with a family clustering in the kitchen drinking wine and eating home-made cake, the living room serious with the tick of a grandfather clock and the little parlour cosily jammed with upholstery and ornaments. One day. Maybe. But not for him.

He dragged the air bed from its slowly deflating position in the little bedroom and set it up downstairs under the big window in the kitchen. It beat sitting on flagstones – he was sure he could feel the coming of incipient piles even after only a fortnight of those chilly floors – and the natural light made it easier to read his scribbly handwriting and the hastily made printouts. 'British Organisation for the Investigation of Unidentified Aerial Phenomena.' 'Right. Yeah, bet they introduce themselves as members of Boiwap,' he muttered to himself. 'They must have a really *great* PR person.'

But the print blurred even with his glasses on. His eyes skipped over the text, drawn irresistibly to the doorway, through which he could see into the old office, and those shoes side by side, backlit by a glorious March sun like a magazine illustration.

A sudden bad-tempered gust rattled the windows and one of the shoes fell sideways. As the wind continued to agitate through the gaps in the ancient wooden frames, the shoe scuffed its way along the stone ledge and Phinn leaped through the room just in time to catch it before it made its draught-assisted way to the floor by way of a serious amount of dust and a pile of mouse-droppings that looked as though they had been passed down through the generations.

'Oh, all right! I'll take them back.' He found himself shouting into the emptiness. 'Satisfied now?' His words rang back at him from the stone but he thought the echo held notes of quiet complacency, as though the house itself was feeling smug about forcing him into a task he'd thought he could delay at least until he could be sure that Molly was out.

Only because you're tired of looking such a complete dork in front of her. Not, for example, because you quite like that sparky look that comes into her eye when she winds you up. Or because those eyes remind you of something you once felt, someone you once felt for. Or you wonder what it would be like to touch that delinquent hair, or because you're intrigued by her shape. Or even because she's already seen you naked twice and not laughed or thrown up, which has got to be a good thing, no?

Wishing he hadn't promised Link that he'd stop drinking – because a couple of stiff vodkas would have put paid to that irritatingly shrill voice inside his head – Phinn stuffed the shoes into a plastic carrier and went back outside.

The wind had knives in it. The sunlight which had looked so soft and pleasant from inside was now revealed to be all style and no substance, a pale yellow wash over ground hard as rock and a fake blue sky. He hustled quickly along the street, past the shop where he could swear the same two women stood gossiping every day and onto the row of little cottages, with his footsteps loud against the chilly pavement. To his left the river ran dark and deep, sluicing under the bridge like blood down an artery. The sound of its gurgling process made him shiver and shrug deeper into his jacket with the bag swinging on his arm as he thrust both hands into pockets and raised his shoulders to his ears.

It didn't sound any less scary with the noise half blocked out. Phinn tried to tell himself that it was just a river, made suddenly deeper by the rain falling higher in the moors. Water on the move. Nothing sinister about it. But when a tree trunk came sailing down, borne swiftly by the power of the waters, one branch raised to the sky like a drowning victim going under for the third time, his breathing increased until he was nearly gasping. His hands were sweating on the plastic handles of the bag and his pace increased until he was almost running by the time he reached Molly's front door.

For the second time in two days he knocked, waited, heard nothing. But this time the sound of his heartbeat was loud in his ears and a panicky sweat was sticking his T-shirt to his back and he didn't really care whether she was in or not. He turned the handle and the door opened and he half-fell into the hallway, the carrier bag bobbing at his elbow and the shoes inside repeatedly kicking him in the hip.

He heard Molly laughing as soon as he was inside and, despite himself and his nameless anxiety, he found he was smiling. 'Molly?'

No answer. But the soft giggle came again from the living room and he put his head around the door to look in.

'What the ... where did you come from?' Molly leaped to her feet removing the earphones she'd been wearing. She had her laptop open on the table, had obviously been listening to something, not able to hear his knock or his voice.

'I ... it was ...' Phinn held up the bag. 'Shoes.'

'Shoes?'

'I did knock, but you were ...' He waved a hand at the computer. 'I'll just leave them here, shall I?' He bent to disentangle the handles of the bag which had spun themselves tightly around his arm and locked into place in a plastic cat's cradle. He was trying to rotate them in the opposite direction and ignore the pain of the sharp heels as they spun and gouged his hip, when Molly moved towards him.

'Phinn. Look. Earlier. I'm sorry. Really sorry. I didn't know.'

The bag spun a dizzying dance and he found he couldn't look away from its green and white logo. 'About what?'

Without speaking again Molly pressed a couple of keys and turned the laptop. He stopped fiddling with the bag, pushed his glasses up his nose and focused on the screen. She'd Googled him and pulled down a news piece with the headline 'Physics-breakthrough Doctor's Wife drowns'. There was a picture of Suze too.

'You knew she died.'

Molly shook her head. 'Not like this, Phinn. This is ... horrible. I thought, when you said she died, it was, like, I dunno, illness or something. Not this.'

'But you were laughing. I heard you.'

'I Googled you to find that YouTube clip you were on about. I wanted to take a look before I told Mike. It's very funny. *You* were very funny. It's a brilliant talk.'

Phinn remembered it well. A somewhat dumbed-down version of his recent research results, given to an amateur astronomers' dinner when he'd been so white-hot with happiness that he could have made a discussion about serial killers amusingly entertaining. That feeling of having everything come right, the world being in perfect balance and everything so good that it shone like diamonds. That feeling. The one he'd lost and never looked for again.

'Yeah, well. Shit happens,' he said, standing awkwardly in the doorway. Didn't want to talk about it. Didn't want to think about it. Didn't want to remember that river running past outside, black and thick like blood or nightmares.

'Not like this. *Phinn.*' She came over and touched his arm and all the tape that held him together came undone.

'We'd split up. She didn't like my work, my friends, my style, my *life*. She'd thought I was going to be famous, that *we* were going to be famous, like she'd be some kind of scientific It girl, travelling the world and wining and dining the glitterati while I won Nobel prizes and discovered new theories and solved the world's problems through a telescope.'

The words came out in a rush. He had no way of stoppering them, they seemed to have been dammed up there behind his brain for *so* long now. 'She walked out when it wasn't like that. When I wasn't there, when I wasn't famous, wasn't getting my picture in the *Times* every week. I wasn't what she'd signed up for, she said.'

His legs gave way and he folded down onto the sofa. At his side the green and white bag rotated and settled snug against his leg.

'But you said she came back?' Molly's voice seemed to come from a long way away. Years away. From a future he'd never planned.

'She was gone about six months. I'd ... I was surviving. Thrown myself into my work, y'know?' He raised his head to catch those blue, blue eyes on him, gave a stupid smile. 'Typical bloke, me. But she came back, Molly. Said it had all been a mistake, that she wanted me, even with my imperfections.' Another grin, little more than stretching his mouth. 'Oh, she had a list of those. I'm not perfect, who'd have thought?' He stretched the arm out and watched the bag rotate again, feeling everything being dragged around inside him as though his internal organs were being re-arranged. 'About two weeks later she told me she was pregnant.'

'Phinn, don't. It's none of my business.' Molly sat beside him. Her eyes were on the bag too now, he noticed, as though looking at him was too painful.

'Doesn't matter. It's not as bad as it was. Still hurts, here,' and he jerked a fist towards his breastbone, wanting to punch himself for doing this, for spreading the pain in her direction. 'But it's fading. She died over a year ago now.'

'Yes, it said. On the ... thing.'

'December. The twenty-first of December.' He gasped in a breath that hitched. 'We'd argued. We kept arguing. Everything was – broken. The love wasn't ... I can't explain it, Molly. But she told me the baby wasn't mine, she'd been with a couple of guys while we'd been separated, she wasn't sure whose it was but it certainly wasn't mine and ... she didn't want it anyway.'

That awful, blazing night, when the frost had concreted the ground and the stars had been hard and lifeless in the sky. Suze, hands on her hips, lips drawn back to make her almost ugly, telling him things ... things about himself that

123

he'd never even suspected. Over a year ago. And it felt like yesterday.

'And then she got in her car and drove away. They found her the next morning. Car had skidded on some ice, gone into the river and she'd drowned.' Another deep breath. 'Trapped in the car.' *Ice in her lungs, water holding her down like arms until she was blank-faced under the surface …*

The silence fell so thickly around them that Phinn felt the world had bubble-wrapped them both.

'And that's why you're depressed? And the drinking?'

'No. Yes. I don't know, Molly, it wasn't like I was … I just started drinking to help me sleep and then it got to be a habit or something. I never drank *that* much, only enough to take the edge off, until … Actually, until I came here. Until that first time with the lights. The depression … that's a lot of stuff that Suze … that what happened, brought to the surface. Childhood, stress. I see … I *saw* someone, back in Bristol, once a week for six months, and it was helping.' He ran a hand through his hair, pushing it back as though he could push the memories back with it. 'My life has been pretty screwed up all along, really.'

Molly stood up. He felt the chill against his body where she'd been sitting as though something precious had been taken away. 'Molly? Where are you going?' He hadn't meant to have that note of slightly high-pitched desperation in his voice but she didn't seem to notice it.

'Phinn, I'm British, where do you think I'm going? To make some tea.'

'Oh. Right.' Stand down girlie-panic.

'You want some?'

This time his breath reached his lungs. 'Please.' And when he moved his arm the bag slid sweetly over his hand, landing on the carpet with the shoes upright and side by side again as though neatly positioned in their plastic transport. 'And whomsoever the shoe fits ...' he muttered with a sudden flashback to childhood.

'Sorry?'

'Nothing.'

She came back bearing two mugs of orange tea and a small plate of custard creams. He was mildly reassured to find that she hadn't taken British Woman in Time of Crisis to the extreme of forming the biscuits into a flower-petal pattern on the plate.

'Where did you get those?' She was looking at the shoes, then at him, with an expression that seemed to imply that she thought he'd been rummaging in her wardrobe.

'You sort of ran out of them last night. I didn't like to leave them out in the rain so ...' He gesticulated with his mug and tea slopped gently over his arm. 'Then I worried about them getting damp or nasty in my place, so I brought them back.'

'Oh.'

They sipped tea genteelly, taking the occasional biscuit but not speaking. Phinn was surprised that the unease he'd been feeling for weeks now seemed to have dropped away, as though telling Molly about Suze had exorcised some demon he'd been carrying unawares. It felt as though a tiny little light in the back of his soul had finally been switched on.

'By the way,' he said, dunking his custard cream. 'I'm sorry about earlier. In the car. I shouldn't have pried into your life like that. It's nothing to do with me how you choose to live, or where, or what your family is to you. I should have known better, I mean it's not exactly as though I'm one of the Waltons myself. So. Yeah. Sorry.'

Molly shrugged. 'Did your wife really think you were going to win a Nobel prize?' She picked up one of the shoes and examined the heel.

'Maybe. I did some work a while back on the multi-universe theory, where I proved that light moves through more dimensions than our four, and if we ever work out a practical application for that then I guess I'll be in line. Behind the guy who invented edible soap probably.'

'Wow. You *are* really clever.'

'What, as opposed to just knowing a lot about galactic rotation curves? Nah, not that clever. I have a brain that works in a particular way really, really well, so that I can work out solutions to problems that people don't even understand to *be* problems. It's more of a knack than massive intelligence.'

'You still have her picture in your wallet.'

Phinn looked at Molly. She was carefully avoiding his gaze, concentrating fiercely on her tea. 'Yes,' he said softly, wondering why she'd brought it up.

'You must miss her.'

'Sometimes. Mostly I miss the life we had together. You know the sort of thing, Sunday breakfasts, going to the cinema – all that. Walking hand in hand in the rain. Not that we ever did walk hand in hand in the rain, but it's the image, isn't it? Being with someone, I miss that. Not always, because I'm a real bastard when I'm working and I just want to be left alone but … oh, wet knickers on the radiators and Tampax in the cupboard and cup marks on the carpets.'

Someone to hold me. When the theories don't work, when the numbers don't add up and I want to hide, someone who's there, quietly on my side. He didn't say any of that, of course. He didn't need to tell her about his emotional neediness – Suze had thrown that in his face with such force that it had probably left an indelible mark that every woman could read.

'I've been thinking.' Molly put her cup down with such

126

finality, such clarity of purpose that Phinn was almost frightened as to what she was going to propose. God, she wasn't going to suggest something physical, was she? Some kind of friends-with-benefits thing? Something inside him trembled like a plucked wire.

'What?'

'Those lights. We need to track them somehow. Which direction they come from, which way they disappear – we need to be up on the high moor when they come over so that we can get a better view.'

'Oh.'

'Not a good idea?'

'Oh, no, no, it's a great idea. Excellent.' *Baxter, you prat. And now look at you, you're disappointed, aren't you? Even though if she had suggested anything you'd have run so fast you'd have hit escape velocity five minutes ago.* 'No. Really.' Phinn tried to look alert. 'How do we do it?'

She gave him a grin which made him wonder, for a brief, hot-skinned moment, whether she knew what he'd been thinking. 'I'm glad you asked. I've got one or two ideas.'

After Phinn left I found myself watching the YouTube clip again, trying to transpose the man I knew with the man on the screen. *That* Phinn Baxter was a shorter-haired, neatly dressed version, clean-shaven to reveal a nice jawline and wearing contacts to show off those big, black eyes. He moved with a certainty that my Phinn never used, as though his body was obedient rather than wilful, spoke quickly and with precision but also with well-timed humour and his smile had a charismatic wideness that had the audience hanging on his words.

And he was funny, intelligent and glamorous, moving around the small dais with his computer clicking from slide to slide in a PowerPoint of perfection. Not a word wasted or a pun misplaced. So what the hell had happened to turn this together guy into the self-conscious, inept man that fell into cesspits and passed out drunk on the moors? *That* Phinn looked a million miles away from the person who didn't shave and wore musty old T-shirts. But then, *that* Phinn worked the room with his smile and was clearly enjoying himself in the middle of a rapt crowd.

What had happened?

It couldn't only have been the loss of his wife. Okay, the shock of that might have wiped out his confidence, and the way she'd left him had obviously knocked him completely flat, but it wouldn't have taken away his belief in his own abilities, his own sense of himself. Something else had gone on, something he hadn't wanted to mention. I found myself frowning at the spot on the sofa where he'd been sitting as though I could interrogate his imprint on the cushions for answers.

But what business was it of mine, really? Doctor Phinneas Baxter was just someone who had breezed into my life on a temporary basis. He made no demands on me, wanted nothing from me and I, in my turn, was slightly reassured by my purely physical reaction to him. I'd been beginning to think that Tim ... that what Tim had done ... had turned my sex drive off at the mains switch. I'd not managed to work up a healthy case of lust for any man since, even the so-called hunks on the TV left me limp with a lack of appreciation, but something about Phinn made my eyes want to follow him.

Maybe there was still a residue of the man he had been lurking under the accident-prone surface, maybe a trace of the charisma still sparked now and again. There was certainly *something*.

Which was nice for my libido, and the rest of me didn't care.

I wrote a quick email to Mike, included the link to the YouTube clip, and pressed 'send' before I could change my mind or start analysing anything. Phinn could write articles for Mike, course he could. Nothing to do with me, I was merely the agent. Then I made myself a mug of coffee and sat down on the sofa, legs tucked up under me and the remaining custard creams close to hand, to carry on reading Caro's father's local folklore book. I'd just found out that the farm had once held a Screaming Skull that had vanished unexpectedly and I wondered if anyone had connected it to Howe End's Moaner. But even Phinn would have mentioned a skull kicking around one of those dusty rooms, wouldn't he?

The phone rang. Caller display showed my mother's mobile. I ignored it, and it rang out, leaving my palms sticky and my jaw aching.

'Knock knock, are you in?' The front door creaked as Caro came into the hall.

'In here. Reading.' I steadied my voice and wiped my hands down my thighs.

'Ooh. I just dropped by to ask if you wanted anything from town. I'm off into York in a bit to buy a new rug for Stan. So, can I get you anything?'

I laid the book down on the adjacent cushion. 'Look, we both know you came over to find out how last night went, with a possible side-order of where was I off to this morning with a car that sounded like the coming of the undead.'

'Yeah, I know. So? Come on, spill.' Caro picked up my mug from the sofa arm, sat down on the chair opposite me and kicked her boots off into a distant corner. 'You were seen heading out of the pub off to parts unknown with the gorgeous scientist – at a run, I may add.' She sipped from my cup, pulled a face at the lack of sugar, then carried on drinking, watching me from under her eyebrows as she did so.

'We were investigating something.'

'Then I hope you had your good underwear on. Jeez, this is horrible coffee. Right, so you've, ahem, *investigated*, what's the next step? If it's a threesome with that well-built blond lad then I want you to take notes, do you hear?'

I stayed quiet, knowing this was just Caro's way of trying to get information out of me. If I refused to confirm or deny she'd be forced to take another tack. Which she did. 'Is that Dad's book?' She leaned forward and slid the little paperback from my hands. 'Are you enjoying it?'

'It's a bit of a hotchpotch, but some of it's quite interesting.'

'There's apparently something in here about how he and Mum got together. I used to ask him about it and he told me that the secret was in the book, but I never found it. But then, Dad wasn't exactly Dan Brown in the edge-of-the-seat stakes, and my eyes used to glaze over about four pages in.'

'I look forward to reading about it then.' I held my hand out for the return of the book. Caro stared at the print for a few moments then passed it back.

'You are no fun, do you know that?'

'Apparently not.' I watched her stand up. 'Oh, Caro, by the way, have you got any wire up at the house? Something I can use to fix the exhaust on the Micra?'

She looked down at me and her face flickered with something that could have been sympathy. 'Since when did you become little Miss Handy? Moll, you barely know the front from the back of a car, and now you're bandying about terms like "exhaust". You know that's the really hot pipe underneath, don't you?'

I shrugged. 'It needs doing.'

Her expression reached her eyes and they softened to something even gentler. 'You really can't fix an exhaust for long with wire. It needs to go to the garage.'

I gave a long blink. She was right. I wasn't the most practical person on earth, I'd never really had to be. One of the advantages of dating men who drove fancy cars and had loads of disposable income had been their desire to do the 'manly' thing and sort out any functional problems that arose for me. I'd only had to flutter my eyelashes and mention that odd noise my car was making and it had been taken care of.

Maybe Caro was right, maybe it was more of a 'father fixation'. Maybe I really hadn't wanted to grow up.

'It'll have to do until Mike pays me for the Halloween contribution.'

Caro smiled an awkward smile. 'If things are tight I could … maybe … just sort of wait for the rent?'

I took a deep breath, tempted. *Grow up, Molly. You've discovered that you can find men your own age attractive, perhaps that's your brain telling you it's time to cut loose from the person you used to be.* 'Thanks, Caro, but I can manage. It's not even as if I use the car that often anyway, it'll wait.'

'If you say so. Just remember that you're going to look a proper berk trying to get back from Morrisons with a week's worth of shopping on Stan, apropos of which, are you sure there's nothing you want from York?'

'You mean am I sure I'm not going to suddenly break down and tell you all about Doctor Baxter and his action in the sack? About which, incidentally, I have no idea?'

Caro's face softened again. 'I'm sorry, Moll. I'm beginning to sound a bit motherish, aren't I? It's only because I care, you know that.'

'The words "mother" and "care" should not be used in the same sentence where I'm concerned.' My fingers had closed so tightly on the cover of the book that it made a squeaking sound. 'Trust me.'

She shrugged. 'Well, you're probably the nearest I'm ever going to get to kids, so forgive me for coming over all parental.'

'Don't be daft, you're only ten years older than I am!'

'I didn't mean … ' Caro sat down again. 'I care about you, Molly. All this refusal to speak to your family and stuff, it hurts me, you know. Seeing you … well.' She leaned forwards so that I couldn't see her face. 'I miss having someone who's known all my nightmares, people who remember my first show, first rosette, first broken leg … It's true, you know, you don't know what you've got till it's gone. My parents have gone, but you've still got your mum and I don't think you realise how much she means to you. I just feel you should, maybe, put things behind you a bit and try …' She twiddled her socked toes on the carpet.

Caro had loved her mum and dad. She'd had a happy family upbringing, all ponies and puppies and Christmas concerts. She just didn't realise it hadn't been like that for all of us, but I couldn't say that without getting into territory that hurt

'I'm sorry. Honestly. Oh, and by the way, I'm not going to tidy my room and I shall stay out as late as I want. So there.'

'Spoilsport.' Caro hunted down her boots and took them out into the hall to pull them back on. 'But you will tell me if you find any interesting stories in the book, won't you?'

I got up and followed her, finding her sitting at the bottom of the stairs yanking at the boots. This change of mood was something we were both working hard to keep going. It felt as though the depth of the previous conversation had scared us both a bit. 'You seriously never read your own father's book, Caro?'

'He wrote it when I was fifteen! You show me a fifteen-year-old girl who'd rather read stories about hobgoblins and mysterious white hares than about Jason Donovan and Bryan Adams!'

'Who?'

'Shut up, child.' With a final savage tug she got her second foot into its tight leather casing and stood up. 'There's no need to rub it in. Who were you reading about in your teenage years then? Take That? Right, see you later then.'

As she left I went back to my seat on the sofa. I'd been a bit shaken by her revelation that she wanted children – I'd got used to Caro as a repository for my angst, finding out she had angst of her own was slightly startling. It felt like a step forward into a different kind of friendship, maybe something deeper. More enduring?

I ate another custard cream and tried to put my thoughts in order. Caro. Pushing our friendship forward as though she'd had inside information that I was staying. Phinn. Who hadn't shown any desire to push any kind of relationship further than we'd already managed to limp. So why the *hell* did I keep getting these flashbacks to tiny things he said or did? Why did my mind feel the need to linger over little details like the persistent line of stubble along his jaw, or the weight of his hand when he'd held mine to help me barefoot through the mud? Was he something to do with the reason I was starting to think of some kind of a future?

Behind me the telephone rang. Again, the familiar number that I associated with postponed meals and broken promises. This time, in my spirit of 'starting anew', I picked up the receiver. I didn't speak, but my mother's voice rang out around the room. 'Molly, I really need to see you, to talk—'

'No.'

'This is important.'

'So was what you did. It was important *to me*. You might

just think all you have to do is explain, be all *practical*, and everything will be all right, well it won't. Never. Things will never be all right again as far as you are concerned. So please stop phoning me and trying to justify yourself to me, *Mother*.' And I slammed the phone down again, my mouth drying and my vision breaking so that the room looked like a badly done jigsaw. As though she could see me down the line I flattened myself against the wall, heart beating so hard that it made my head thump against the plaster with each pulse. The cord hung from my fingers and I found that I was winding it around my hands so that the plastic wire cut through my skin and beads of blood burst onto my palm.

Why did I answer? Now she'll think I'm talking to her again, that all she has to do is to keep trying, keep phoning and eventually I'll give in and we'll be back where we were. When I know that we were never in a good place to start with.

Chapter Thirteen

'All right, git-features. What have you done now?'

Phinn looked up. Link was lurking over him, rolling himself a cigarette and pretending not to be staring into the bag. 'What do you mean?'

'Packing.' A hand, trailing wisps of tobacco, waved at the holdall. 'You cutting and running on me again, man? Because I am a guy of limited patience these days.' His lighter flared into life and he lit the tube, sucking smoke into his lungs with every evidence of enjoyment.

'Oh, this? No, this is just a few bits and pieces, camera, video, gear like that. Molly and I ... well, we thought we might try to intercept the lights.' Phinn saw Link's eyebrows raise and his heart jumped with a quick moment of guilty pleasure. 'We're going to watch tonight, and if they come, well, we're heading up onto the moors to try to get a fix on them.'

The eyebrows stayed up. 'You are one slick mover, my friend.' A hand clapped Phinn on the shoulder and a small heap of hot ash sprinkled the back of his neck. 'She is a cutey. Fantastic arse on her too. Ask her if she's got any sisters, would you? Hot ones, obviously, I don't want to know if she's got some humpster in the family tree.'

'Link, you aren't just a prat, you're a sexist prat.' Phinn slid the battery unit under a rolled up blanket for security and tucked it into a corner of the bag. 'Molly and I are trying to find out what the hell the deal is with these mysterious lights, the ones that you *say* you can't see. That's all. No romance, no sweaty nights of passion, no condom-related panics, okay? Whatever your fevered little brain might be coming up with, it's wrong. Some of us can see a woman without being seized by the urge to drag her into a dark corner – it's called "evolution".'

'Woah.' Link puffed a bubble of smoke and watched it scribble away into the air. 'That's a whole load of words just to say she doesn't fancy you.'

'She …' Phinn saw the slow smile arrive on his friend's face and dropped his head so that his face was hidden behind his hair. 'How did you enjoy your horse-adventure?'

'Cool. Nice to be aboard again.' Link sat lengthways on the window seat, his feet braced against the opposite wall. 'And that Caro is hotter than a mince pie on Christmas morning, know what I mean?'

Phinn leaned back on his heels and looked at his friend. He and Link had known each other – how long now? Since their parents had dumped them together in that not-quite top echelon pre-prep school aged … God, four? That meant – he did a quick calculation in his head – that they'd been friends for twenty-eight years. A whole generation. Moving to prep school, then on to that ghastly private place where Link had managed to get the whole fourth form expelled and it had only been the fact that the school had been so keen to have Phinn on their roll that got them all readmitted.

Link glanced across. 'What the hell are you smirking at?'

'Just remembering. Us as kids. That thing with the headmaster's Range Rover and the donkey.'

'Gods, you on some kind of nostalgia kick?' Link swung his legs around so that he was sitting upright. 'What made you think of that?'

Phinn shook his head. Link had been in his life so long that he couldn't remember a time before they'd been friends. Or rather, he could, but it was part of that whole barren wasteland of memories that attached to anything concerning his parents; he'd shut that all out a long time ago. 'Just, you know. Wondering why the hell you left everything to come looking for me up here?' *And what I'd do without you ...*

The question had haunted his mind for days now, ever since Link had turned up in this kitchen to hand him the kettle and scare him into a new set of underpants. He really, *really* hoped that there wasn't going to turn out to be some underlying homoerotic thing that he hadn't picked up on, the fear that Link would declare undying love for him was the only thing that had stopped him asking so far.

'Oh, really?' Link leaned forward, elbows on knees and smoke trailing from the inadequate roll-up. 'You didn't think that, oh, I don't know, maybe I might be *worried* or something?'

Phinn blinked. 'Worried? Why? What about?'

'You stupid bastard.' It was said mildly, but the emotion was on Link's face, not in his words. Phinn saw it, registered it like a punch to the lungs. 'I see it as my mission in life to get you sorted before I can rest.' Link sprawled back against the wall, feet and legs forming a triangle. 'Anyhow, without me you'd still be wrapping yourself in newspaper and lighting matches to read by.' He waved at the Arctic-quality sleeping bag Phinn was sitting on. 'You're not the most practical guy on the planet, admit it.'

'I can't help who I am, Link.' *I tried, for Suze I tried, but ... I couldn't even do that, couldn't even pretend.*

'Yeah, yeah, gotcha on that, but ...' Link secured the cigarette between his lips and dug a hand into a pocket. 'Look, man. I want to see you out there again. Like you used to be, okay, no, you're not exactly the one-night-stand king, but, hey.' He shook his head. 'You used to be fun, or, maybe not fun but you used to talk to people.' Out of the pocket came a tiny foil packet, like a very small condom.

'What the hell is that?' Phinn had his suspicions but, knowing Link, it could be anything from heavy-duty mood changers to the flavouring from a Pot Noodle. *Why am I even listening to this?*

Link shook his head, dismissive. 'A touch of mood enhancer, kick of self-confidence, squeeze of front-it-out. Oh and a pinch of Viagra. Just a little helper.'

Phinn stared at the tiny package. 'Don't be stupid,' he said, and even to himself his voice lacked conviction. 'I'm not going to start doing drugs just to be able to do what you seem to manage to pull off so effortlessly, which is being a dickhead, by the way.'

'Hey, man, no harm in keeping it in your pocket, though, eh?' Link pushed the metallic square into Phinn's jacket and patted it into place. 'You never need it, all well and good. But if you find yourself needing a little bit extra … well, this'll give you a touch of the Tarzan's when you want it most. Suze was right about a lot of things, y'know. You exist in your own little bubble, your thoughts, your feelings, and no one else's even crawl into your consideration, do they? By the way, heading back to the main topic of today's conversation … I was scared for you, man. The anti-D's, the booze, the whole not-sleeping-walking-the-streets thing? And then when I came over to the flat and there's just a bunch of students living there, who said that you'd let them have the place rent-free, just packed up and gone? What did you *think* I'd do, shrug and wait for a postcard?' He shook his head.

There was a creeping cold in his soul. Phinn felt it settling at the edges, freezing off, shutting everything down. 'I didn't realise,' he said stiffly. Knew the words were inadequate but what could he say? What could he do? He tried for a smile. 'Sorry, Link. I'm glad you're here, really. But you don't have to worry about me, I'm okay now. Better, anyway. You could go back.'

'What, and miss the next instalment?' Now the smoke

followed the grin and formed a Cheshire Cat smile in the air. 'You are better than the telly, man.'

Phinn shook his head and concentrated on the holdall, checking the contents. 'But what about your love life? Aren't you after a bit of action? I haven't seen you without a woman attached to some part of your anatomy since you were about sixteen. Or are you still in hiding?'

Keep it steady, Phinn. Don't let him know what he's said … Don't let him know that he's finally confirmed your greatest fear.

Link shrugged. 'I'm giving the old man a bit of a rest before I start my onslaught on the female masses again. Don't want him worn out before his time.' He patted his groin affectionately. 'Moll's friend Caro in action on a horse, phwoar, I'm hoping that translates to humans. And round here they're not exactly spoiled for choice in the male market, I've *seen* the local blokes. Like shooting fish in a barrel, mate.'

'If you say so.'

'I do.' Link carelessly stubbed out what was left of his cigarette on the wall. 'You want coffee? I'm going to put the kettle on and dream about central heating. You know they're forecasting snow up here soon?'

'Snow?' Phinn forgot the racket of emotion in his chest. 'But it's March. That's ridiculous.'

'That's Yorkshire, God's Own Country. Apparently God is some kind of masochist Eskimo. Yeah, falls of up to six inches on the high ground, which is us, 'cos you can't get much higher than Riverdale Moor without being in, like, orbit or something.' He strolled across to the primus and began the business of trying to light it. 'I'll head out to town again later, lay in supplies.'

'I'll … I'm going to get some writing done.' Phinn collected his notepad and pen. 'I'll sit in the old office, it's a bit warmer in there.'

Need to think. Need to work on this. Need to be alone.

Link shrugged. "Kay. I'll catch you later then.'

Phinn took the sleeping bag, went into the small room and closed the door. He huddled himself inside the down-filled quilting, curled around his pain. *It's just Link. He didn't realise what he was saying, didn't realise what he was doing. Come on, you've known him forever, he's more family than your actual family. Remember, remember those Christmases, the pair of you blind drunk in the flat watching TV with a takeaway, jeering at all the old films and the kids under the tree-ness of it all? Remember each and every time he's been there for you. Hold on to that.*

But still. Link. What did you do?

Chapter Fourteen

As arranged, we met as the sun vanished behind the hunch of moorland, staining the clouds a bright red and the ground a sinister blueish tinge.

'Through here.' I led the way up the drive into the stable yard. 'Here.' The bolts slid open and Stan stepped towards us, half a haynet hanging from his lips, wearing the same expression that I would expect on the face of a lifer receiving an unexpected reprieve. 'This is Stan.'

'It's a horse.' Phinn hung around outside the loose-box, outside biting range. 'An ugly one.'

'He's not *that* ugly,' I said, affronted. 'And he's better than any kind of All Terrain Vehicle. He'll get us up onto the moors faster than walking, and we can go direct up the bridle path instead of having to drive up the road and then walk. So? What do you think?'

Phinn's eyes looked deep. He didn't really seem to be listening to me or even seeing what was in front of him and his face had a haunted kind of look. 'Er, yeah. Okay. I've never really liked horses much. Bit unpredictable. I deal with things that happen over millions of years, horses tend to act a bit quicker than that.'

'Can you ride?'

'Dunno. Probably. I can calculate wavelength shifts to two decimal places, so I shouldn't think riding a horse can present much of a problem.' He put the holdall he was carrying down onto the cobbles and took his time about straightening back up, flipping his hair away from his eyes with a gesture that looked unnecessary, as though he was trying not to have to speak to me. 'Except for the horse element.'

'Phinn, are you all right?' I nudged Stan out of the way and took a step forwards. 'If you're upset about earlier ... I said I was sorry.'

'What? Oh. no, Molly, it's not you. And there I was thinking I was being all subtle ... no. This is ... something else. Some*one* else.'

Stan poked his nose forward and showed his teeth, which made Phinn flinch.

'And you're not all right,' I said quietly.

Phinn stared at the ground. 'I just ... oh, I probably misunderstood or something. It's nothing, Molly, me being stupid, that's all.'

I touched his sleeve. 'But you're not stupid, are you? You might be all those other things you call yourself, but you certainly aren't stupid.'

He spun round to face me properly. The last light from the sun caught the angles of his cheekbones, made his face look wild and despairing. 'Please let me be stupid, just this once. Let me be wrong, let me have jumped to a conclusion that won't turn out to be right, *just this once*. Otherwise ... everything's gone.'

'Phinn ...'

'Are we going to go look for the lights? Because we'll need to be somewhere more open, somewhere we'll see them coming, it's too enclosed here with the roofs and everything.' Speaking quickly he moved away, talking over his shoulder as he headed out of the yard and down towards the village street. 'So far they've come from the south west, if we direct ourselves towards that quadrant and do occasional sweeps of the whole sky we should see them approach in good time. And then, I'm guessing, we bring out the errr ... four-legged transport, I suppose.'

By now we were both standing in the road. 'Perhaps if we stood on the bridge?'

'No. Not the bridge. It's too ... the water is too dark. Can't ... there's too much water.' With a dismissive wave of the hand he started walking again, hands in pockets and shoulders hunched up to his ears. 'Here.'

'What, on the village green?'

'It's a good clear space.' From his jacket pocket he produced a camera. It was slick and black with a long lens screwed to the front and it sat in his hand like a malignant growth. 'I'm sorry. I'm not very good company tonight, Molly.'

'It's okay.' In the dying light I could see the way his fingers clenched around the camera strap, the irregular beat of his pulse in the gap between his jacket and his T-shirt neck. Every line of him was tense, wary, he looked like a horse about to bolt. 'You've been through a bad time. You're allowed to have rough days.'

I was having to fight the urge to move in and give him a hug, he looked as though he badly needed some kind of physical comfort, but I didn't dare. There was something dangerously attractive about his edginess and his guarded words and I was slightly afraid that, if I touched him, I might not be able to stop at a hug. Damn the return of my sex-drive, without it I'd have been able to offer at least a little reassurance.

'Thanks.' A slight smile. 'I mean, I don't need your permission to be a miserable sod, obviously, but it's nice that you can appreciate that it's nothing to do with you. I mean, it's not your fault, not that I'm telling you to mind your own business. Shit, I'm going to shut up now.'

'Maybe we should—'

'—watch the sky. Yes. Good idea.'

But I was still watching him as he tipped his head up and scanned the far horizon. YouTube told me that under that scraggy overgrown stubble was a sexy, firm jaw, and that body looked terrific in a carelessly-worn designer suit. It also had things to say on the subject of his ability to project himself, to appear as a capable, dynamic educator with a grin that was wide with confidence and eyes that were alight with mischief and fun.

And yet. Here the real man stood. Scruffy and ungroomed, his only confidence seemed now to come from holding a conversation and his grins were almost diffident, as though he was waiting to be slapped down or reprimanded for being enthusiastic. Even his stance was different. Now he kept his hands in his pockets, his body averted, he seemed to be waiting for the final punch, the one that was going to lay him out.

'Phinn.'

'Mmmm?' His head came round and, just for a second the Phinn from the stage was there in a focus behind the eyes and the tilt of the head, until he seemed to remember himself and bring everything back down. 'What?'

'Nothing. Sorry, I just thought I saw something.'

'The stars are coming out.' One long arm swept the heavens. 'Look. Aren't they beautiful? All those distant suns, all those other planets sitting up there. When I was little I used to think that the night sky was like a blanket and the stars were the lights that shone through from the day on the other side.' A shy smile. 'God, I must have been a whimsical little bugger, no wonder my parents sent me to boarding school.'

'That's a bit harsh. Did you enjoy it? Boarding school?'

'Nothing to compare it to. It was all right, I suppose. Better than – well, the alternative.'

'What, being with the rest of us plebs at an ordinary comprehensive?'

'Being dragged around by my parents on the lecture circuit. A series of hotel rooms and theatres with a shedload of travelling in between, not really my style. It's no way to bring up a child. If I ever have children I—' A sharp half-laugh. 'Christmas stockings and beach holidays with buckets and spades and *being there*. That's how it should be, not being raised like some rare plant in permanent education-compost. Kids need love and attention and games and bedtime stories and all the other stuff I never got.'

'Yes,' I said faintly, past a lump in my throat. *You might have been raised as a genius, Phinn, but your wishes for childhood sound a lot like mine.*

We stood back to back for a while. He seemed to have relaxed a bit now, wasn't holding himself aloof as he had been. In fact, to my wishful thinking mind, it almost felt as though he too was leaning in against me, returning the pressure of body against body. I started to wonder what would happen if I turned, if I let myself move into him. Would he move away, or would he turn too, would we end up face to face? Would those soul-black eyes search mine for permission before that quirky mouth touched mine, or would he go straight in for the macho lip lock? Would his hands ...

'There.' He spoke, quickly erasing the whole of my fantasy in one syllable. 'Coming in fast from the west.'

'I'll get the horse.'

We ran towards the yard, Phinn occasionally pausing to point the camera at the sky and fire off a series of shots with the whining of the camera ricocheting around the chilly night air. We reached the stable, I flung the door open and dragged Stan out, flipped his rug back off onto the hayrack and leaped aboard.

'Jump up behind me. He can carry both of us easily.'

Phinn's face was a masterpiece of doubt. 'Are you sure?'

'He was purpose-built for carrying eighteen stone farmers around the hills, of course he can carry both of us, unless you've got lead bones. Grab the bag and come *on*.'

I shuffled my way forward, until I was sitting almost on Stan's neck.

'I don't know.' Phinn was practically rotating on the spot. 'I don't do horses. Or animals of any kind really, we didn't have pets.'

'He won't hurt you,' I said, and then, remembering it was Stan. 'At least, he might nip a bit but he's pretty well meaning really.'

'Can't I walk?'

I glanced up into the sky. The lights were moving slowly, drifting in a breeze we couldn't feel. 'I thought you wanted to keep up with the lights. Riding Stan up the hill is the fastest way.'

Phinn was pacing tiny circles now, the bag clonking against his legs. 'He might, I dunno, run away with us. What do we do if he runs away with us, Molly?' There was a note of panic in his voice that was bordering on real fear, so I indulged in some snap-psychology.

'Phinn, it's not Stan you're afraid of, is it? This is a control thing. Well, I've been riding since I was ten, and I can tell you that if there was ever a horse that was most emphatically *not* going to run away with us, it's Stan. Besides, I'm the one doing the steering and the starting and stopping and after eighteen years I've pretty much got a handle on the whole thing. You just have to sit here and hang on, all right?'

'You sure you can stop him?' Phinn stopped pacing, but stood out of reach of Stan's front end.

'It's more the getting started that's the problem. Honestly.'

Phinn looked dubious but, with a good deal of 'oomfing' and awkward rearrangement, got up behind. 'Now what?'

'Now we find out if you can ride.' I turned Stan using his halter rope. I hadn't bothered with saddle or bridle to save time, and I'd ridden him this way often enough for him to get the message that if I was hauling away at his headcollar then I probably wanted him to do something. He set off out of the yard at a swift, bone shaking trot. 'Which way?'

Phinn's hand came from behind me. 'That … way. Ouch. Do you mind if I … grab hold?'

'You can grab anything that doesn't wobble. And if you grab something that does wobble but shouldn't, then I'd be grateful if you didn't mention it.'

I steered the horse towards the steep bridle path that led along the edge of the moor and was the fastest way up onto the high ground. Stan knew the route, and even broke into a canter along one of the even stretches. Phinn wound both arms around my waist, put his forehead down on the base of my neck, and swore all the way.

When we reached the top of the path where the moor flattened out in front of us, I pulled Stan up and Phinn inched himself slightly further back. 'Oh God. I thought falling in the septic tank was bad but at least my balls didn't get alternately punched and squeezed.'

'Sorry. Where have they gone?'

'Into my body cavity, I suspect, never to return.'

'The lights, you fruitcake.' I scanned the skies. 'I can't see them.'

'That way. Heading over towards the east, just before the horizon.' The camera grazed my neck on its way up. 'No point getting the video out, they're too far away. We need to be *faster*!' Snap snap.

I caught sight of the tail end lights whisking almost joyfully away over the moor and forced Stan to stump around in a circle in order to watch them as they dropped away over the curvature of the earth. Phinn muttered and grabbed a firmer hold with one hand, using the other to keep snapping but I could tell the camera was wobbling wildly around from the way it kept poking me in the neck. 'Sit still. You won't wobble so much.'

'Ha! That's easy for *you* to say.' Another wobble and Stan reacted by shifting his weight to counteract the lack of balance, there was a moment of anxious grabbing at my body and then Phinn slid sideways and parted company with both of us, landing on his back in the heather with the camera held up above his head. 'Ow! Shit!'

'I thought you said you could ride a horse.'

'*Probably.* I said *probably.* And that ...' he waved the camera at Stan, '... is not a horse, that is an instrument of the devil. My genitals haven't been this pummelled since—'

'Since your wedding night?'

A wry smile. 'Not even then I don't think.' He sat up and began to get to his feet, rotating his shoulders and checking his limbs. 'I'm walking back. I'm sorry but I don't think horses and I were meant to be acquainted.'

'You did all right,' I said, staring away in the direction the lights had taken in case there was still anything to see. 'Tim fell off first time out and he had a saddle. And a neckstrap. *And* we were only walking.'

Phinn stopped waggling his elbows as though he was trying to take off. 'Tim. Was he your ...?'

'My fiancé, yes, he was.'

Phinn started checking over the camera. 'What was he like?'

'Successful. Clever. Rich. You know, all the things a girl looks for in a potential mate.' My hands started plaiting at Stan's mane. 'And, in the end, a bastard. Well, no, not really a bastard but a cheat and a liar and ... all the things a girl calls her ex.'

He was staring at the camera screen, looking back through the pictures he'd taken. 'And he is why you're here, is he? Why you're hiding? What was he, some kind of mafia boss?'

'He was ... *is* a journalist. You might have heard of him, Tim Arnold.'

Phinn's eyes flicked to mine. 'The Tim Arnold that won the Anderson Prize? *That* guy?'

I looked away. 'Actually, we both won the Anderson. It was a jointly authored book, but Tim picked up the award because I had flu and couldn't get to the ceremony. I didn't care at the time because we were a couple but since then – well, he's pretty much pretended that I had nothing to do with it. And I won't stand up and say "oy, I won too", because … I never want anything to do with him again.' Beneath me Stan sensed my tension and shuffled his feet. A knife-edge of wind slid under my jacket and I shivered. 'We should go back.'

'So why are you living way out here? I'd have thought that winning the Anderson would make you in demand – what was it you did again?'

My stomach tightened. 'It was exposing the waste and corruption in government. I was working as a sort of freelance reporter based around the Houses of Parliament, picking up bits and pieces of stories here and there, and then, one day I … Look, it doesn't matter. I worked with Tim on the book, we won a prize. We got engaged, we split up. I don't want to go back to doing what I did, but writing is all I can do, so working for Mike, for the magazine, it's making the best of it and can we talk about something else now, please?'

I turned Stan's head for home and prodded him into walking back the way we'd come, my hands buried deep in his mane to hide the fact that my fingers were digging into the palms in my attempts not to think about it, not to remember what had happened.

'Wow. That has got to be the most simplified version of someone's life I've ever heard.' Phinn started walking alongside me, a careful distance away from Stan. 'I did something, I won a prize and then I stopped doing it.

Are you deliberately trying to be enigmatic or something, Molly?'

'I just don't like talking about it, all right?'

Phinn stopped. 'No, not really.'

'What?' I tugged on Stan's rope until he stopped walking, then tugged a bit harder until he turned a small circle to face back the way we'd come.

Phinn was leaning against a standing stone, one of the many which jutted from the moor like broken teeth, with his arms folded and one leg bent, his foot resting on the step of stone at the base. His pose was casual but I could see him shivering, the leather jacket clearly wasn't providing much protection from the niggling little splinters of wind. The darkness lent him a magazine-cover glamour; the way his hair blew back from his face, that stubbled jawline – he looked like a Burberry advert.

'What?' I repeated, irritated for some reason I couldn't put my finger on. 'What do you mean?'

He chewed his lip and tipped his head back. Those incredible eyes, accentuated behind his glasses, seemed to be reaching into my brain, slowly unpacking all my tawdry secrets and I felt my palms get a little sweaty. There was something in that look, something uncalled for and yet something I half-wanted to see, a cool appraisal of me as a woman. 'I told you about Suze. It would be nice if you felt you could tell me a bit about yourself in return.'

I felt my hackles rise. 'Sorry, I didn't realise it was some kind of "tit for tat" confessional thing we had going on. I thought you told me about your wife to stop me wasting unnecessary sympathy on you, not so that I'd be obliged to give you chapter and verse on my own nasty little secrets.'

Stan, seeming to sense that this one was going to run and run, put his head down and started to graze. Phinn didn't move. 'We don't have a "thing going on" as you put it, as though you've been possessed by some kind of Spirit of Nineteen Fifty. I told you what happened because … because you seemed to care. And because I thought you needed to know that relationships are – well, they're not all good. You aren't alone in having screwed up yours, it happens to all of us some time or another.'

'I did not screw up! I did everything right, everything that I should have done. It was Tim who screwed up.'

Phinn just raised his eyebrows and uncrossed his arms so that he could shrug. 'Yeah, okay,' he said, with disbelief in every line of his body.

I slithered down off Stan so that I could confront him better. 'Yes! He cheated on me, he ran off and left me, and the worst of it all is that he didn't even go off with someone young and sexy and gorgeous; he ran off with *my mother*,' and then I'd said it and it couldn't be unsaid and I was left standing biting my tongue, trying to decide whether I wanted to burst into tears or kill the man in front of me.

He stepped away from the stone. 'There,' he said, and his voice was gentle now. 'That wasn't so hard, was it?' Then he patted me on the shoulder and headed off down the path.

'Wha—wait a minute, is that *it*?' I trotted after him and, after a moment's consideration, Stan trotted after me. 'You trick me into saying something like that and then all you can do is *walk away*?'

Phinn stopped again, so quickly that I bumped into him. 'What were you expecting me to do?' he asked over his shoulder.

'I don't know! A small show of concern might be nice.'

His jacket brushed against me as he turned round. He was so close I could smell woodsmoke and soap from his clothes and feel the trace of warmth he was giving off. 'Concern, hmmm. Okay.' Chilly hands touched my face, his eyes hung before me like holes in the sky, and then his lips brushed against mine bringing a warmth greater than the sun. 'Enough concern?' He stood back.

I stared at him. 'You kissed me,' I said with, I think, understandable aggrievement.

'Yes, I know. My face was on this side of it.'

'Why?'

Now I got the first hint of uncertainty from him. 'It ... You wanted concern. It was either that or phone Crimewatch. Why, what did you *think* I was going to do?'

'I didn't know! Not that!'

Stan nudged me between the shoulder blades and I turned around to fuss with his headcollar, anything to avoid having to look at Phinn. Even that brief physical contact had made me pink and sweaty under my coat and I was having to restrain myself from running a finger over my lips in a bewildered way. 'I just thought you might say something.'

There was no reply and when I looked back I found that he was ten yards away, moving swiftly over the soft heather and bracken like a ghost.

We walked back to the village in silence. At the bottom of the track, Phinn, still a little way ahead, stopped and turned. 'I'm sorry. It was wrong of me to ... I'm feeling a bit shaky, my responses are a bit off and I'm seriously not behaving normally. Believe me, kissing women without at least a written invitation in triplicate, is completely atypical.'

Stan got more fussing. He gave me an 'am I going to die?' look, and then bit my shoulder in response, but it was useful to have something to look at that wasn't Phinn. 'No. You were right, you were just showing concern, I'm completely out of the loop on ... well, being kissed like that.'

'What the hell did Tim do then, Masonic handshakes?' He hunched himself against the wind and poked his hands into his pockets. I wasn't sure if it was the weather conditions or the subject of the conversation that was making him so uncomfortable.

'My boyfriends ... even before Tim ... they've all been, well, older. Than me, I mean, not, like older than God or something,' I added, hastily. 'I was a bit of a ...' I tried to think of a way of summing up my teenage years and early twenties without making me sound as though I'd never worn knickers, '... a bit of a wild child. I liked older men.'

Phinn gave me a smile that looked pulled down at the corners. 'I think you'll find, physiologically, we're pretty much the same. Lips, teeth, noses, all that. Age doesn't really come into it much. Unless,' and his smile went a bit oddly-shaped, 'we're talking dentures.'

'I meant ...' I said, and stopped. How did I sum up the difference between all my previous kisses and the one he'd given me? The difference between a kiss that had always had something of the business transaction about it, trading my youth and energy for financial solvency and solid security and Phinn's almost tender tentativeness. 'I have to go and put Stan away.'

Phinn sighed. It made him sound empty. 'Of course. Goodnight,' and with an additional hunch to his shoulders he turned towards Howe End, walking as though he'd given away a fortune.

'Phinn!' Driven not to let it end this way, I called after him, watched his stride break as though he couldn't make up his mind whether to turn, stop or walk back to me and his legs were waiting for a final decision.

'We'll talk about the lights later. Tomorrow. Another day. Goodnight, Molly.' He spoke without turning round, raising a hand in a loose-wristed farewell gesture, and I watched him all the way down to the bridge before I turned Stan and headed him back to the yard and possibly the most energetic brushing session he'd had for months.

Chapter Fifteen

Phinn sat in the farmhouse kitchen without switching on the big torch that Link had thoughtfully left for him. The darkness felt appropriately heavy and he stretched his arms out over the table and rested his head on them, letting its weight settle over him like snow.

Every time he thought about kissing her, enough conflicting emotions arose for a small war to break out in his chest. Had he really done it? Had it really been *him*? He'd kissed women recklessly before ... well, all right, not recklessly, he was a physicist and physics and recklessness tend to go together like cats and explosions, but he'd kissed without due care and attention. Some of those women had even kissed him back. But Molly ...

He groaned as the embarrassment flooded his face with heat, and then buried his head deeper in his arms. *Whhhhhhhyyyy? Oh God, please let this all have been a terrible dream.*

He'd first kissed Suze in the park on the hottest day of summer. And she'd kissed back, oh, had she ever, they'd barely made it back to his flat before ... Phinn slammed a fist on the table and the sound echoed around the bare room, filling the corners with his hurt. *Was that what I wanted Molly to do? Drag me home with her and strip me slowly in that little bedroom? Pull me into her bed and whisper me into making love?* The squeeze in his groin was purely physical and wasn't reaffirmed by his brain, for which he felt curiously glad. *No. That's not Molly. That was Suze, sex used to overcome the distance between us. Molly is ... I don't want it to be like that with her.*

But that just begged the question, what *did* he want it

to be like? He groaned again and banged his head on the tabletop to try to knock some sense into his brain. *Nothing. I don't want it to be like anything. I don't want it, full stop.*

I lay sleeplessly watching the moon-thrown shadows of my curtains slowly moving down the wall as the hours passed. Every so often I would fall into a doze only to be thrown back to wakefulness by the memory of Phinn's cold hands cupping my chin and the warmth of his mouth on mine. Then I would be forced to punch the pillow until the hot, hard feeling of embarrassment went away.

What had I expected? I sat up in the bed, hugging my knees, horrible little flashbacks projected against the dark walls of me as I'd been before. I closed my eyes but they were still there, running in the back of my brain, the memories of the way I'd used my vulnerability to persuade men to help me, to comfort me, *to save me.*

And then, Phinn. Who looked far more in need of comfort and saving than I ever had, and yet I'd still tried the same trick on him, that old 'I'm just a likkle girlie who needs a big, strong man's arms around her'. Oh God.

I should cut myself some slack, I really should. I thought I'd found the right man in Tim, he'd ticked all the boxes. Older, financially stable, nice car, heading for the top of his career – not that investigative journalism really had a 'top' as such, simply not getting shot was usually good enough – and seemingly sufficiently fond of me to propose and start making wedding plans.

Bastard.

I punched the pillows again. Small downy feathers drifted from the pillowcase where my stress-relief methods had perforated something and I decided to get up and make tea. Anything which might distract me from this constant loop of shame and horror that I seemed to have locked myself into.

Halfway down the stairs I was once again assailed by the memory of Phinn's face, looking slightly shell-shocked as he'd moved away from me, letting his fingers trail the length of my cheekbones before falling to his sides. His eyes, huge and full of starlight. His expression, not of pity but of understanding, as though he could somehow comprehend how utterly humiliating it had been to find that my fiancé had been having an affair with my mother; that he'd called off our wedding not because of the mythical 'overseas job offer' that he hadn't been able to turn down but because he couldn't work out how to explain things to his friends. Because, oh yes, he'd managed to run the whole double-life thing for six months, escorting me to journalistic functions, taking me around to whatever 'do' required the presence of his co-award winner. Whilst, at the same time, quietly dating *her* and, when the school at which she taught had a Christmas dinner-dance for the staff, turning out in a tuxedo and jiving the night away.

This time I kicked the wall. The pain was like a message from another world telling me to concentrate, not to let myself get sucked in to reliving that horrible, humiliating time; that Phinn wasn't Tim. That I should just accept the kiss for what it was – sympathy and understanding portrayed in the only way that made sense at that moment – forget it and move on. The girl I'd been before … that wasn't me any more. I should realise that just because Phinn had kissed me didn't mean there was any obligation on either side to leap into bed, relinquish my existence to please a man for as long as it took for me to see the next best opportunity.

As I hopped down the rest of the stairs and into the kitchen, holding my injured toe and swearing slightly, I made up my mind. Yes, I kind of fancied Phinn, but that was all it was. A physical attraction to someone with a good body, a cute face and a nice smile. That was all. It was allowed. It didn't have to be acted upon. We barely knew one another, and as far as I could tell, the only thing we had in common was a preoccupation with the mysterious lights. Hardly even a basis for a flat-share, let alone the exchange of bodily fluids.

I fetched a packet of frozen peas from the freezer and stuck them on my foot while I staggered about making the tea. The big hot flushes of shame were dying down now, probably because it's hard to overheat with three pounds of petit pois on your instep, although I was still getting the occasional memory-rush that made me sweat ... *Daniel driving me to work every morning and waiting to drive me home; Simon, who took me for a week to the South of France where he got tired of my flirting with his friends; Marcus who owned the polo ponies and let me ride his best horses whenever I liked* ... I'd used every one of them. Slept with them for what I could get, and never really cared a damn about anyone. *Had I really cared about Tim? Or did I care more about what he'd done to me?*

I made the tea, took it back upstairs, and was asleep before I'd taken a single sip.

Next morning I got back in from raking another six inches of hair off Stan, who was either losing his winter coat or attempting to grow himself a friend, then sat down to chill my now throbbing foot and grab another densely-packed chapter of folklore. It was fascinating. There had been a sighting of a giant black dog outside the building that was now the pub. It had followed a man all the way along the street only to vanish into the wall of my cottage. I stared at the wall for a few moments, almost as if I expected it to reappear, then read on. There was an entire chapter based on the well-known-in-the-village fact that the hill I regularly rode over supposedly housed a dragon nursing its hoard of gold. I gave a little shiver and the bag of frozen peas fell off my foot.

I carefully rebalanced them and read on, a short and rather thin-on-detail paragraph about a ghostly white hare which haunted the village fringe where Riverdale adjoined the moorland. My pleasurable frisson of fear was curtailed by the ringing of the phone.

'Hi, Mike.'

''Ow did you know it was me, babe?'

'I've got caller display. What's up?'

There was a rasping sound, which was probably Mike scratching his cheek with his pencil. ''Ow're you goin' on the folklore thing? Can you run to a long piece or shall I just shove some more pictures in?'

'It'll be fine. I've got lots of material.' I looked at the thin book lying on my chair. 'Well, quite a bit anyway. Don't worry. It's not like you to start badgering me; you know I'm good for coming in before deadline. What's up?'

'It's not so much you this time, love. That guy you asked about a column for? The one in the YouTube clip? 'Ow well do you know 'im?'

And all the carefully structured arguments came rushing back into my brain on a tide of blood which heated my face to near-ignition point. 'Why? What does it matter? I mean, we're just friends, of course, there's nothing more in it than that, in fact I'd hardly even say "friends", more like casual acquaintances. If that. Barely know the guy.'

'Oh.' Mike sniffed. 'Okay.'

'Why?' If I sounded suspicious it was with good reason. How could Mike *possibly* know anything about Phinn and me? Had someone been spying on us? Had the kiss reached as far as London?

'You know I works for the Beeb sometimes? Nature

programme stuff? Well, I've got a mate makin' this kind of real-world look at sci-fi,' which Mike pretentiously pronounced 'skiffy'. "E'd got some guy lined up to front it all, cheap version of Brian Cox or summin', guy's only gone and fallen down some bloody mountain or another, six months in a specialist unit they reckon. My bloke came to me and I showed 'im that clip you sent me ... d'you reckon your man would be up for it?'

'What, *Phinn*?'

"E's got the "look". Apparently. 'Ee don't look no different to any other bloke to me, but then I'm not some steamin' poofter from Production. Get 'im to give us a ring, love, will ya? I can put the two of them in touch. Hey, your man there could be lookin' at fame, fortune and beatin' 'ot girlies off with a stick!'

The thought of Phinn being faced with hot girlies made the bag of peas fall off my foot again. 'I'll pass the message on,' I said, my voice a little on the quiet side. 'I can't promise anything though.'

"S fine, babe. Look after yourself.' And Mike was gone, leaving me with a supernaturally red face, a swollen foot, and the need to call round at Howe End. I debated various other methods of contacting Phinn which didn't involve facing him, but eventually had to concede that none of them would work and limped down the road in a pair of sandals, my toe being too sore to accommodate my usual boots.

When I got there Link was sitting outside with a spiral bound notebook on his lap and his mobile on the grass beside him.

'Morning.' He looked up at me, narrowing his eyes against the sun. 'Bax has just gone down to the shop, ran out of milk. You haven't got any more bacon on you, have you?'

'Sorry, no.' I looked down at the notebook where he'd

been working, lines in pencil scored through, overwritten, circled around and with additional words written in the marginated edges of the page. 'What are you writing?'

Link rummaged a hand through his hair. 'You're not going to laugh, are you?'

'I don't know. I suppose it depends. I mean, if you're writing love letters to Nigella Lawson or something, then I might snigger a bit.' I crouched down beside him, carefully propping my foot to one side. 'But if it's the creative outpourings of a mind filled with angst, then no I won't. Probably.'

'Well, I'm not. Writing to Nigella, that is. Although, phwoar, I wouldn't say no to a bite of her ravioli ... okay. No, this is my job, only it's not exactly the most macho of earners so I tend to keep it all a bit quiet. I write greeting card verses.'

'What, that "roses are red, violets are blue, you are a nutjob and I smell of pooh"? That sort of thing?' I was trying to read his compositions upside down but the combination of terrible handwriting and faint pencil was defeating me.

'Almost exactly nothing like that. Why is there no mobile signal in the village?' He changed the subject with an adroitness that told me the subject of his creative talents was closed. 'It's ridiculous. I can't even text. No Snapchat, nothing.'

'You see that hill up there?' I pointed. 'It's supposed to have a dragon living under it, sitting on a huge pot of gold.'

Link's eyebrows shot up. 'And that stops the signal?'

'I think it's more that it's four hundred and fifty metres high that does it. Not much gets over that.'

'How the hell do you all *live*?' He shook the phone to emphasise our technological poverty. 'It's barbaric! Not even *texts*.'

'We're used to it. And we live in the same way as people lived for hundreds of years before mobiles were invented – we talk to one another. Ow.' My foot bent underneath me and my toe was subjected to more pressure than it could accommodate.

'What did you do?' Link looked down at my unpedicured feet in the sandals, ridiculously summery for March. My unpainted nails stared back. 'Looks sore.'

'I kicked something. It's all right, it's only bruised, when you work with horses you learn to recognise a broken toe just by the shading, and this isn't that bad. It'll just hurt for a day or so.'

Link reached out and lightly touched my rapidly blackening nail. 'I've got some Arnica cream you could put on it.'

There was a commotion of disturbed blackbird in front of us and then Phinn appeared. He stared for a second and then dropped the four-pint plastic container of milk he'd been carrying. It hit the stone path and split, sending a fountain of white liquid spraying up over Phinn's legs which he didn't even acknowledge, he just kept staring at Link and me. Then, paying no attention to the lactic accident pooling around his feet, he walked past us, keeping his eyes on the front door until he'd gone through it. It slammed behind him with such force that the windows sang in their loose frames.

'What the hell was that about?' I stood up, wincing.

Link shrugged. 'Dunno. Think he's off on one. He's been really odd with me. Can't speak, doesn't want to go out, can't even drag him to the pub for a meal and, considering all we've got in is tinned macaroni cheese which tastes like Play-Doh, must mean there's something up with the man.'

'Have you tried talking to him?'

Link pulled a face and pointed to his groin. 'In possession

of a full set, which I'd rather like to keep. Anyway, testosterone exempts me from all that "touchy feely" stuff, that's your department.'

'Great. Thanks.' Now resigned to having to have some kind of conversation with Phinn I levered open the door and went into the house, where there was no sign of him. I wandered through the downstairs rooms which mazed around a central passageway, making me realise that the door we all used wasn't the main front door to the house but the side kitchen door. The real main door lay to the west, where the old driveway used to run and it opened into the impressive entrance hall, tiled and panelled, with a huge oak staircase ascending from it into the dark heavens. My failure to find Phinn on these lower levels drove me up the stairs, which creaked and muttered with each footstep, as though I walked through a field of ghosts.

The upper landing was equally darkly panelled. All the doors were shut so no light penetrated and I had to grope my way around using the handrail. 'Phinn? Are you up here?' I called softly. There were shadows here, things which moved independent of light sources, creaks and groans that reminded me of skulls that screamed. Somewhere above my head a door slammed and I jumped. All I could think of now was the Thing That Moaned, and I ran until I found myself at the foot of another staircase, pine this time, cheaply made and installed to give access to the attics. I shot up the stairs and past an internal balcony towards the door at the far end of the house, which must have been the one that slammed, although it was standing open now.

And on the other side of it, resting his forehead against an almost impenetrably dusty window, stood Phinn. He had his eyes shut and his arms wrapped tightly around his ribcage. As I stood just inside the doorway, panting and trying to quiet my heartbeat, my footsteps silenced by the dust, I saw him raise a hand and scrub at his cheek, then flick his fingers across his eyelids as though chasing away tears. 'Phinn?'

He jumped so hard that his head bounced off the windowpane. 'Molly? Ow, what the hell are you doing up here?'

He was trying for composure, trying to pretend everything was normal but I could see the tracks of moisture down his face and the clumpiness of his eyelashes. His eyes looked like walkways into hell.

'I came to see if you were all right. You looked … if this is about last night then it's stupid. Unnecessary. That was just a … a nothing.'

He went back to resting his face against the window. 'No. It's complicated, Moll. I've got no right, no claim, nothing.' A deep breath in made the cobwebs dance. 'Just one question though. *Did it have to be him?*'

'I don't have the faintest idea what you're talking about.' I walked right into the little room now. It looked as though it had once been a nursery or a maid's room; bare boards showed a pale square where a rug had once stood in front of a rusty iron firegrate and there was just room for a small bed or a cot against the wall. The dust lay thick and stifling, but the cold was like something solid.

'You and Link. I shouldn't be surprised, I know. I mean he's worth, what, two mill a year? Enough to turn any girl's head, and most of her other parts as well, but I thought, well, with last night …'

I'd finished the extended limp that had taken me right across the floor and now I stood behind him. Watching his reflection in the dirty window. 'Writing greetings card rhymes is worth two million pounds a year? I am *so* in the wrong job.'

A half snort of laughter misted a single pane. 'No. Writing

poetry is just what he does to make him look sensitive. He's a Trust Fund boy, our Link. I'm surprised you didn't know, it's usually the first thing he tells women. And if you know the *second* thing he tells them, I'm surprised you're still here.'

'Is it groin-related?'

Now he turned round completely to let me see the devastation on his face. 'I'm just thick, Molly, that's all,' he said wearily. 'Thick and ignorant and tired. You're welcome to him, course you are. Best of luck.' And he waved a hand which then fell heavily by his side.

'Why are you being like this? I'm nothing to do with Link. Bloody hell, he's still stuck somewhere around the Stone Age where women are concerned, isn't he?' Cautiously I touched his shoulder. 'What's this really about?'

Another huge breath in which I could feel by the way his shoulders moved. 'Jealousy, betrayal, guilt, oh, you name it I've got it. I'm like a walking psychological diagnosis, Molly.' And now he sighed that breath out. 'Yesterday Link said something. He didn't even realise what he'd said, he just carried on as if … it was something Suze told him. Something about me.'

I felt my stomach flip as though the feel of him moving under my hand had closed some circuit around my body. I wanted to clutch at it, to stop it betraying me like this, to reassure myself that it was only hunger or anxiety or even pity making me feel as though my innards were falling into a bottomless pit dragging my heart with them.

'So Suze talked to Link about you, so what?' I heard myself say, whilst my brain fought to push my organs back to their rightful places.

'No. You don't understand. Suze and Link … he was my best man, course he was, who else would I choose but … they didn't talk, him and her, not really. Not like that. *But he still knew.* He quoted her, like what she'd said was important enough to remember. And it made me think and ... you know what I think?'

'You think your wife and Link were having an affair?'

He raised an arm and, with his forearm he rubbed a clear stretch of window. Dust scraped along his skin like a bruise. 'I've been wondering for a while ... when she left me, she went to someone. I knew Suze, she'd have got an escape route all lined up before she ran out on our marriage, some guy she'd been running as a second string all along in case things went bad.'

'I'm sorry, Phinn.' I gave his shoulder a quick pat. 'But you might be wrong, you know. You should talk to him.'

He gave a short, hard laugh. 'Would *you*? You won't even answer the phone ... talking to Link won't make it better, it'll just make me want to curl up and die even more than I do now.' He turned away from the window and caught at my hand as it slipped from his shoulder. 'I can feel my whole life sliding away from underneath me, Molly. Everything I was ever certain of, everything I worked for, that I wanted, it's all moving under my feet so that I can't tell which way I'm facing any more.'

I looked at his hand where it held mine in a loose grasp. 'There's still your work,' I said tentatively.

'No. There really isn't. I walked out on them. Oh, I know I said it was a sabbatical and all that rubbish but ... look, I was drunk, I chucked it all in. Wasn't thinking straight, wasn't thinking at all, all I knew was that I didn't want to be there, staring at yet another download from the space telescope and trying to get a bunch of students interested in dark energy measurements. I couldn't keep doing it, and that's the truth. So now, here I am, no money, no job and a house that's so full of ghosts and memories that I can't tell which decade I'm in.'

He used his sleeve to wipe his eyes as I stood mesmerised, held rigid by the feel of his cold fingers and the soft brush of his sweater sleeve against my arm.

He was half turned towards me, our bodies touching down one side. I could sense the rise and fall of his breathing and see each fine hair where his overlong stubble was struggling to turn to beard against his cheeks. I wanted to step right in, to let his arms close around me. It felt as though I was poised on the edge of some terrible precipice, safe for the moment but at any second and with any movement I would fall. As my heart already had.

'I need a friend, Molly,' I heard him say distantly, as though he already lay at the bottom of that immense drop. 'I just need someone … something right now.' The grip on my hand tightened.

Various scenarios played through my head. Did I let him know how I felt? Did I tell him that I was afraid that I was falling in love here? Or did I let my body do the talking for me, slide myself inside that dark zone around him until he couldn't mistake my intentions? And then his words trickled through that pink hazy mind-set, slowed my heartbeat and cooled my brain. *That's how you worked it, not him. You were the one who did the 'save me, save me's', don't put your MO onto him. He wants a friend. Not a lover. Just a friend.* Be told.

'Mike rang me.' I let those words blurt out, safe in the knowledge that they'd stop anything else coming through, anything I might regret. 'He wants you to call him back. Something about, maybe, a job with the BBC?'

Phinn let my hand drop. 'You are joking.'

'Nope. A show about science fiction? Something like that. They need a presenter, stat.' I told him about my sending the YouTube clip and Mike's Beeb connections and all the while I watched as Phinn's head came up, his spine straightened and he became the man who'd stood up on that moor with the wind in his hair and the stars in his eyes.

'Wow. No, really, Molly. *Wow.*'

'Yes, wow. Good timing or what?' I hooked my hair back behind my ears and turned away from him so that he wouldn't see the slightly desperate look that I was sure must be radiating out of my eyes. 'You can use my house phone. Better do it soon, I think they're pretty worried at that end.'

And I limped my way out determined that Phinn would never find out the extent of the way things had suddenly changed for me in that tiny room.

Chapter Sixteen

Phinn leaned his head back against the train seat and watched as the world moved backwards past him, pulling him towards Yorkshire again.

That has to have been the most bizarre few days of my life, he thought, letting his lids block out the scenery top to bottom. Scrubbed up, dropped in front of camera with a script that had made no sense until he'd rewritten it, screen-tested with his credentials checked until they squeaked. And then they'd ummed and aahhed and poked him and tied his hair back then let it loose again, tried him without his glasses and with and finally sucked their teeth as though they were about to buy a second-hand car and offered him the job.

His spine crept as he remembered accepting, giving them provisos that they'd nodded through, and then they'd enthused about his expertise and his looks, how 'right' he was for their programme, prodded him a bit more and then sent him shopping with his new 'assistant', Annie, a woman who looked like a very thin shark, to buy 'cutting edge' clothes. Now he was dressed in razor-sharp jeans with a collarless shirt under a Prada jacket, clothes he loved so much that he refused to take them off after the trying-on session and they'd had to let him walk away in. He'd never felt so ... so ... *cool*.

He'd shaved too and the make-up girl had trimmed his hair, then told him he looked like some rock star guy he'd never heard of. He'd been baffled but had still let himself feel that tiny tickle of unaccustomed vanity, spared a very short moment to wonder what Molly would say when she saw him, then dismissed both pride and prognosis. It was stupid to wonder and even more stupid to care.

He flipped open his laptop and continued his research into the subject which haunted him more than it had any reason to. The lights. Those weird, almost sentient lights which came from nowhere, seemed to display themselves purely for his and Molly's bemusement and then vanished into equal nothingness. Lights which didn't seem to tally with any UAP sighting recorded anywhere, in fact the nearest equivalent seemed to be—

'Earthlights.' He didn't realise he'd spoken aloud until the woman sitting opposite him raised her eyebrows. 'Like the Berwyn Mountains case? But …'

He tapped a couple more keys, slightly worried when the woman smiled and kept her eyes on him. It was one thing to know you looked cool, but it was quite another for other people to appreciate it, so he crouched down a bit, putting his screen between him and her. Kept tapping keys so as not to get engaged in conversation whilst letting his mind fret over the problem of what he was going to say to Link when he got back.

Molly had been right, he had to talk to him. Had to find out, one way or the other, what Suze and his friend had been to one another, if they'd been anything. And if they had been … lovers, if she had run to Link when she'd had enough of trying to be a good wife to a man who lived so much inside his head … what else had she told him?

He felt that cold wash of shame as he typed away, it raised a blush he could see reflected in the screen, making him lower his head until his chin almost touched his chest to avoid his red cheeks being noticed. Suze had been so right about him, he was needy and emotionally desperate. Pathetic.

'Hopeless,' he said aloud again. This got him a sympathetic smile.

Suze knew me inside out. She knew my fears, my foibles,

she knew my frailties. And she enumerated them to me that night, took all my inner uncertainties and made them certain. Made everything I secretly suspected about myself a huge, concrete absolute. Because I'm not a man, not a real man. Not like Link, with his disposable attitude to women. I should love 'em and leave 'em, not wrap my heart around them. It's needy. It's useless. I shouldn't care, however much I want to, because women want men who can survive, who can carry them through a swamp on one arm whilst killing bears with the other hand. Short-sighted, depressive guys whose only expertise is in theoretical science need not apply.

He sighed and let his head fall back onto the cushion. It was darkening outside, trees had become sketches against the sky, and he felt a curious desire to be home, at Howe End. Cold, almost furnitureless, bare floored – home. Maybe Molly would let him borrow her bath again, if he promised not to break in to use it. Maybe she'd read through his research into the lights and make some suggestions. Maybe she'd at least give him the time of day and not notice how his blood pressure rose a little every time she came into the room. Or into his mind. Maybe she'd be kind.

'Your man's back.' Caro threw straw around the loose-box as I wheeled the full barrow out to the muck heap, calling over her shoulder as I passed.

'Which man?' My load wobbled and threatened to spill across the yard and I had to concentrate to keep it level.

'Your sexy scientist.' She leaned on the door watching my ferocious attempts not to care. 'I just saw him when I opened up the barn.'

'He's not a "scientist". He's a physicist,' I said pedantically, fighting the weight of the barrow as it oscillated, using its distraction to keep my mind steady.

'Yeah, but saying sexy physicist sounds like I'm learning

to whistle. Anyway, he's back. But I can clearly see you're not interested from the way you've gone all pink and that barrow is starting to get away from you. Look, let me do it, you go and find out what he wants.'

I stopped wrangling the barrow and straightened up. 'Why would he want anything?'

Caro gave me a level look. 'Well, he was standing at your front door. He either wants to talk to you, or to have another illicit bath, and either way I think you ought to be there.'

The metal supports of the wheelbarrow gouged the cobbles as I stepped back, brushing my hands down my jodhpurs. 'I ... yes, you're right.'

'And you look fine. Glowing. Nicely healthy.' She raised her eyebrows at me. 'Mind, you might smell a bit.' She had to call that last bit after me as I dashed from the yard and across the road, dropping back into as nonchalant a saunter as I could manage when I saw the back view of Phinn still standing outside my front door, poised to give the knocker a little more punishment.

'The door's not locked,' I said mildly. 'You could just go straight in, you usually do.'

He jumped, flinching like a bitten horse. 'Molly!'

'Hi.' Wow, he looked good. Tidier, a bit sharper round the edges. And his clothes were fantastic. 'How long have you been back?' I walked past him and opened the door, kicking off my boots on the step. He hesitated, then copied me.

'Got in last night. Apparently the BBC want me, so I have to go back next week to do some filming and I'm not sure how long I'll have to stay down in London then.' This was all said with a new edge of confidence, an air of belonging somewhere else. Not to this little crowded valley any more.

I felt my heart acquire a tiny frozen edge. 'Oh.'

'So I thought … might be my last chance to sort out those lights.' He swung the bag he carried in my direction. 'I got this.'

'A holdall. What are you going to do, take them on a weekend away?'

He flicked his hair out of his eyes. He'd got new frames for his glasses, narrower ones that made his cheekbones look stellar, and a haircut that accentuated his expression. 'It's a tent.'

'You're going to take them on a *cheap* weekend away then.' I walked on through into the kitchen and began to fill the kettle, trying not to let myself feel anything other than curiosity.

'It's for us.' He was still behind me, I almost walked straight into him as I went to the cupboard for biscuits. 'I thought if we camp out up on the high moor, it needn't be for long, maybe one, two nights. We'll take it in turns to keep watch, we'll be in exactly the right place then to see where they come from, where they go! Good idea?'

He's going back to London, Molly. He's going to leave Riverdale, he's going to leave you. Even friendship won't save you from that. 'I suppose so.'

'You "suppose so".' Phinn hitched himself up onto the work surface. 'You were keen enough to get up there the other day, when you made me ride that evil glue-stick on legs. Why have you lost interest now?'

I opened my mouth to say that we ought to leave it alone, let mysteries be mysteries. That he'd got a glossy new persona now, new job, new confidence. And then my gaze travelled down, down those long legs in their designer jeans to his feet. Toes protruded through a sock seam that looked as though it had given way decades ago, and the heels were worn thin enough to read a broadsheet through. He was still Phinn. Glossy on the outside, but on the inside, still the carelessly dressed, painfully emotion-filled, so-clever-it-hurt, Phinn.

'Oh, all right then. But it might get cold, it's still only March.'

'It's one of those new Polar Explorer tents. All insulation and anti-walrus netting. Got it off a guy in the Natural History unit. They'd been to the Falklands and he reckoned it kept him warmer than his house.'

I eyed up the small bag. 'You didn't happen to ask what sort of house he lived in, did you? I mean, Howe End is technically a house but the internal temperature goes up every time you open the front door.'

'True.' A grin that made my own lips twitch in reply. 'So. You up for it?'

'Yes, all right.'

'But no horses. You understand that, don't you? No horses, not ever again. Not even if the whole of civilisation crashes and we're driven back to living in the Mesolithic era and I lose a leg. I'd rather hop.'

'No horses. Got it.' I poured the water onto the coffee. I'd made him one without thinking, which stopped me in my tracks for a moment, then I got over myself and handed it up to him, where he sat perched on my granite-look work surface like a big black punctuation mark. 'So when do we do it?'

'Soon as you like.' He smiled now, his eyes creasing at me through the steam over his mug. 'Before I go back to London would be best, unless you fancy sitting up there solo and trying to stay awake all night.'

I sipped my drink. It was far too hot but it gave me something to do with my face while I worked out how I felt. 'So, when will you be gracing our screens then, Doctor Baxter?' I managed to get my voice to sound light and unconcerned.

'Thinking about it, I'd rather pogo stick my way round Europe than ride a horse again. Actually, riding that horse was remarkably *like* pogo sticking round Europe.'

I threw my dishcloth at him. 'Stan is not like a pogo stick. He's an endangered species.'

'Good.' Phinn caught the cloth in the air. 'And if you make me get on him one more time, the species will make the "critical" list.'

'Horse riding is very good exercise, I'll have you know. Very aerobic.'

'Yeah well, so is sex.' A momentary pause. 'And *that's* all kinds of trouble too. Oh, and to answer your question, I think the programme is scheduled for autumn. *The Science Behind the Fiction.* Or something. I'm actually looking forward to it. Apparently I'm a natural, or so they say, although I did notice that they didn't specify a natural what.'

'You're going to be famous.' I tried to put the same teasing note into my voice that he had in his, but I didn't think it was working.

'Molly, I'm already famous. Well, famous-ish. If you're into theoretical physics and dark matter investigations then you'd know me, know my work anyway. All that will happen here is that I'll get more attention from people who know about life outside the lab.' He dunked a biscuit. 'So what about tonight then?'

'Tonight?' I wondered if I'd made some promise, some date that I'd forgotten. 'What about tonight?'

Another grin. He was positively Mister Smiley today. 'Up on the moors. I was thinking, we get up there as it gets dark, what, about fiveish, maybe a bit before so we can pitch the tent, get set up, see what happens. Okay with you?'

'I'll need a bath,' I said meaninglessly, while all I could think was – *all night? In a tent? With you? How do I play it, cool or do I pretend that sitting in a space a little bit bigger than a hamster cage with a bloke I think I might be in love with who looks on me as a friend is the best offer I'm ever going to get? Even if it is the best offer I'm ever going to get.* 'And to put some warmer clothes on.'

'No hurry,' and he dunked again, distracted this time by the end of his biscuit falling into his coffee.

I finished my drink and washed up the mugs. Phinn eventually swung back down to earth. 'I'll go back to the farm, fetch the Primus then. Maybe a jacket.'

'All right.' I didn't turn round, although I could see him hovering just behind my shoulder. 'I'll meet you back here at half four?'

'Well ...' Phinn looked down, wiggled his bare toes against the lino. 'I was going to come straight back. Things are ... with Link, I don't know what to say to him. He's carrying on like nothing has happened, he obviously doesn't know what he said, doesn't know that I know.'

'Or you *think* you know. There may be a reasonable explanation, Phinn, you do realise that don't you?'

His head dropped lower. 'I want to believe that. Really, I do, you don't know how *much* I want not to think of my best friend and my wife together.' He rubbed his hands over his face, smudging his expression. 'I don't want to know the worst, is what it is. This way I might suspect, but I don't know. A kind of Schrödinger's affair.' A sudden glance up at me, as though he was waiting for me to tell him to pull himself together, to give him an order, and when I simply smiled he nodded slowly. 'And I don't want to open the box. But you're right. I have to talk to him.'

'Okay.'

'But, later. After tonight.'

'Right.'

He left the tent on the floor and walked silently in his

holey socks to the front door. 'Thank you,' he said, the words having more weight than if he was just thanking me for the coffee. 'I'll see you in a bit.' The door closed gently behind him and I left a decent interval, then ran upstairs to break the world record for bathing, hair washing and leg shaving before changing into some decent jeans and a warm thick jumper.

When I came down again Caro was lounging on the sofa. 'So? What did he want?'

I gave a disbelieving giggle. 'We're camping out on the high moor tonight. Both of us. One tent.'

Caro whistled. 'Way to *go*. By the way, your phone was ringing just now.'

'Yes, I heard it.'

'I picked it up. Thought it might have been important.' She gave me a straight look. 'It was your mum.'

The giggly warmth that the thought of spending a night with Phinn had engendered evaporated like water hitting the sun. 'You had no right to speak to her.'

Caro gave a long, slow sigh. 'Your *mum*, Moll.'

'I don't ever want to speak to her again. I wish she would fall off the face of the planet, just go away and just … just *stop.*'

Caro leaned forward. She clasped her hands around the back of her neck. 'Look, Moll, it might be none of my business …'

'It isn't.'

'… but my mum died when I was fifteen. Do you know how much I'd give to have her back here today? *Do you?*' Caro sounded almost as though she was close to tears. 'Anything. Molly, I would give anything.' Her voice was not much more than a whisper. 'I'd trade the rest of my life for one more day with Mum.' Her head dropped and her hands came forward to cover her face now. 'So it makes me

176

angry when you won't even spare a couple of minutes to chat to yours.'

Caro was never angry. She never lost her temper or shouted, she never even so much as kicked a bale of hay in annoyance. It was one of the reasons she was so good with the horses, however badly they behaved, she always knew they didn't mean it and kept her sense of humour. How could she be angry with me?

'My mum ran off with my fiancé, Caro. They were having an affair behind my back.'

Caro took a deep breath. 'I knew it had to be more than just your boyfriend cheating on you. You should have said.'

'I didn't know how to.'

Now she stood up and was suddenly very tall. 'To me, Molly. You should have said something to me. I'm your friend and you couldn't tell me something that important? D'you know something? It makes me feel a bit like you've been using me.'

I felt my heart drop suddenly down onto my stomach, then further. Like a huge, heavy weight was falling through the centre of me. 'No,' was all I could say.

'You'll tell me the superficial stuff but not anything that really matters underneath. It's like you've been keeping me at arm's length, and that's not a nice feeling, Molly. Not nice at all.'

'I ...'

Caro's voice grew cold. 'Eventually it's going to sink in, you've been looking for replacements for the parents you never had. You've used me to replace your mother and the men – they've all been father figures. I'm hoping you've finally grown up and started looking for someone to be an equal, not someone who's going to tell you how to live your life. Because, from what I've heard from Link, Phinn is not the kind of man you muck around with.'

She didn't give me a chance to reply, just pulled her jacket from where she'd draped it over the back of the sofa and went out, suddenly much more of a stranger than she ever had been since the moment I met her.

I sat and stared at the door after it had banged shut behind her. I'd got so used to Caro being quiet and uncritical about my life choices that her abrupt anger had left me not knowing which way I was facing. *But I'm right not to speak to my mother. After what she and Tim did to me, I'm right. If I don't make contact, then they can't hurt me any more, can they?*

"I'd trade the rest of my life," Caro had said, "to have one more day with Mum." But then her mum had wanted her, hadn't she? Brought her up with love and attention and all those other things? While mine ...

The door banged again and Phinn was in the room, wearing a big coat. 'Hey. Are you all right, you look a bit – shocked.'

'I've just ...' No. This wasn't the time. 'It's fine. Perhaps we should go now. Get the tent pitched and everything.' My voice sounded a bit squeaky, probably because of the way my stomach was trying to hijack my vocal chords. 'It's only an hour or so until it gets dark.'

'All right.' Phinn swung the tent bag onto his back. 'It might take me that long to get the damn thing up. I've never pitched a tent before. But, on the plus side, I do have a down-filled sleeping bag here.'

One sleeping bag? 'Only the one bag?' I tried to think my way through this one. It was a bit ... well, *blatant* for Phinn, surely?

'One on watch, one sleeping,' he said, giving me a look. I hoped he hadn't picked up on what I was thinking. 'Why?'

'Nothing. Just wondering how big the tent is. Thought there might only be room for one person at a time,' I improvised hastily.

'It's fine. Plenty of room. We could hold an orgy in there if we wanted to – which, of course, we don't.' He swung the bag from one hand to another. 'Shall we go?'

'Oh, yes, I think so.'

Outside the wind was changing direction. The metal fox on the top of the maypole was swinging to and fro with a noise like an angle grinder at work and a bank of cloud was moving in from the coast, sending sudden trails of darkness out as it covered the sun.

We hit the steep part of the slope out of the village and Phinn puffed a bit. 'Sorry. Theoretical physics isn't much of a preparation for the real world.'

'Maybe that's a good thing. The real world isn't so great when you get into it, is it?'

'So you *are* hiding here?'

I stopped and looked back. Phinn was about twenty yards behind with the tent bag slung across his shoulders and the last rays of the sun tinting his face and hair before it sank behind the huge hump of moorland to the west. It caught his glasses and blocked out his eyes, replacing them with reflections of the scenery, making him look as though he'd been possessed by the spirit of the moors.

I thought of Caro, of her sad, accusatory expression and the fact that she hadn't waited for my explanation, and gritted my teeth at Phinn. 'Look. I've had enough of this today. If we're going to be spending any length of time together in a small, inflammable container, then you'd better learn to stay *off* the topic of my private life, all right? We're here to track those lights, not do an Oprah.'

Phinn struggled closer up the hill. 'You said it.'

'Good.'

'Fine.'

We walked the rest of the two mile trackway in silence.

Chapter Seventeen

Phinn frowned and swore quietly to himself under his breath. *Oh gods. Why didn't I pay more attention when that bloke showed me how the damn thing went up?* 'Maybe this bit goes in here?'

But Molly wasn't paying any attention to his increasingly feeble attempts to erect the tent. She was staring out over the hills with dusk snagged in her hair, and his heart snuggled itself away behind his stomach to hide.

He flicked the tent again and this time one side stayed up for long enough to get the ropes tight and he managed to get the securing pegs dug into the earth, screwing them in with the kind of vicious energy that displacement activity lent to any action. 'There.'

Molly turned just in time to see the tent tug gently against the guy ropes and collapse back to earth like a shy ghost. 'Oh. It seems to have deflated again.'

It was almost completely dark now. Phinn stumbled over the groundsheet in his attempts to locate the peg he'd just managed to dig into the banks of heather and bracken, caught both feet in the fallen tent and fell full-length on top of the failing structure. The huge, hot weight of humiliation tucked itself around him like a blanket of shame. '*Bugger.* Sorry, I really should be better at this kind of thing.'

To his amazement Molly laughed. 'Why? I can't imagine quantum physics requires you to camp out much, does it?'

'Well, no, but ...' *But real men can put up tents.* 'I've got a doctorate,' he finished, berating himself for the non-sequiturial nature of his follow-up. 'I mean, I thought these things were designed to be foolproof.'

Molly looked down at the tangled mass of ropes and

shiny, weatherproof fabric. She shook her head as though casting off unwanted thoughts. 'Yes, but it's a tent. Don't they have their own kind of cunning intelligence? So they can only be erected on dry sunny days, during the hours of daylight?' She poked the canopy with her toe. 'It is clearly in keeping with the rest of its kind. Violence is probably the only language it understands.'

She seized the poles and shoved them through the fabric sleeves which gave the tent structure, then rammed the first of the pegs into the ground. Obediently it remained up for long enough for the rest of the ropes to be tightened and the pegs to be forced into the peaty soil. 'There. Told you, sometimes violence is the only way.'

Phinn stared, amazed. 'That's incredible.'

She grinned. 'Yeah, well sometimes Stan can only be steered if you get off, run round to the front and lean against him, so I'm used to having to use force.' She walked around the tent checking the ropes were all taut, leaving Phinn staring into the darkness.

The wind cut like glass and a few gust-borne particles sliced at his cheek. He tipped his head back to greet the sky and hoped that the lights would put in an appearance soon. If he had to spend any time at all in that tent with Molly he wasn't sure what he'd do. If they came in the next hour then he'd be able to strike camp and head back down to the relative warmth of the valley rather than hovering around up here in this liminal wasteland.

Phinn shivered. The dead felt so close in places like this, he could almost sense Suze hovering over his shoulder, muttering critically. He had a sudden image of her body as she'd looked when he'd identified her, greenish-pale, her hair dried to strings around her head. And even then, even in the mortuary, she'd seemed to him to have a half-smile of derision on her lips, as though she was mocking his tears.

When Molly touched his elbow he leaped into the air, so lost in his vision that he half-expected Suze to be standing there, dripping water and accusing him of sending her to her death with his last, desperate words.

'Phinn? Are you all right?'

He became aware of the scalding feeling behind his eyes and turned away to hide his face in the dark sky. 'I'm fine, yes. Just, you know. Wind in my eyes.'

You see, Molly? Suze was right about me. I cry too much. Sometimes everything hurts, even memories.

'So, do you want to take first watch, or shall I?' She'd moved back, whether to give him space or because she was disgusted with his exhibition of emotion, he didn't know. 'Actually, if you do it I'll make us some food. I brought some of the camping packs that I had to try out for the magazine. They're not bad as long as you don't expect cuisine. Oh, and if you light the Primus.'

'Sounds good. Thanks.'

The sky is constant. Space is infinite. Focus on that, on the never-ending nature of nature itself and remember that nothing else matters. Love is a matter of fleeting hormonal shifts, but space endures, Baxter, the universe and all its mysteries are yours, so stop angsting about things you want but can't have. Shut up and watch the skies.

The tent had a little vestibule area, so I hunched over the Primus out of the wind and let Phinn scan the skies whilst I stirred a bottle of water into a tinfoil container of something that looked like horsefeed. But at least it would be warm, and with the way the wind was cutting through the ripstop material of the tent like Wolverine through muslin, we were going to need that heat. It was distracting too, keeping me busy so I didn't have to think about any of the things that Caro had said. We'd never argued before. I'd come to think of her as all-accepting, so it felt a little bit as though I'd been savaged by my duvet.

'Molly.' Phinn's voice blew in sounding professional. 'They're coming.'

I scrambled to my feet, switching the Primus gas bottle off and resigning myself to losing the meal. 'Which way?'

'From the south. Quickly, I need you to man the video.'

The wind was manic outside, punching into me armed with pellets of ice. 'Where?' I had to shout over the noise of it. 'I can't see.'

Phinn's glasses were frosted over. 'There.' He took me by the shoulders and turned me bodily around, pointing with the camera. 'Up. Higher.' His hand left my shoulder and tilted my chin. 'See now?'

As though the wind flustering down below didn't reach any higher than us, the lights hung unbothered. In fact they seemed to be making stately progress towards us, coming diagonally from the south, skirting the edges of the village and drifting towards the high moor as though on a leisurely outing.

Phinn shoved a piece of machinery into my hand. 'Point it up and press this.' He cupped his hands around mine, indicating a glowing blue button. 'Keep it steady.'

I tried to comply but the wind was buffeting me from both sides, swirling and skirling around us, and my hands were shaking. Phinn was clicking away with his camera, periodically glancing down to make a quick pencilled note on pages which whipped and drummed as the wind flipped them. Flurries of sleet obscured my vision and I had to keep lowering the camera to wipe my face.

'You okay?' Phinn called, his words rising over the gale. 'You're doing all right, keep going.'

I looked at him. The storm was dragging his hair away from his face, pushing his glasses sideways and threatening to tear his clothes from his body, but he looked as though he didn't care about any of this. Head thrown back, eyes fixed on the lights, he looked almost elemental himself. 'And here they are.'

Directly above us the lights seemed to halt. 'How are they doing this?' I asked, my mouth filling with little gobbets of ice which cut my tongue. 'It's like they're watching us.'

'Earthlights!' Phinn yelled at the sky. 'Got to be earthlights! So why does it look intelligent?' He lowered his camera but kept his face turned to the stars. 'You bastards! What's the point of all this?'

His face was pulled out of shape by the wind and by the emotion inside him. I suddenly had the sense of a kettle that had simmered for so long but was now reaching a full boil, feelings erupting into the cold air like escaping steam. 'Hey.'

He ignored me. 'Is it you, Suze? Are you doing this somehow? Is this you coming through from the other side to make sure I understand what kind of a loser I really am? Was it not enough that night – you have to make sure that I carry on knowing that I'm a waste of space?' And in an act of sudden violence he raised his arm and flung the camera across the rapidly whitening heather in an overarm throw that sent it tens of metres into the darkness. 'D'you know something, Suze? I really don't give a flying fuck about what you think any more. See? That's how much I give for your opinion of me now!'

He strode suddenly past me, head still up despite the now driving sleet, and ducked into the tent which was humming and flapping like a restrained bird.

I followed him. What else could I do?

At first I thought my eyes had deceived me and he'd gone past the tent and headed off into the night, but as my vision adjusted to the eerie new dark inside I saw him. He was huddled up against the back wall.

'Phinn?'

'Yeah, I know. I blew it.' His voice was tight as though he had rocks in his throat. 'Sorry.'

'Why are you apologising?' I advanced cautiously. 'It wasn't exactly a procedure we could practice, was it?'

A high laugh. 'Oh, I just apologise first and explain later. It saves time. It's always my fault, when it comes down to it, after all.'

I didn't know what to say, how to play it. I'd never really had anyone break down and lose control like this. I was used to people being very stiff-upper-lip about disasters and tragedies. 'That can't be true,' I said carefully.

'Oh, can't it.' He sounded tired. 'Okay. If you say so.'

'Phinn—'

'We should go. Get out of here, get down into the village. They won't be able to see us down there, we can hide indoors.' He stood up, unfolding himself until his head brushed the roof of the tent. 'Come on.'

But as soon as he opened the tent flap wide I could see we weren't going anywhere.

'It's a bloody blizzard! We can't go down in this. We'll freeze and get lost and die.'

'I thought you knew these moors?' He was lit by the weird blue light of the falling snow, it made his skin look dead. 'You can find your way down, surely?'

I sat back. 'Not in a full-on white-out I can't. There's no real path to follow and everything looks different in the snow. We'll have to sit it out. You can't cross untracked moorland in snow without a compass and a map.'

Phinn stepped outside into the tugging wind. 'I'm prepared to give it a shot.'

'No!' I crouched in the vestibule and pulled my jacket close around me. 'You don't understand, it's brutal up here. Feel how cold it is? In ten minutes you'll have lost all sense of direction and even a bloody genius brain like yours won't be able to cope. You'll just lie down exhausted and freeze to death.'

Snow splattered him, settling on his shoulders, his arms. He threw his head back and I could see the feathery flakes touching his eyelids, his lips, like dead kisses. 'Okay, and why is that such a bad idea?'

'Oh stop being so bloody overdramatic! It's a bad idea, all right? Come back in here and we'll wait until it stops.'

He turned his head to look at me and the expression in his eyes was hot and hard. 'I think control over whether I live or die is mine, don't you, Molly?'

There was a curious moment of stillness as though we stood at the fulcrum of something huge waiting to see which way the lever would move. Even the storm dropped and the snowflakes started falling straight down, dizzyingly white.

'Phinn.' It was all I could say. I hoped that my voice sounded neutral and cool but I rather suspected that there was an undertone of longing slipping through. 'Don't.'

He moved, a minor snowdrift outlined where he'd stood for a moment, and then he was gone, walking into the falling flakes. His dark shape stayed visible for only a second and then was swallowed up by the renewed wind chasing white flurries across where he'd been and blanking him out to my view.

I scrambled to my feet and rushed outside the flap. 'Phinn!' Even his footprints were filling in as though nature was trying to expunge him from the world. 'PHINN!'

The snow cut across my vision with dancing lines, blinding me, driving into my face with a force that made the softness just a story; this snow cut and lanced and drove itself home like an armed troop. I took a stumbling step forward. 'Phinn, please. Where are you? Don't do this. You can't do this, not to me … please.'

My voice sobbed into silence. There was no answer but the wind's echoing cries as it dragged at the tent and hurled fistfuls of snow to earth. I was alone in the whiteness, the man I was now pretty sure I'd fallen in love with had walked away to almost certain death.

'I wasn't aware I was doing anything to you.' Phinn's voice came from behind me. I turned so fast that my feet slipped from underneath me and I landed on my backside, legs akimbo, gazing up at the dark shape approaching rapidly from out of the storm. 'Certainly not from back here, anyway.'

And there he was again, snow melting against his skin and lying half an inch deep across his jacket. He raised an arm. 'Had to fetch this.' He waved the camera by the strap. 'Losing my temper is all very well, but I don't want to lose all the evidence too.'

'I thought ...' I scrabbled my way to my feet. 'I thought you'd ...'

Phinn pulled a face. 'I'm not that noble.' He reached out a hand and grabbed mine to help me to stand up. 'But I *am* interested in why you'd take it so personally.'

'You're my friend. Of course I care about what happens to you.' I used the excuse of brushing the snow away from my face to cover my rapidly heating cheeks with both hands. 'And for God's sake, let's get back inside the tent before we end up soaked and frozen.'

'Okay.' Phinn held open the flap to let me in first. 'And thank you for not mentioning my outburst back there. I'm not sure what happened.'

'It's those lights.' I unzipped my jacket in the new warmth. 'They're doing something to us.' At least, that was my reasoning. It had to be some external force that was making me feel like this, as though my stomach had turned to marshmallow and my heart was a weak, frail thing barely managing to beat.

'Some kind of psychic thing?' Phinn removed his jacket now, sending a spray of melted snow splashing across me. We were both tinged pink from the small amount of light from outside filtered through the red nylon of the tent. It made his hair look orange and his skin healthily blushed. 'Could be, I suppose.'

He sat down and pulled the camera onto his lap, switching it on and flicking through the photographs on the screen. 'None of these are much good. They're always too far away to show up as anything other than blobs which could be anything.'

'So you don't think it was the lights that made you lose it.' To occupy myself I began stirring at the rank, turnip-smelling mass still sitting lukewarm on the Primus, hoping that the light wasn't making me look heart attack purple. My trousers were sticking to my wet buttocks and chafing unpleasantly. 'What was it then?'

Phinn stopped moving. Sat very still, looking down at his knees. 'Would you tell me something, Molly?'

'Tell you what?'

Now he looked up. Beads of water hung in his hair like diamonds. 'Would you tell me the truth? Whatever I ask, will you tell me, honestly, what you think?'

'I ...' How could I promise when I didn't know what he was going to say? What if he asked if I really thought of him as a friend? My woolly jumper was suddenly a size too small. 'I suppose so.'

'Okay.' Back to looking at his legs again. 'Do you think I'm a wimp?'

'A ... *No*. No, of course I don't.'

'No "of course" about it. Do you think I'm a pathetic excuse for a man, then?'

'Phinn ...' Without knowing why I was doing it I reached out and touched his hand where it held the camera. 'Why would you even say these things? Have I ever ... do I make you feel like that?'

Slowly his eyes came up to mine. He looked tired, beaten, and his eyes had a bruised kind of look to them. 'No. But life does.'

'Your wife—' I started, then realised I had no idea where I was going with the sentence. 'You're a lovely guy, Phinn.'

'My wife told me I'm a wimp, just as she was leaving for the second time. In other words, just before she crashed and drowned, she told me I was a pathetic example of manhood. Introverted, a waste of what little testosterone I had, as she put it, a weak, ineffectual geek whose only saving grace was that he knew how to put the toilet seat down after he'd used it – and she even said *that* as if it was a bad thing.'

'She was wrong,' I said definitely.

A shrug. 'Maybe.' Now his gaze moved across my face. 'I've never done anything particularly manly, never known how to.'

'This is all crap. Why should you have to be all butch and masculine. There's plenty of women who like their men a bit less macho. I mean, look at Johnny Depp, he's not exactly going to be playing rugby any day soon, is he? And he's not short of the odd female admirer.'

'Wow.' Phinn smiled and the smile drove the haunted look from his eyes. 'Me and Johnny Depp. At least I'm in good company.'

'And you're kind and sweet. You took my shoes home so that they wouldn't get wet and ruined, that's not something that a typical man would even think about doing. Sometimes thoughtfulness trumps being able to bench press a hundred pounds where women are concerned.'

'I had to resort to medication, Molly. Real men, apparently, don't get depressed either.'

'It happens. It's not your fault, Phinn.'

'Thank you,' and he sounded genuinely grateful. 'I'd been … dwelling, I guess, on what Suze said, and the business with the tent and everything … it just rattled me. Being up here, all so wild and empty and miles and miles of nothing, it felt like she was right behind me with her sarcasm and her cheap shots.'

'Why did you stay married to her?'

I stood up and found the two spoons I'd brought in the pocket of my jacket. Hauled the rapidly congealing food from the stove using my sleeve to insulate my fingers from the hot packet and held it up. 'Dinner, by the way.' I used my jacket to insulate my lap and rested the foil on top.

'She seduced me, you know.' Phinn took a spoonful of glop. 'I've never been particularly … a PhD doesn't make me an expert on … I don't really know what women *want*. It's like … having a penis doesn't suddenly qualify you to know how to unhook a bra and when to do the tongue thing. It just complicates matters when all I really wanted to do was take it slowly, talk, find out … but Suze really took it up to new levels, and then … it was just easier to hang in there than to try and get off and face her. I know that makes me an even bigger coward, the fact that I'd stay with a woman rather than put up with the unpleasantness of divorcing her, but … it wasn't all bad. Suze wasn't all bad. And I had a home, you know? Someone to go back to, a place that was fixed and permanent and *mine*. It might be stupid and it might be wimpy but … all I really wanted, all I've *ever* really wanted was a home.'

I felt my skin prickle. I knew how it felt to long for a proper home, lights on in the windows and food cooking; a cuddle before bedtime … I wanted to go outside and pound my fists against the earth until the feeling went away.

'But you must have had other girlfriends, ones that didn't

treat you like that. Women that made you feel good about yourself?'

His spoon hovered near his mouth. 'There were a few. But my previous girlfriends were all colleagues, workmates. If we had nothing else to talk about there was always the research. Those relationships just kind of petered out, or they'd move on to another programme.'

'So what did Suze do for a living?'

'She was a model.'

I swallowed a mouthful of the greyish food without tasting it, although the gritty grains stuck to my tongue. 'That figures,' I muttered.

'But I'm good at what I do, Molly. And I love it. Trying to prise the lid off the universe, find out what makes it tick, what fills all those spaces ... I can't explain it, it's like ... did you ever do jigsaws? You know when you find that piece that fits so perfectly that you can't believe you didn't see it before, the piece that makes sense of everything you're looking at? *That* is how my job makes me feel.'

He looked up at the roof of the tent, a taut nylon screen above our heads onto which he seemed to see an image of the sky projected. 'It's full of all the possibilities that there ever could be, Molly,' he said, his voice only just above a whisper. 'There could be *anything* out there, from *Star Trek* spaceships to *Dune*-style sandworms. Life could all be connected through invisible holes we can't even sense. We might even be able to reach out and touch it.' He raised a hand and brushed my cheek with his fingers. 'If we knew how.'

I closed my eyes. Everything inside me had risen into my throat, and I couldn't entirely blame the awful food. *What should I do?* He didn't know how this went, he'd said so himself. But what if I did something and it turned out to be a misunderstanding?

'Phinn, I ...' I opened my eyes again and he was looking at me now with those eyes that looked like a black hole.

'Molly.'

'You wanted me to be your friend. You said, you needed a friend.'

His hand dropped away and he went back to scoop another spoonful of mixture from the foil container. 'Friends. Yes, you're right. We're friends.'

'Is that still what you want?' I could feel my heart beating so hard that it felt as though it was trying to drill its way out through my shoulder blades.

'I want ... shit, Molly, that's not a fair question right now.'

Very carefully he placed the food brick at the side of the tent and then turned back, kneeling in front of me so that our faces were level. 'I've never known what I wanted. My parents had me as some kind of thought-experiment, brought me up as a prodigy then sent me off to school. There was university and the doctorate and the research programmes and then Suze – and all that time, no one asked me what *I* wanted. I was just this super-thinking-brain, y'know? I was meant to have all the answers, not the questions. And now ... now life is all questions. What do I want, where am I going, what the hell is *happening* to me? I ...' He raised both hands and let them fall onto his thighs. 'I've got nothing.'

I bit my lip to stop myself touching him. *He won't make the first move – but if I do, then I'll always wonder whether I forced him into something.*

'Your wife said some terrible things to you. It's not surprising that you're questioning everything now, I suppose. But you are a fabulous guy, Phinn. You're intelligent, wow, yes, I don't have to tell you that, *incredibly* intelligent. You're sensitive and funny and sweet and—'

'And nice guys finish last. Yeah, I know.'

'I was *going* to say, and you're amazingly attractive, actually.'

'How can I be? I'm the original ten-stone weakling. In glasses. There's more muscle on a biology wall chart than on me.'

'Are you angling for a compliment, Doctor Baxter?'

'What, another one? No, don't worry about me, Molly, I know my limitations. And, as a friend, I have to say, thank you. Thank you for being honest, for making me feel – oh, I dunno, less of a freak.' And he straightened his legs to raise up onto his knees, leaned forward, and kissed me.

Outside the wind howled like a cheated wolf.

Chapter Eighteen

When Phinn woke up he found Molly's head resting on his chest. They'd managed to make the sleeping bag fit both of them by lying on their coats and using it as a glorified duvet, but this had meant they'd had to squeeze up so tightly together that trying to get comfortable had been a little bit like a dry humping session.

Her hair smelled of strawberries. It was all he could focus on, the sweet fruity smell that made him think of summer and also, incidentally, brought to mind the horrible humiliation of sports days but that wasn't her fault. He shifted his weight, uncomfortably aware of pins and needles in the arm that Molly was lying on and that he really needed a pee, but loving the feeling of having her so close that he could feel the gentle snores she exhaled into his shirt.

And he'd kissed her. Properly this time, not a fleeting peck on the cheek. A full-on-the-lips kiss that had gone on for longer than simple gratitude dictated, that had softened her mouth under his until he'd felt the light pressure of her tongue. A kiss that had aroused him to the point that he'd had to move back and break contact so that she wouldn't notice his groin hardening against her.

And now, here he was, waking up with her. Both of them still dressed and his groin still … yep, still hard. Very, very carefully he slid his arm out from underneath Molly's shoulders, receiving another brush-past of her berry-hair as she muttered and settled deeper into him, nestling her face against his ribs.

He wondered how the knocking of his heart hadn't woken her. It was leaping up and down and trying to call attention to itself like an under-exercised Golden Retriever inside his chest, so filled with need and want and longing that was only partially soothed by having the object of its affections so physically close. He felt ... yes, purged was the only word that fitted. Last night's very ... *unusual* outburst, so unlike him, had left his mind feeling cleansed. *No, not cleansed. In fact, quite a lot dirtier than usual.* Phinn twisted his lips to stop himself swearing aloud. Okay, it would have ruined everything if he'd pushed it last night. It would have spoiled their friendship; all the cosy calling round and eating biscuits would have been ended in an explosion that would have made the Big Bang look like a soggy party popper. And maybe she'd have despised him now, looked on him as just another one of those asshole men who directed her life for her, told her where to go and who to talk to.

But sometimes he hated himself for being a gentleman.

Unable to resist, he moved forward, dropped a quiet kiss on her sleeping head and let himself relax for a second into the fantasy that she was his. Sleeping with him, laughing with him, giving him a reason to come home. An anchor in the increasingly unstable seas that theoretical physics was becoming. And they'd live at Howe End – only with heating and more furniture – she'd write and he'd commute to London for filming; they'd snuggle up together on the putative sofa and she'd giggle at his TV persona in its sharp suits and trendy shirts.

Yeah, right. She won't want that, will she? She's hiding here from the pain of rejection, the last thing she needs is to get involved with someone whose idea of a happy future sounds like something out of the nineteen forties. She's used to men who excite her, dynamic men with drive and ... all those other things Real Men have.

Phinn was surprised at the sheer physicality of the pain. Suze leaving, yeah, that had hurt but it had been tempered with huge amounts of relief. The marriage may have failed but with its passing he'd lost that confused feeling, the awful sensation that he wasn't quite keeping up with what was expected of him. Her return had made him happy for a while, she'd changed a little and become softer, more gentle ... pregnancy hormones obviously had agreed with her, even if the whole idea of having a baby hadn't. But then ... Had he really been such a pathetic specimen of humanity? He shook his head quickly and, disturbed, Molly gave a sigh which quietened him to almost statue-like stillness.

Don't wake up. Not yet. Let me lie in this fantasy world for a bit longer. Where I'm in charge of my own destiny and you're not just sleeping in my arms wrapped in seventeen layers of wool but naked, sated. Happy.

The thoughts of her naked and sexually satisfied drew his attention back to his groin and the knowledge that he really, seriously needed to pee.

I woke up to a cold foot and a gradual realisation that I was alone. Next to me, where he'd lain, the cover was still warm but there was no sign of Phinn. I gave my hair a quick tidy with my hands and made a furtive check on my cheeks for dribble, knocked the sleep from my eyes and sat up. 'Phinn?'

The tent flap waved in reply but nothing else moved. The air coming in was chilly but had lost the diamond-blade effect it'd had last night, so I eased myself out from underneath the down-filled sleeping bag.

The previous evening played on my mind. His kiss had, by several orders of magnitude, outdistanced the polite cheek kiss and gone right into the territory of preceding-sex, but he'd moved away just as I'd been about to touch him. Backed off and cleared his throat, changed the subject away from anything personal and made me talk about my cookery lessons, prompted, I think, by the setting concrete nature of the camping food. And I hadn't dared do anything, although every instinct told me that he wanted me. The way his eyes had become unfocused, the way his hands had moved across my shoulders as though unwilling to let go, the quickening of his breathing – it had all said 'this is going to end in sex'.

And now I was, to put it mildly, a bit cheesed off.

'Phinn?' I burst out of the tent entrance and found him standing a few yards away. The ground was covered with a sprinkling of thawing snow and the air was unnaturally quiet. 'Why are you out here?'

'Ssshhh.' Phinn waved a hand at me. 'Stand still.'

'What?'

'Look up.' His voice was hushed, almost awed. 'It's the lights. You can hardly see them in the daylight, but they're there.'

I looked. High above us, in the sparkling blue of the clear air, hung a sequence of lights so faint that they looked like facets of diamonds, mere distant winks and sparks. 'In the daytime?' I breathed, copying his low tones. 'Do you think they were there all night?'

Phinn tipped his head right back to look directly overhead. 'Dunno. Maybe.'

'Do you want me to get the camera?'

A shake of the head. 'They are so beautiful. You know, I don't think I really appreciated that before. What the hell are you, eh? If you're earthlights then we must be in for one hell of an earthquake.' His gaze dropped from the heavens and settled on me. 'Molly, last night—'

'Phinn, look—'

'No, let me finish.'

'I really should go first.'

'Last night, when I kissed you. I don't want you to get

the wrong impression of me, that's all.' He spoke quickly, trying to beat me to it. 'I don't do that kind of thing, like I said, I'm not that kind of guy. I don't know why I ... what is it?'

'Please. If we're going to have this discussion, can we have it when you've done up your fly?'

'Oh *hell.*' He turned away and fumbled with his zip for a moment. 'Sorry! Sorry about that. I'm a bit ... did I wake you?'

'No, it's fine. At least it's stopped snowing.'

Phinn looked around him as though noticing the world for the first time. 'It's so amazing. Is that Riverdale down there?'

'Yes. You can just see Caro's fields from here.'

'Can you see my house?'

'Howe End, you mean?'

He gave me a quick glance. 'Well, if you can see Bristol I think you just broke a world record. Yes, Molly, Howe End.'

I pointed and then waggled my hand at the end of my arm. 'It's sort of round the corner. You can just see the chimney, kind of. Is it your house then?'

Phinn shielded his eyes with one hand from the glare of the newly risen sun, which was catching the snow and glittering and glimmering like some kind of fairy rave. 'Well, Uncle Peter left it to me in his will. He was my mother's brother, not that you'd ever have known it, over-intellectualised neurotic that she is.' He took a deep breath. 'I wanted to make love to you last night, Molly, but I was scared. I don't want to repeat the experience I had with Suze, falling in love with someone only to end up terrified. And that's what it would be for me, y'see.' He turned back to face me and his eyes were huge. 'I'm too emotional to go down the casual sex route.'

I inwardly cursed the woman that had made him like this, so self-doubting and afraid. 'I really like you, Phinn. I mean, seriously.' Several yards of snowy moorland separated us, it felt wrong half-calling sentiments like that, so I moved a little closer. 'You are so ... so ... different.'

'Yeah. And there's the problem. Where I come from, that's not different, it's weird. I'm odd, Molly, even odder than your average physicist, which is saying something. I feel things too much.'

I thought of Tim and his offhand reactions to my fears for his life. 'Better than not feeling at all.'

'Maybe. But it makes me – well, half my department thinks I'm gay, put it that way. Look, there's one last thing you need to know about me and Suze and that night she ... She was standing there, screaming things at me. Terrible, awful things about how I was more like a half-set custard than a man, and I—' He stopped. Hid his face in his hands. I could see the clouds of his breath strained through his fingers.

'Phinn, it's okay.' My heart belted my chest, squeezing me hard enough to bring tears to my eyes. God, this man.

'No, it's not. Listen. This is the kind of man I am, this is how *pathetic* I am. Suze was throwing all this at me, and do you know what I said?' His words ended half-choked. 'I told her that if she stayed I'd bring up the baby as if it was mine. That no one ever needed to know what had happened, that we'd carry on as before. She could even go back to work, I'd work from home, look after it. That is how *desperate* I was, Molly, to keep my home going. I was prepared to take on another man's child *just so that I'd have a home. Something solid, something to hold on to.*'

The cold was nothing now. All that existed in the whole wide universe was this man, with his self-doubt and his self-loathing, not seeing that his offer had been the single greatest sacrifice he could have made.

'You'd have done it? Pretended the baby was yours and ...' I was about to tell him how I really felt about his wife, about the woman that had told him such lies about himself that they'd stained him soul-deep. But then I stopped myself. He'd loved her once. It wasn't up to me to tell him what he already knew in his heart; that she'd been confused and angry and let down and that she'd taken it all out on him.

He shrugged, and the shrug took in the sky, the earth, everything. 'That is the kind of spineless guy I am. You needed to know that. To stop me making the ultimate fool of myself by stepping into something new, something with you. I'm sorry, Molly, really I am. I behaved badly last night.'

He was working so hard to hold on to the shreds of his dignity that when he turned away from me and started walking I didn't have the heart to stop him. I watched him search uncertainly for the path in the newly-melting snow, then set his shoulders and head down over the lip of moorland towards Riverdale and as soon as he was out of sight I flipped the tent down.

It wasn't his fault that I knew about tents – writing about outdoor stuff in *Miles To Go* meant I'd had more experience than an outward bound instructor at putting these things up. *It's not your fault, Phinn. You're sweet and gentle, and nobody should ever have made you feel less of a man for being kind.*

I rolled the tent back into its carrier, then sat back into the snow, wondering about Tim. About all my previous boyfriends, who'd been cast in the role of alpha male to my cutesy girlie act. Had they wanted it to be like that? Maybe, just maybe they might have appreciated me being in charge sometimes. Or had I deliberately chosen men who would let me get away with it?

Phinn was so different. But maybe I was ready for that now.

I trailed him all the way down into Riverdale and caught up with him on the bridge, where he was staring with a shocked look on his face down into the racing waters, as though he was terrified but dared not look away.

'Snow's thawing, that's why the river is so high,' I said, being as matter-of-fact as I knew how. 'It's all coming down off the high moors.'

Phinn just jerked his chin at me in acknowledgement. He looked haunted, with the newly emerged stubble breaking out on his chin again and he'd lost that glossy, high-performance polish that London had given him to a kind of dark, inward-looking depth and silence. It was like walking down the road with night.

'I'll make some coffee.' I went to turn up the road and walk towards my cottage, but he caught my arm and stopped me.

'I don't think … maybe it's best if we don't. I'm going to London, I'll sell Howe End and the fees from the programme will pay me to—'

My whole body chilled and prickled as though a thunderstorm was about to break. 'You're going? Phinn?'

'It's for the best. I can't … you make me want things, Molly. Things that I'm not fit to have.'

I stared up into the war zone that his face had become. His eyes wanted me, they held a heat and a promise that, if things had been different, he'd have been dynamite in bed, with all those repressed emotions pouring out and me there to receive them. But his brain, his mind, was telling him that – what, he didn't deserve me?

'This is …' I was about to say 'stupid' but bit the word back, along with the urge to wrap myself around him. It might make me feel better, he might even stay for a while, but it wouldn't help him. Wouldn't give him back the self-respect he'd had shot down in flames, it would just delay the inevitable. 'Sad,' I finished. 'And what about the lights? Are you going to leave me alone with them?'

He didn't return my smile. 'I have to. I'm sorry.' And then he turned on his booted heel and walked away from me over the bridge, without looking back.

I watched him all the way to the Howe End drive, where he disappeared into the gap between the flowering currant bushes. Then I waited for a ridiculously long time in case he changed his mind, waiting to see his lanky figure amble back out onto the road again, hands in pockets and mind elsewhere. But he didn't. Nothing stirred in the village at all, until Caro rode around the corner out of her yard on China, who shied quite dramatically at seeing me standing in the middle of the Green.

There was a moment's awkwardness, and then the Caro I'd known since I arrived rushed to the fore. 'Molly? Are you all right?'

I wanted to be cool. To ask her how she dared pretend that she cared, after what she'd said about my mother. But the truth was that I needed her. I needed that steady presence in my life, making up for the parental one I'd never had, even if she didn't always understand why I did what I did. It was Caro, she wasn't my mother, and she didn't come with the background layer of resentment and disinterest.

'Yeah, I'm fine. I will be fine, I'm just a bit ...' I sniffed hard and blinked harder. 'Yes, fine. Phinn is ... he's going to London. I don't think he's coming back.'

Caro walked her horse over to me and slithered down to the grass. 'I did warn you about Doctor Sexy. Not the kind you muck about with.' She looped the reins over her arm. 'I'm sorry,' she said, with her back to me, fussing with China's forelock. 'About yesterday. I stepped over the line and I have no right to tell you how to feel about your own mother, Moll, of course I don't. Especially after ...' She coughed and rubbed the mare's nose. 'After what they did to you. It was a shock. I never thought ...' Her hand hesitated on the pink muzzle, as though the softness of the horse's lips made her think of something else. 'You should have told me.'

'Yes, you're right. I should have.' I wiped both hands over my face. 'I'm sorry too, Caro. I felt stupid, that's why. Stupid for trusting Tim, for believing the things he said and for letting it happen. She ... my mother ...' I remembered her words about her own mother, and tailed off. 'And now I've lost Phinn too.'

'Maybe not. I mean, he really seems to like you a lot and London is a big place with not much to recommend it.'

I half-smiled. 'I like him a lot too.'

'Well, there you go then.' She rested her cheek for a moment along China's grey face. 'If anyone can persuade him to stay, it's you.'

'I don't think that's a good idea. Phinn's had people manipulating him for a long time and now he sees undue influence in everything. He's so panicky about loss of control that he didn't even want to get on Stan.' I gave a deep and unflattering sniff that totally failed to communicate my being all right with Phinn leaving. 'And, let's face it, Stan's only ever out of control when it comes to food intake.'

Caro sighed. 'Life is never what we think it ought to be, is it?' It sounded rhetorical. 'Mine ought to have had a brood of kids and some patient bloke with loads of cash and a love of horses. Instead ...' She shrugged. 'Not as bad as what's happened to you, but still.' Then she dealt me a gentle punch on the arm. 'You and me then, Moll. Horses and a future of staring into wine glasses and wondering where the time went.'

I nodded, slowly. 'You're right. It could be worse, at least I've got you.'

'And Stan.'

'Oh, yes, there will always be Stan.' I gave a teary half-laugh. 'Nobody else would have him.'

Caro put a tentative arm around me. 'Not to upset you or anything, but ... Phinn's friend asked me out last night,' she carried on conversationally. 'That Link boy. He's been out on Wenlock a couple of times this week. Charming and cute and absolutely *loaded*.'

'He told you that? Before he even asked you out he told you about the money? Good God, he must have nearly as big a rejection complex as Phinn.'

We started walking towards my cottage, China striding peacefully alongside without attempting to take chunks out of the grass or the hedges or people. Stan should start modelling himself on her rather than Hannibal Lecter, I thought.

'Well, he was quite drunk. Actually, make that *very* drunk, but I'm still going to hold him to the date. It's so nice to be going out with someone I haven't known since they were at school. It'll never come to anything, of course, he's got other places to be, but it's still a pleasant change. Is he ... you know, a nice guy?'

'I think so. I can't see Phinn hanging around with anyone who'd hurt someone for the sake of it.' *But he'd hurt Phinn, hadn't he? He and Suze, and then he thinks he can carry on being his best friend, just say nothing, keep quiet and hope it never comes out?*

'But then I don't really know Link very well, so you should be careful. And if Phinn sells Howe End then I guess Link will leave with him, so don't go losing your heart to that one, Caro.'

She pulled a face. 'I'm too old and wise to pull that stunt,

Moll. But your man's going to sell up? That'll be sad, the place has been in that family since … God, I think it's in Dad's book somewhere, hundreds of years, anyhow. It'll be the end of an era.' She leaned, thoughtfully against the mare's shoulder. 'Although it's a family house really. You know, filled with lots of kids who all need to learn to ride.'

'Mercenary? You? Who would ever say such a thing?' I gave her a grin that I didn't really feel like, as she hopped back aboard again and turned China's head towards the moors.

'Me for one. Money first, sentiment second, otherwise you've got no business.' Caro straightened her stirrup. 'Are you really all right, Molly? About Phinn, I mean. The way you two have been hanging around together, I really thought you might … well, get a shag at the very least.'

I blinked up at her. 'His ex did him a lot of damage. Said a lot of stuff he can't get over and I don't think he's ready for a relationship of any kind yet. Not until … well, until he realises what he's capable of.'

'Screwed up men, eh? So attractive and such hard work. Hey, you want to get Stan out and come with us for a gallop? Clear your head? The snow's all melting fast and it'll be completely boggy for weeks afterwards, this could be the last chance to get a good fast ride before July.'

I hesitated for a second. What if Phinn changed his mind? What if he came looking for me? But then I shook my head at my adolescent silliness. I'd never waited in for a phone call, why the hell should I wait now? And Caro clearly wanted to make sure that our argument was completely forgotten. 'Hang on there for a moment, I'll go and tack him up.'

'You'll need to use Poppy's saddle,' Caro called after me as I ran towards the yard. 'He's eaten his again.'

Chapter Nineteen

If he had to do one more 'establishing shot' Phinn thought, as he stood staring up at what purported to be the night sky but was, in fact, a giant green screen, he was going to drop down dead of boredom.

'Just one more, Doctor Baxter.' The director, who persisted in using Phinn's full title at every opportunity, waved a hand. 'Turn a bit more this way for this one, thank you.'

Phinn sighed and blinked hard behind his third new pair of frames this week. These glasses were going to be a continuity nightmare, but They, whoever They were, wanted him to wear different sets depending on whether he was talking to camera, interviewing or in long shot. Making a TV show was like making a patchwork quilt, they'd told him, all the bits would be stitched together and put into an order which would make sense of everything. He was really glad about that because the stuff he'd filmed so far made no sense at all, even to him, and he'd written it.

He leaned back against a strategic bit of scaffolding while a girl, who surely wasn't old enough to have left school, rushed in and dabbed at his face with a brush. *Was I right to leave? To make that decision so firmly, so finally? Maybe I should have thought more about it, taken advice, not let myself be panicked by the fear of what might have been and the longing for something to be again.*

He shook his head, willing himself to keep focused, and his assistant, Annie, touched his shoulder. 'Stay with us, Phinn,' she whispered. 'Soon be over. You up for a drink later?'

'Sorry, can't make it tonight,' he whispered back. 'It's the last day of this block of filming, isn't it?'

She checked her iPad, surely unnecessarily, she'd been organising him all day, she'd know the schedule if anyone did. 'Well, yes, but we usually go on somewhere …'

He had that curious feeling in the pit of his stomach again. As if he stood at a crossroads and could choose his path, but one way was full of pitfalls and snares. He wished he knew which track was which. 'Got a train to catch.'

'Right.' She leaned in and tweaked the collar of his jacket which had wilted under the lights, much as he was doing. 'Do you need me to get the tickets for you?'

He smiled. 'I think I can just about manage to do that myself, Annie, thanks.'

She gave him a slow nod. 'Okay. Anything else you need me for, just call, all right? If we're not going for a drink, I'll get on home, relieve the childminder.'

Phinn shook his head, more at the image of this impossibly chic, impeccably tailored woman having a child than at her words. Annie was so cutting-edge that she was practically a razor. 'That's fine.'

She gave him a grin and walked out of shot and Phinn was cued up to gaze at yet another portion of featureless sheeting. But it wasn't the screen he saw, it was Molly's face, scrunched up in sleep, nestled into his chest and the feeling of loss made him tip forwards and screw his eyes shut, ruining the take.

I was snuggled up in bed with the folklore book, listening to the rain spattering against my window in the gusty breeze. Warm, cosy … and with a mind that wandered more than a tomcat. I'd battled my way through three-quarters of the book so far and started drafting up my article based around some of the more blood-curdling episodes, like the ghost that held its severed head in one hand while it wandered the lanes, screaming at passing locals and presumably frightening the local wildlife into scarcity, and the Moaning Entity at Howe End.

But it wasn't enough. Not distracting enough. When I slept my dreams were all of black eyes and hot kisses, of strangely drifting lights sent from weird cloud-countries, and I watched the skies every night with increasing desperation. But the lights didn't come. At least, while I was watching, anyway. Perhaps they came late at night when I'd given up hope and gone to bed. In the six days since Phinn had left, I hadn't seen so much as an unidentified gleam in the direction of the sky.

There was a knock at the front door, and then a pause. This was odd, usually everyone just tapped once then walked straight in, in the case of Caro she'd have kept going until she got to my bedside. 'Hello?' I opened the window and looked out.

'Oh, hi. Sorry, you still in bed?' Link stood on the garden path, rain plastering his hair down and making him look even more like an overgrown schoolboy. 'Only Caro said that you'd got a laptop I could maybe borrow? Only for five minutes, just to submit this stuff.' He brandished a rather soggy notepad. 'I've got a deadline,' he finished sheepishly.

I pulled on some random jeans and a fleece and went to let him in. *I won't ask,* I told myself. *If Phinn Baxter has fallen down a mineshaft or got a place on* I'm a Celebrity ... *I'm not interested.*

'Have you heard from Bax at all?' Link stood in the living room and looked around. 'How's he enjoying the fame and fortune game?'

'No idea.' I showed him to my laptop, already plugged in and online. 'Isn't he in touch with you?'

Link shrugged. 'No mobile signal. And if he's emailing, well ... it'd mostly be a waste of time, wouldn't it?' He rubbed his hands together. 'Any chance of a coffee, Moll?

It's like living in the middle ages in that farmhouse.' He sat at the table and stared at the laptop. 'Although a mysterious consignment of furniture arrived the other week. Either Bax wants the place more comfortable for some reason or we've got a poltergeist with an Ikea account.' His lips slid across each other with a series of unspoken thoughts. 'Before he went, did Phinn say anything to you?'

I stopped in the kitchen doorway. 'He said a lot of things.'

Link looked at me. His hair was beginning to dry and fluff up like a chick's feathers. 'Only I thought he might have taken you with him. What happened to you both that night you camped out? I mean, I know he's a bit ... quiet, but he's not usually the love 'em and leave 'em type, not like this. Hell, he still gets postcards from a girlfriend he had when he was seventeen, and most of the others send Christmas cards.'

'Nothing happened. Well, nothing physical.' I tried to keep my back to him, fussing with the kettle to stop my blush from becoming noticeable. 'Phinn is very messed up, Link. His wife ...' I stopped talking and began spooning coffee like a madwoman.

'Suze. Yeah, she was a case.' Link looked down at the keyboard, grinning. 'Serious fruitcake.'

'He knows,' I said quietly and watched Link's reaction. The grin faded and his cheeks looked as though they fell in a little.

'Oh.'

'Is that all you can say? "Oh"? That man, *your friend*, is so seriously screwed up by what she did that he started drinking himself to sleep, and all you can say is "oh"?'

A key tapped. Delete delete. 'We never meant to hurt him. Shit, Moll, I'd never hurt Bax. We grew up together, he's virtually my *brother*. But she ... God, Suze could be so ... Look, she saw something she wanted, she'd take it. That's how she was with him, with Bax, saw him, wanted him, and jeez, he was something to look at back then, and she homed in there and she took him. He never saw it coming, never knew what hit.'

The kettle boiled and I ignored it. 'Didn't she ever stop to think what she was doing to him?'

Link stood up now but kept on tapping that key as though his finger was stammering. 'That was Suze. She never thought things through, she was ...' He raised his hands and ran them through his hair, sighed. 'She was like this kind of force of nature. She was beautiful, Molly, so, so beautiful, and if she wanted you, you had to be *fast* to get out of her way.'

'And you weren't fast enough either.'

He looked at me, serious now. 'No. I wasn't fast enough either.'

'You bastard.'

He nodded. Kept on nodding, while a single tear ran down his face. 'Yeah. You don't need to tell me.' A deep breath which seemed to help and then he wiped his face with both hands. 'So. How much does he know?'

'That she went to you when she left him. That she was probably running back to you the night she died.' And probably a whole lot more, given how clever he was, how much he'd been able to work out about me, simply from how I lived. Like ... 'That the baby was yours.'

Link took two steps towards me and then crumbled. He rested his forehead against the wall and went silent, the tears now streaking in a continual line. I could see them rolling down to land on his collar where they stained his shirt a darker blue. 'I *tried* ...' It sounded as though his teeth were gritted together. 'I wanted ... But she blew me out. Went back to him while she decided what to do, and then ...' A sadly simple little gesture with one hand which illustrated a life cut short.

'Did you love her?'

A head tilt towards the ceiling. 'I don't know.' Then infinitely sad eyes met mine. 'I'd have tried, Molly. For her, for the baby, I would have tried. But I think ...' He scrubbed at the tears with the back of his hand. 'I think it was the money, not me. With Bax it was the glamour, the whole "wife of a famous man" thing she wanted. It was all so *stupid*, like she was looking for vindication through a man, you know?'

I felt one short, horrible moment of affinity with her. Wasn't that what I'd done, wasn't that how it was with the men I'd dated, with Tim? The successful man syndrome? 'She must have been quite insecure.'

'She'd had a shit childhood, I know that much.' Link walked past me into the kitchen and used one of the mugs from my mug tree to get himself a drink of water from the tap. 'It wasn't really her fault, Molly. It was the only way she knew how to be. And she had the looks ... no one called her out on her behaviour, no one ever told her that she didn't have to be that way.'

'Did anyone ever try?' *Like Caro tried with me, telling me that I didn't have to look for a father figure? That maybe Phinn was nearer to what I needed than Tim or any of the others had ever been?*

Link shook his head again and straightened his shoulders. 'I dunno, Molly. What Suze and I had, it wasn't anything real, you know. It was like she was *looking* for something, something that nobody could ever give her, not me, not Bax, not any of the other guys she'd trail around after her.'

'And then she took it out on him, on Phinn? Made him think he was too pathetic to be loved, what, to make sure that no one else would ever have him?'

He shrugged. 'You didn't know her, Molly. You can't judge her.'

211

'No. I suppose not.' I poured the water onto the coffee, the bitter smell spiralling out of the cups on a conveyor of steam. 'You never know what goes on inside other people's relationships, do you?' I fetched the milk from the fridge and nudged both mug and bottle towards his hand. 'I just wish he'd … I dunno. Realise that he's not a wimp.'

'Weeelll …' Link gave me a red-eyed smile. 'He is a bit.'

'Maybe. But it's the nice bit. The bit that doesn't come over all macho and try to be in the right all the time. The bit that's kind and gentle and sweet.'

Link blew steam. 'Wow. You really are gone over him, aren't you? Are you sure it's not the body? You know, we practically have to cover him in talcum powder to be able to see him when he takes his shirt off?'

'Shut up you. Do you want the laptop or not?'

He gave a deep, broken sigh. 'Yeah. Yeah, I'd better.' And then, quickly, with his words coming in a tumbled rush, 'I know you think I'm just a trust-fund kid who doesn't care about anyone but himself, but I'd die for Bax, Molly, you should know that. What happened – it was wrong, I knew it when it was going on, and it wasn't just Suze's fault. I was just so bloody *jealous*.'

'Of Phinn? Why?'

He sat back at my keyboard again, and his fingers found the delete key irresistible once more. I wondered if he knew he was doing it, or whether it was some subconscious urge to wipe out what had gone before. 'Oh, not his background – his parents are like the two biggest weirdos on the planet. D'you know they don't even have a house? They spend all their time on the lecture circuit. Dad's some kind of hotshot in the world of nanoparticles and his mother built the first neuro-compatible computer. But he's incredible, Bax, he's so clever and quick and brilliant he makes me feel like I'm … I'm like the really dumb friend that he keeps around to reassure himself of how intelligent he is. Like keeping a dog, or a fish, so that you can know that, however stupid you might be, there's some form of life lower than you are?'

I stared at him. 'He doesn't. No, Link, he doesn't think of you like that.'

Two fingers now. Delete and backspace. 'No. But that's how I *feel*. When you see him work, when he's making connections ... He doesn't just push the envelope, he shoves the whole fucking Post Office. And then he upped and married the most stunning woman that I'd ever seen – it's like he had *everything*, Molly. And maybe ... maybe I just wanted to see a little tiny rip in that wonderful life.'

I opened my mouth to scream at him. To ask him how he dared to sit here and tell me things like this. I'd bunched my hands up and I was a hair's width away from punching him, yelling and shouting, until I saw his expression. He'd lost all the flirty winks and cheeky grin and was sitting with his eyes closed, one arm hugging himself and the other hand still flipping between those two, telltale keys. He wasn't being brutal, he was being *honest*.

'Thank you,' I said quietly instead of screeching abuse.

'Don't tell him, will you?' Eyes still closed.

'No. No, of course I won't.'

'He's all I've got. All I've ever had, really. My parents aren't much better than his, to tell the truth, but at least I got to spend Christmases at home. He'd either come with me or have to stay at school.'

'It's like a bloody Dickens novel,' I said, trying to make him smile.

It worked. 'Hey, nothing is quite *that* bad. And, you know, a trust fund makes up for quite a lot.'

We shared a moment of complicit silence during which he stopped trying to wipe everything out and rested his hands on the main keyboard.

'You'd better ...' I nodded at the notebook.

'What? Oh, yeah, sure. You're right. Wouldn't want to keep the happy birthday grandma market waiting, would I?' There was that tinge of bitterness again.

'Link ...'

'No. It's okay.' A renewed cheeky grin. 'Honestly. It's really okay.'

While he was tapping away at the keyboard with a look of concentration so intense that it even made *me* poke my tongue out of the corner of my mouth, I went upstairs and sat on the edge of my bed. My stomach was rolling and my head hurt, not through any physical cause but because I'd started to see myself through someone else's eyes, and what I saw wasn't pretty.

Mine hadn't been a shit childhood, whatever Link had meant by that. Not really. Plenty of my schoolmates either never knew, or had never met their fathers too. Plenty of us were raised by mothers who had to work all hours, lots of us wore second-hand uniforms and at least I'd had the riding lessons – I'd joined the school pony club and fallen in love with all things equine, and Mum had paid.

My mother had fallen pregnant during her first year of teacher training. To her credit she'd never considered giving me up, she'd worked extra hard to afford childcare while I was small, and then had simply worked around my school hours. But she didn't seem to have considered my feelings in any of this, she'd simply carried on the life she'd always wanted without taking into consideration that a child might feel a little ... well, left out of things.

She'd sit up late writing reports and lesson plans, and while I sat in our little front room working on essays about the causes of the Second World War, she'd been in the kitchen with a pile of exercise books, marking. I think she'd positively encouraged me to ride because it meant I spent my Saturday mornings at the local riding school and she could spend those hours drafting out schemes of work for her department.

And when I started dating, it wasn't boys that attracted me. Not for me the hours spent sitting in a teenage boy's bedroom while he stared at a games console and perfected the art of ripping the heads off things in 'Silent Hill'. While my friends were standing cheering on chilly touchlines or sharing single student beds with earnest, acned lads, I was being driven in natty little sports cars by men who should have known better.

All of them older. Considerably, sometimes almost *ridiculously*, older.

All of them wealthy, or at least by my standards. Flattered, usually, by the attentions of a moderately attractive, fairly intelligent girl. Easily manipulated.

I felt myself blush, and lay down to hide my face in the pillow. Suze and I hadn't been a million miles apart really. Although I hadn't consciously damaged anyone, I was beginning to see how I'd tried to find something in each of these men that none of them had to offer, that I had, as Caro said, been looking for a father all that time.

A man who would love me uncritically, unconditionally, however badly I behaved, however much I rode roughshod over his feelings or desires. Suze, and her longing for a famous, eye-catching husband with an up-and-coming career, really wasn't very different to me.

From downstairs I heard a tentative throat clearing. 'Molly? I've done with the laptop, thanks.'

I stood up. My skin felt tight, as though it might split and shed at any moment. 'Good. Yes, okay.'

Another bout of throat clearance. 'And what I said earlier … all that stuff?'

I poked my head onto the landing to look directly down

the stairs at him, standing uncertainly in the hallway. 'Don't worry, Link. I'm not in any hurry to hurt him any more than he already has been.'

Link's face seemed to inflate, the chubby innocence coming back to his cheeks and the spark to his eye. 'Right. Great. Thanks, yes.'

'But I think you and he ought to talk about it.'

'I've been thinking the same thing myself. Maybe I'll head on down to London, try to meet up with him. Or I could go back to Bristol, he'll probably head home when he's done with the filming. Try to catch up with his research or something.'

He paused, as though about to say something else, then jerked his head sideways as though the thought was too petty to put into words, and let himself out of the front door.

Chapter Twenty

Phinn sat in front of the enormous TV screen in the hotel bedroom, cursed his cancelled train and tried not to think. But, it turned out, even *Babylon Five* repeats weren't enough to block out everything, despite the sound being up so loud that the people in the next room knocked on the wall. He kicked his shoes off and drew his knees up to his chin, forcing his eyes to remain on the Vorlon ambassador striding up and down in forty-inch HD glory across the flat screen.

He wanted someone to talk to. But someone *real*, not one of the programme crew or some plastic-faced publicity person, someone who'd understand what he was talking about and not keep smiling and telling him that he was doing a great job and this series was going to be the success of the decade. He *knew* he was doing a great job. He was wired up to do a great job. Not to fail, not to slack off and cruise on past success but to keep on expanding knowledge, studying, researching. That was what he *did*. Not to walk away from an unknown situation but to patiently work at it until he could comprehend its parameters, then scrutinise those until a workable theory could be reached.

And in television, that was *easy*.

His treacherous brain slithered towards those thoughts he didn't want to have and he curled his arms around his legs, trying to use motion to distract them. On the screen a Minbari ship floated by and he amused himself for a while trying to work out where the still shots of the external universe had come from. It didn't help. Of course it didn't help, even standing in front of a full film crew hadn't helped, there was no way that sitting alone in this room with a television, however large, was going to take his mind off things to any extent.

He stood up. *I could go down to the bar. Have a few ... no. That way led to ripping all my clothes off and begging to be abducted – hardly my macho moment of the year. I'll just have to sit it out, catch the morning train to Bristol. After all, it hardly matters whether I get there tonight or tomorrow, does it? There's nothing there for me, apart from the university and I shouldn't think they're desperate to see me, given the way I carried on over the last year.*

It hit him hard, again, the feeling that no one knew where he was, and even fewer cared. Oh, the BBC people sort-of cared, they didn't want their new leading light to be involved in anything that might produce the wrong sort of publicity, but that was where their concern began and ended.

He flicked at his camera-friendly hair, took his glasses off – interview frames today – and polished them on a corner of the sheet. Wondered what Link was up to. Wouldn't let himself wonder about Molly, it was bad enough that he could still feel the weight of her head against his heart, still smell that sun-ripened berry scent of her hair. Thinking about her wouldn't help this loneliness. Nothing would.

She's my unknown parameters. Something that I should have worked on, worked out. But the equation for something like that ... good woman, strong woman who's got her life under control and really doesn't need a fuck-up like me falling into it; the horses, and the river and why am I so bloody SCARED all the time?

He opened his bag and looked at the left over antidepressants, innocently bubbled in their plastic, that he carried like a talisman. *20mg per kilogramme of bodyweight is a toxic dose. Why do I know that? Why do I even care that I know that? Why have I really kept them?*

Why am I so pathetic?

And then he found the little foil packet that Link had shoved into his pocket. He'd taken it out and slipped it between the sheets of prescription drugs, hadn't wanted it to fall out at some inopportune moment and show him up as the kind of man who, not only can't ride in and do the 'white knight' thing, but a guy who'd need chemical help to get his armour on.

Four tablets. Enough.

His hand shook as he unfolded the metal foil, and he closed his eyes as he swallowed.

It rained all night, I knew because I didn't sleep. Oh, I tried, lay in my bed with the covers pulled up to my face, but whenever I closed my eyes instead of the peaceful darkness all I could see was Phinn's smile. Not his rather tense, wary smile but the one he'd had when he'd addressed those diners on YouTube. That wide, confident grin, the one that reflected mischief in his eyes. The smile he smiled when he was happy.

And I knew he'd been right to go. Knew that I could never make him smile like that, me, with my background in passive manipulation, my use of men as status symbols, my hopeless power kick. I'd been stupid to ever think that beautiful man ought to be within a million miles of me – I was only slightly less bad for him than botulism.

My cheeks flamed again. He'd been right, all the time, he'd been right. If we'd had sex in that tent up there on the moor, surrounded by the lights and the snow, we'd have fallen into something that neither of us could handle. For all Caro's assertions that I'd grown up and moved on from the needing-a-daddy thing, I would still have used Phinn. And him? Maybe he was too weak for me, too insular, too cerebral, maybe I did need someone who'd challenge me, face me down, argue with me.

But Phinn does that too.

And I'd just let him walk away. But what else could I have done? Been all controlling and demanding, thrown a temper tantrum and made him stay? Seduced him? *Been like his wife?*

I breathed out and the duvet puffed around me like a living skin. No. I'd had to let him go. For the first time I'd done the right thing and let a man walk away from me when every line of his body had said that he wanted to stay. I'd been strong, we'd *both* been strong. It had been the only way.

So why did it hurt so much?

In the morning the rain was still grumbling across the windows and dawn hardly bothered getting started under skies stacked with cloud like folded linen. I had a long, hot bath and contemplated wandering over to see Caro, give her a hand with the mucking out, even being up to my shins in wet straw and horse muck would beat skulking around in my kitchen.

But in the end I just dressed in my most comfortable old clothes and curled back up in the armchair with the book of folktales in my lacklustre hand.

I couldn't focus. My eyes were tired and the print so small that it blurred and danced and refused to be pinned into words. Coffee. I needed coffee.

As I padded into the kitchen on softly socked feet, I heard a knock at the door. Waited for the inevitable bursting in amid flurries of drizzle, but it never came, so it wasn't Caro. Thinking it must be Link again, sufferer from the archaic form of manners as taught in all-boys boarding schools, I slithered my way along the lino to open it.

'You can just walk in, you know. It's not like you're going to catch me naked or anything,' I said, and pulled the door to reveal a plump, glossy man dressed in clothes that would have suited someone twenty years younger, standing on the step. We stared at one another for a moment.

'So you are here,' Tim said. There was almost a note of accusation in his voice, as though I'd been deliberately pretending to be elsewhere, rather than deliberately pretending to have ceased to exist. 'May I come in?'

I hesitated. Glanced over his shoulder to where the brand-new sports car was precisely parked, currently having one wheel-arch piddled on by a small scruffy dog. 'Why?'

'Because I've taken considerable trouble to come here, and because I know you have the manners to at least let me over the threshold to discuss our business in private, rather than yelling it from the doorstep.'

I held the door wide and he moved past me into the hallway. As he went I noticed the smell of cigars which moved along with him like another skin, and the memories that came associated with that smell made my heart squeeze just a little.

'How did you find me?'

Tim gave me a cool look. 'Does it matter, Molly? I came to talk. Through here?'

'No! Anything you want to say, you can say to me in the hallway.'

A wry cocked eyebrow told me that he'd expected this and that my behaviour had fulfilled some kind of promise he'd made to himself. Or a bet. 'All right. But why not put the kettle on?'

Fussily he peeled himself out of his jacket and turned to hang it up on the end of the banister rail, patting its folds into place as though reassuring it that it wouldn't have to hang in this lower-class establishment for much longer.

Had he always been this prissy? I knew the answer to that too, as I knew the answer to so many questions suddenly.

'Maybe I will later.'

'Oh, do stop sulking,' he said, carefully positioning himself against the newel rail, arms folded. 'It doesn't suit you and it doesn't do either of us any good.'

I noticed suddenly that Tim was fatter and balder than he had been, or maybe it was simply my exposure to a man who made coat hangers look a little plump and whose hair struggled even to fit on the 'unstylish' continuum.

'I'm not sulking,' I said carefully. 'I'm angry. And do you know the stupid thing? The person I am most angry with is *myself*.'

All of a sudden the front door flew open so fast that the inner handle banged against the hallway wall with a noise like pain. There in the doorway, with his hair plaited by rain and his jacket streaming, stood Phinn.

'Shit,' he said. 'Sorry about the door. No, not sorry. Not sorry at all.'

Tim looked him up and down. 'Oh dear Lord. Is *this* how you chose to replace me, Molly?'

I ignored him. Looked instead at Phinn, whose eyes were wide, pupils huge and blazing, in his pale, pale face. 'What are you doing here? I thought you said it was better if you went?'

'Went. Came back.' Leaving a trail of watery footsteps on the lino, Phinn advanced towards me. 'I can't do it, Molly, can't walk away like this. Wanted to see you again, wanted to explain properly.' A sudden shake of his head sent water flying, splashed my cheek and made Tim wipe ostentatiously at his forehead. 'I *can* do this. It was stupid to leave, to think I should just go, without facing up to what was happening.'

'Oh, bravo.' Tim started clapping. 'What an excellent performance, very touching.'

'Phinn,' I said, a bit weakly, 'this is Tim.'

Phinn turned slow, heavy eyes. Water was pouring from his Prada jacket, teeming in little rivulets from the AllSaints jeans. He looked like he'd walked right out of the river.

'This.' His voice broke off and I saw him turn his fingers inwards, pinching at his palms. 'This. Is. Nothing. To. Do. With. You.' The anger weighted his words, made them drop and bend the atmosphere around them. 'I think you should go.'

Tim straightened but he was a good head shorter than Phinn, whose lanky body seemed to have acquired more substance suddenly. 'I need to talk to Molly.' But the words sounded reedy, apologetic. 'It's important.'

'Not so important that you couldn't hang around to sneer at me. No, if it was really important you'd have said it already.' Phinn gave Tim a steady stare. 'Go.'

'Phinn …' I went to touch his arm, to reassure him, calm him, I don't know what, but he jerked the wet leather sleeve away from my hand and stepped to the door which still stuck open, the handle half-embedded in the wall. With a wrench that made more water torrent from his shoulders he pulled the door free.

'Out. If you really want to talk to Molly, come back tomorrow. Afternoon. We'll be in then.'

My mouth opened but refused to say anything.

Tim looked from me to Phinn and then at the door, but the smugness was gone from him now. 'But I—'

'Tomorrow. Now piss off.'

Tim fussed towards the door, looking anxiously at the sky. He pulled a face as he stepped outside and the rain began to hit him. 'Er. Could I have my jacket?' He gestured to his pure wool coat, hanging from the banister as though he, not I, lived here.

Phinn moved, picked up the coat and flung it out through the open door past Tim, who failed to catch it, and out into the garden, where it hooked itself on the hedge and trailed a dismal, expensive hem into the mud. 'And that's for the *fucking* cordon bleu lessons! Learn to cook yourself!' And Phinn swung the leading edge of the door so that it flew across in front of us and slammed resoundingly, leaving my last impression of Tim's expression as one of complete surprise.

I stood speechless as Phinn leaned against the door and closed his eyes. He slid, slowly down the painted wood leaving a snail-trail of dampness behind him until he came to rest on the floor, knees pulled in and head thrown back. 'That was amazing,' he said. 'Why did I never do that before?'

'Because you're the nice one.'

'Yeah.' He scooped his dripping hair back. 'And look where nice got me. Sitting in a hotel bedroom contemplating ... never mind. Nice got me nothing, Molly. Got me a wife who cheated, a best friend who lied. Nice gets you shat on from interstellar space. While *that* ...' he indicated Tim by bumping the back of his head against the door gently. 'That got you. That fat, officious, patronising git had *you*, Molly.'

'He's bald as well,' I added helpfully.

'Not making it better. But seeing him walking into your house ... I knew who he was, you didn't have to tell me. He even *looked* like the kind of bloke who'd make you take cooking lessons, and pick up an award that you both won! And he was walking in here like he owned the place, like he owned you still, after everything he'd done.' Phinn sighed a ragged sigh and closed his eyes. 'I'm sorry. I didn't mean to interfere, I just felt ...' His eyes opened, blinked, and he pulled his glasses off to shake them free of water. 'It wasn't *fair.*'

I gazed down at him for a moment. Water was puddling

slowly around him, his boots were caked in mud and the hems of his jeans were ragged where they touched the floor. 'It's not like you to be so macho, Phinn.'

He put his glasses back on and looked up at me. His pupils had shrunk back to nearer normal but were still wide, outlined by the deeper black. 'I know.' With one smooth movement he stood up. 'I just needed to know that I could. If I *had* to, I *could*.'

I wanted to touch him. To know he was real, not some water-zombie sent to taunt me, no kelpie risen from the deeps. I reached out and laid a hand against his stubbled cheek. 'Phinn ...' Moved my fingers down to touch his chest. Stopped. 'Why are you so wet? It's not raining that hard but you're soaked to the skin.'

He smiled that smile and I felt my blood press against me. 'Got the early train, no buses, no taxis, could only get as far as Pickering. Had to walk the rest.' His hand came up and his fingers cupped mine closer against him until I could feel his heart under that cold, damp T-shirt. It was keeping pace with my pulse.

'But that's fifteen miles!'

'Nine. I came over the fields.'

'And you didn't get lost?'

'There are two ways of looking at that question.' Phinn took half a step forwards and under my fingers his heart began to gallop. 'One answer is no, obviously not. And the other ...' He leaned to close the gap between our lips, touching my mouth with his very gently, 'Is yes.'

The kiss deepened and time stretched. I eased his sodden jacket from his shoulders but wouldn't go any further. I could sense from his reactions that he wanted to make the running this time, to set the pace. To seduce.

'Molly.' He spoke my name against my skin, his breath raising all the hair along my neck. 'I'm soaked.'

I moved back a fraction to look at him. 'Yes.' All my weight felt as though it was in my tongue.

'Do you know what I need?' He was smiling down at me with that slightly wicked look in his eyes that I'd seen on the YouTube clip, that look that said he knew what was coming next, and he knew I'd enjoy it.

I took a deep breath and felt the lever move, the switch flick, the pathway change under my feet. 'You're the one with the answers now, Phinn. I think you'd better tell me.'

His hands moved, down from where he'd been touching my face, down over my shoulders, brushing down my arms until he took my hands. Linked his fingers through mine and tugged me gently. 'I need a nice hot bath.'

As though he'd never done anything else, he took the lead. Set the bath running until the room filled with steam, then took his glasses and hooked them, very carefully, over the edge of the sink. 'Don't want to break them,' he said, and the promise in those innocuous words made my legs tremble.

Then he was kissing me again, a fog-ghost in that humid room, almost insubstantial under my hands, but he wouldn't let me touch him properly, wouldn't let my fingers find their way under his clothes. Instead he caught my wrists and held them pinned to my sides while his mouth traced lines along my neck and my shoulders and his tongue wrote sentences of fire on my skin.

When he released my hands and stepped back I nearly fell over. 'Molly.' He sounded very serious.

I had to calm my breathing just to be able to answer. 'Yes?' Even then my voice was high and weedy.

'I don't do casual sex. You should know that before we go any further.'

'*Phinn.*'

'It's important to me. *This*, everything we do from here

on, it means something to me. You mean something to me. I don't want you to think that it's all about the sex, it never was, it's about you and me, Molly, finding out what we want.' His look held me while his fingers undressed my body, his eyes seeming to reach right inside my head and strip me of all those moments when I'd let myself be undressed by men before. This time I wasn't letting myself be used, I was letting myself *go*.

And he made me let go. Made the whole universe burst behind my eyes as he touched me, made my body explode into galaxies of whirling dust clouds and solar flares until I shook and gasped and his gravity pulled me back together. His eyes were all I could see, burning in front of me. 'Oh, Phinn.'

He scooped me up off the floor, lifted me and placed me carefully into the full bath. 'I wondered what this would be like,' he said softly. 'Never really had the chance to do this seduction thing before, but I think it's working rather well, don't you?'

The water lapped at my skin, keeping me warm while he undressed. I watched every move, every second of the unveiling, the body I'd seen naked at least twice but so much more than just a body now. He was *gorgeous*. So lean, shaped by just enough muscle to define him, long legs and the finest brushing of hair across his chest and down his stomach. I lay back to give him room and he slithered in to lie next to me, our bodies touching, pressed together by the edges of the bath.

'I am really glad this is a big bath,' I said, trailing a hand down through the water that sloshed up between us. 'This would be impossible in one of those hip-bath things.'

Phinn smiled. 'You think?' Then his hands lifted my waist, I floated to the surface and discovered that, really, the size of the bath didn't matter a damn.

Chapter Twenty-One

Phinn woke slowly from dreams of flying. There was a bed, which surprised him slightly, he didn't really remember much after the bathroom, apart from the sex which seemed to have taken place in most of the rest of the house. 'Wow. All night, eh?' He tried to think past the headache. 'Never done *that* before.' Then remembering, a huge out breath. 'Never done a *lot* of that before. Didn't know I had that much imagination.'

They'd stopped for food, or at least slowed down for it. In fact, there was still a slightly squashed grape in his hair, he pulled it out and stared at it, then ate it, turning his head towards his distinct memory of Molly, flat out and tousled, with her face all pink and her eyes very round. 'You were ...'

Gone, leaving nothing but a warm sheet and that scent of strawberries.

The whole of yesterday thundered in and left him shaking, curling around himself in the bed and clutching the duvet as though it could stop that awful plummeting in his heart and that rise of his blood that trumpeted to itself about what a total stud he'd been. *Oh God. Please. Please let me wake up ... why did I do that? Why did I ever think that anything Link said would be a good idea and why ... for the love of the entire Universe ... why did I take those tablets?*

'Molly?' he called, his voice experimental and cracking under the weight of his remorse. 'Are you there?'

Silence. Without his glasses the room was a series of blurred colours and fuzzy shapes and the glowing face of the bedside clock a collection of lines and angles. He squinted. More angles and lines than he was expecting of a twenty-four hour clock, in fact. All four fields bore a shape ... what the hell time was it?

With no one else there and no glasses to hand, Phinn had to pull the clock up almost to the end of his nose in order to resolve the shapes, and when he did he wasn't sure how he should react. *Fifteen twenty seven? Nearly half past three? In the bloody afternoon?* He ran his hands through his hair. *How much sex did we have? All day yesterday, and then we slept ... Wow. I mean, yes, terrible, obviously but she didn't run off in horror. No, in fact she ...* More memories, the image of Molly's face while he made love to her, blurred with need and then relaxing into open-mouthed bliss. *Shit.* He ran increasingly desperate hands through his hair, the mental images stretching and flexing with the passion they'd shared; the whispered declarations, the brief touches to guide and enhance and ...

Oh God. She enjoyed it. I enjoyed it. It was ... unbelievable. It was soft, it was reciprocal; it was all the obsession and excitement and mutual satisfaction that I always wanted it to be. And her. Molly.

But it was all fake.

So where was she? Careful listening revealed no flushing toilet or running water sounds. No soft footsteps downstairs, or music, or humming. Slowly he peeled back the duvet, wincing slightly at some areas that were more sore than they should be, and padded his way across the floor to the last place he remembered seeing his glasses.

'All right, that's enough walking.' I stopped, my feet sinking into the riverside mud. Beside us the dark waters bowled along with the sucking, slurping noises of someone eating a difficult boiled sweet, occasionally lapping up over the bank in a cappuccino-curl of froth. 'If you want to say something, Tim, then say it.'

Tim inclined his head. He'd managed to regain most of his composure today, mostly by putting on a hat so that his bald spot didn't look so much like a long shot of the rising moon. 'It's ... difficult,' he said. 'Jacqueline asked me to come.'

'My mother knows you're here?' I actually felt a little bit better knowing that. I had been beginning to wonder if Tim was going to work the reverse-affair trick and try to seduce me again, and his overly familiar behaviour hadn't managed to disabuse me of that idea. 'All right, so why did you come?'

He stared ahead at the river racing under the narrow arch of the bridge. There wasn't much clearance now and the darkness of the peaty water running off the moors gave the river the look of bad coffee. 'You wouldn't speak to her on the phone, and she ... *we* needed you to know. The cancer is back, Molly.'

My stomach turned. 'But ...' *That terrible time. Diagnosis, me not knowing what to say while my mother kept the stiff expression that she'd had all of my childhood, and then, after she started treatment, after everything seemed to be going well ... the betrayal.* 'She was better!'

Tim shook his head. 'She was in remission, the doctors hoped. We couldn't talk to you about it, not with, well, everything.' *You wouldn't listen,* ran the subtext. *Too busy being selfish, being angry and running off.* 'And now it's back.'

I felt my feet sink as the world rocked. My mother. She stole my boyfriend. Had an affair with him while I planned our wedding. I looked sideways at Tim. He was frowning slightly and searching with his hands through his coat pockets, a nervous tic of his. My mother. And Tim. And I'd run away, cut my ties, never wanted to see either of them again. But.

'How is she?' It must be hard for him too, I thought.

'Well, chemo and all that, but she's strong.' He tipped back on his heels, still staring at that bridge. 'Yes. She's strong.' His voice broke, just a little and for a second the polished shell that was the Tim I'd been engaged to split a fraction and I saw a glimpse of a man I'd never known.

He cleared his throat. 'Yes,' he said again, firmly now as though his conviction was enough to make it so. 'She's fighting, but it takes time. Thought you should know,' he repeated, as though it was important that I appreciated this fact. 'Thought it was only fair.'

'What, so that I can worry about her? She didn't worry about *me* did she, when she took you away.'

Tim raised his eyebrows. 'Molly. That whole thing ... you and I, getting engaged, it was all a bit of a cock up, wasn't it? Honestly? We were never really suited, you and I. I wanted ... well, I suppose I was flattered really. You were so young, so vibrant, so seductive. And *clever*. When we won the Anderson ... I got carried away by it all. And then, when you introduced me to Jacqueline, she and I just had so much in common ...'

'Well, me for starters.'

'And then, with the cancer, I realised just how much I truly *cared* for her. Wanted to be there, to help her through. And I simply never felt that with you, you were always so ...' He seemed to flounder, struggling for the right word. 'So *self-contained*. As though you didn't need anyone, not truly. You liked all the trappings and the accoutrements associated with a relationship, but you were never really bothered about the person that came with it.'

My mother made me like this, I wanted to say. *How could I ever care for someone, when she never cared for me? When she treated me like an unwanted impediment to her career?*

'And you must care a little, to have left a phone number,' Tim went on, still flipping through his pockets, so that the front of his jacket rippled and undulated like a rising tide.

'That was for emergencies. I never thought you'd track me!' I heard my voice wobbling and fought to keep it level.

'I'm a journalist, Molly. It's what we do.' Tim sighed. 'But you seem to have found someone else without too much difficulty, although I can't say that I liked him very much.'

'Good. Wouldn't want you having an affair with him; you don't get stamps for a full set you know.'

Something inside me was aching, and it wasn't because of the seventeen hours of nearly non-stop sex. My heart, which had sneakily allowed Phinn inside, was trying to stretch. Trying to make room for another person.

'She never really loved me,' I said, almost experimentally. 'She was always so busy.'

Tim sighed again. 'Well, of course she was. She was trying to build a career, trying to raise you without help, running a house and studying … she did her best, Molly, that's all. If you feel she didn't love you enough or give you enough … she did her best. And you were so totally unexpected, did you know? Jacqueline had … problems, some kind of ovulatory thing, so she didn't even know she was pregnant until a matter of weeks before you arrived. She never had time to prepare, and there you were.'

And she, aged twenty, had trained, sat exams, worked hard. All with this unexpected baby lurking in the background. 'Oh,' I said.

'Anyway. Better get back. She worries, you know, when I'm away.' He turned and began to walk away, his chunky body almost comical in the big wool jacket, like a bad imitation of Paddington Bear.

I gritted my teeth, holding back the memory of his lack of concern for me whenever he'd been on an assignment;

his sheer contempt for my anxieties. He'd forgotten it all. Wiped away our relationship as though it had been a fleeting thing, a few quick dates and a few quick romps, not ... *actually, what had it been? A real thing, or just something I held on to for security in a world where my career was rising faster than I could keep pace with, propelling me from a background where hard work had triumphed over emotional connection?*

And then I thought about her. About my mother. Working those long hours into the night, with no company but a sourness-filled child with no empathy, who resented everything. Didn't she deserve something too? If she and Tim felt just a fraction of how I felt about Phinn, could I really grudge them that, now I'd seen how it could be?

Almost against my will I called after him. 'Tell her ...' Then I stopped. Words couldn't do it, they couldn't fill the gap that ran beneath my relationship with him and with her. Nothing could do anything about the way I felt about my childhood, not now.

Tim turned and squelched back over the grey grass. 'It was never meant to hurt you, you know,' he said, and his voice, under the pretention and the officiousness, was gentle. 'Neither of us wanted to hurt you.'

I looked at him standing there, chubby and bald and so, *so* not right for me and wondered what I'd been looking at when I'd decided I was in love with him. 'Yes,' I said. 'Thank you. And I hope ...'

I couldn't do it, couldn't say anything else.

Tim leaned forward and folded me in a damp embrace. 'I know you'll do the right thing, Molly.'

Then he released me and walked off without looking back and I watched him until he got behind the wheel of that overpriced car and closed the door with what seemed like a thankful thud. To think I'd once considered being driven around in a car like that as being the epitome of style. And now … now there was a man who cut through me, sliced through the detachment and the self-imposed loneliness. I was in love with a man who gave me the entire galaxy. Wrapped me round with stars and moons and showed me the heavens as though I deserved them.

Phinn.

With the donning of his glasses Phinn felt all the old doubts sweep back through him, as though having the world in focus once more brought it home to him that his place in it was never going to be among the winners. He sat on the end of the bed and put his face in his hands. *Last night. Did I really …?*

The tattered remnants of a silk scarf, one end still tied to the bedhead, told him that yes, he really had. A riding crop stood in the corner of the room, angled arrogantly towards his hand and he tried to avoid looking at it, shame cascading through him in a hot wash which made the sweat prick under his arms and along his forehead. *Oh dear God. I should never have listened to Link.*

He'd been someone else last night. The man who'd crashed into Molly's house yesterday, that hadn't been him. Doctor Phinn Baxter would have buried himself alive rather than tie a woman to her own bed, wouldn't even know how to go about using a hairbrush along the contours of bare buttocks to raise cries of pleasure from an unsuspecting throat. *I don't do that. I'm not Link, all leather and machismo like a man who got lost on the way to the rodeo. I'm the quiet one. The gentle one.* He sunk his head lower. *The wimp. Last night was false pretences on an unimaginable scale.*

Unable to sit still with these doubts rushing through him he jumped up and began pacing around the bedroom. Every so often another memory would assault him and he started a kind of ritual of once-around-the-bed-and-groan as each new vision of the past came to him. He resisted the urge to knock his head against the wall to drive them out and instead rested his forehead against the chilly moistness of the window. Condensation ran down, softened the lines of outside almost as if he hadn't bothered with the glasses; across the road towards where the village green lay in a smudge of greyish green, he could see a figure.

Molly, it had to be. No one else he'd ever seen had hair that seemed to have an independent existence apart from its wearer. Today that hair looked as though it had been to an all-night party and a renewed flush stung at his cheeks as he remembered just a few of the reasons why it might look like that.

She stepped into an embrace with that bald tosser she'd been talking to. There was a moment of physical closeness – *were they talking? Or kissing? Were things being decided?* Phinn felt that pain again, the pain that had almost become a friend when he was precariously hanging on to his marriage. A pain that said 'you aren't good enough. She's got someone else, someone who's more of a man that you could be, no matter how many drugs you take'. Now she was walking along at the edge of the green where it had been filed down by many years of rising rivers and she seemed to be staring into the water.

She doesn't exactly look like she's covered in rosy glow, he thought. *More like she's thinking really hard. Oh, hell, why did I do it? She liked me before, I know she did, why in God's name did I have to take those tablets and come over all Captain Caveman last night?* The self-doubt was joined by self-loathing as he remembered Suze's reaction the one time he'd tried to take control in bed. How she'd first been startled, then amused by his attempts at being

235

commanding, how she'd started laughing and been unable to stop when he'd tried to throw her down onto the bed. How it had ended, with him pleasing her as she told him to, where to touch, when to stop, at which angle to enter. *But I gave Molly no chance to say any of that.*

So, which course of action now would make him look less pathetic? If he simply told the truth about the drugs, said that he'd been out of control? Or if he apologised, prostrated himself before her and swore it would never happen again? Which was worse, to be thought of as a junkie madman or a sexual control freak?

When he looked up again she was standing beside the fast-flowing river, dropping what looked like pebbles from a clenched fist. He saw them fall, the tight circles of their impact immediately swept away by the water, all trace of their passage gone, erased. *Maybe I should do that. Just go. Vanish.* But she knew he was working for the BBC, she'd probably write to the *Radio Times* about him. *Tell them all how I forced her.*

I need to talk to her. To tell her. To say, what? That I'm really the wimpy guy too scared to make a move? That who I was last night was an imposter?

Before he could chicken out completely, Phinn pulled his jeans on, found a jumper lying over the back of a bedside chair and, in the absence of his own shirt, dragged it over his head. Grabbing his soaked jacket, he shoved his feet into his still-wet boots and headed down the stairs in search of Molly.

For the first time in my life I wondered what things must have been like for my mother. Twenty-eight years ago, having struggled to make herself a life – she'd not got on with her father and I'd never met my grandparents – being accepted to teacher training college, she must have thought things were starting to go right for her at last. And then, one night with a stranger and her whole life had become something else.

I'd never asked about my father. All I knew was that he'd been a student, a passing 'thing', not even a relationship, just a drunken party, a walk home and a mistake. And then, there I was and she'd been forced to deal with another life.

I threw a handful of mud into the receiving river and it swallowed it down. Swirled a deeper brown for a moment and then nothing. I shivered. She could have had me adopted, but she hadn't. Could have just left me in the hospital, walked out with the visitors, pretended she never had a baby, but she hadn't. *Why?*

She did her best Tim had said. So maybe she had loved me? Just hadn't known how to show it, what to do with this awkward, careless daughter that nature had handed her? And now she was dealing with something else she'd never asked for, a disease that no one deserved. One she thought she'd beaten once.

'Molly.' Phinn's voice made me jump. He was wearing his jacket, still sodden, over one of my jumpers, so much too small that it left his midriff bare. 'I'm so sorry about last night. It was … I was … complete aberration. Not me at all.'

I sighed. My head felt full to overflowing. Last night, the way he'd been … 'No, it's okay. It was fun.'

I'd said the wrong thing, I could see it in his face. 'I don't know why … look, I'm not like that, Molly. I'm really not. Look at me.' And he stretched his arms wide. The sleeves of the tiny jumper bunched under his jacket, leaving a long expanse of wrist poking from the leather like an overgrown seedling jutting from the earth. His jeans were buttoned up wrong and his boots had that murky grey patina of seriously wet leather. 'This is the real me. Not whoever I became last night. *This.*'

If half my brain hadn't been full of memories, of new, disturbing thoughts about the way I'd been as a child, I would have smiled. He looked fantastic, even with his glasses at an Eric Morecambe angle on his nose and the ill-advised clothing choices. And last night, with those galactic eyes and that stellar body he'd ripped up every book I'd ever read about sex and rewritten them all. I'd yelled his name more times than I could remember, in more places than I could remember, and the recollection of the sheer abandonment made me blush a little.

'There's nothing wrong with *this*. But last night was … extraordinary, Phinn.'

A smile made the corner of his mouth twitch. 'I'm so, so sorry. I took … never mind, all you need to know is … it was like possession, like some kind of altered state of being. I don't *do* that, Molly. I can't.' A shrug. 'Like I said. Wimp.'

'You're too hard on yourself.'

'Maybe. But some of the things I did … it was wrong. You had no say, I took you …' A head shake now. 'I shouldn't have.'

'But what if I enjoyed it?'

'Then that's worse in a way. Because it's not who I am.'

'I think it could be, Phinn. You could be so much more if you stop thinking of yourself as worthless and pathetic. You're gorgeous, I mean, look at you, all hair and leather and … and …'

'And wet. Wearing, if I'm not mistaken, a pink mohair sweater that doesn't even reach my navel.'

'But why does that matter?'

'Because it does!' he shouted. 'It matters to *me*! I've never done anything normal. I've never *been* normal! Just this freaky guy with a brain too big for him to handle, all thoughts and ideas and theories and nothing of any fucking *use*!' Now his voice was an almost desperate shout. 'I'm in here, somewhere, the me that I used to be. It's like I'm looking out through my own eyes. I'm shut in here, Molly, sealed in with the way I once was, and last night showed me that I can't …' He dropped his voice and stood very still for a second. 'I can't,' he said again, and the quiet tone of his voice held a horrible finality.

I felt my stomach drop. There was a horribly resigned look on his face, as though he'd always known this day was coming and had been preparing for it all his life.

'I don't want you to go,' I said, very quietly. 'I know you don't believe it, but you are an amazing man, Doctor Baxter.'

He gave me a sad smile. 'I just …' and then his words were coming in a rush. 'You deserve so much better than me, Molly. And this really isn't about you, it's about me. I saw you with whatsisname, Tim, and you looked so … and it was the same when I thought you and Link … doesn't matter, still not about you, and I thought – there was guilt and jealousy and you don't need a man who thinks like that. You don't need someone like me. What I'm trying to say … it wasn't me that you had sex with last night.'

I opened and closed my mouth feebly. 'Identical twin?' was all I could ask. His expression was a sort of tortured dismissal that made my heart ache as much as my lungs did.

'Those tablets … Maybe we should look at the multiverse theory, yes, it's the only answer; they let some alternative version of "me" break through for a while there and … and …' He turned his back as though not looking at me made the words flow more easily. 'Not … not me, Molly. I'm sorry, I can't … I just don't do that.'

'Phinn,' I tried to start but he whirled around again, hands wringing around one another and finally cupping his face.

In the odd half-light that twitched and danced over the

river's surface he almost seemed to flicker, as though several of those overlapping universes were trying to claim him at once and he was only partially existing in this one. 'You really are great at over-dramatising everything, aren't you?' I said, finally.

'Over-dramatising. Good way of putting it, yes. I guess … yeah, that's me. But that's …' He waved a hand. 'The universe. It's drama on an unimaginable scale. Makes *EastEnders* look like … actually I've never watched *EastEnders*, but I'd imagine the universe makes it look like an anthill. A really *tiny* anthill. Microscopic, possibly.'

'Well, that puts things in perspective.'

'I have to go, Molly. If I can't even bring myself to trust you, then I certainly can't trust myself.'

I dropped my gaze and stared at my feet. Mud was squishing up around my boots, claiming me an inch at a time for the river. I wanted him so, so much. But not like this. Not scared and disbelieving, and whatever I said here, I knew it could never be enough. He doubted himself too much.

'I know.' I couldn't look up, even though I could see from his reflection in the fast moving water, that he'd started to reach out a hand to touch me. 'Just go, Phinn. Before I crack completely.'

No more words. Just a soft exhalation that sounded as if it wanted to be words but didn't dare, and then his footsteps sucking through the sloppy mud away to the road.

Chapter Twenty-Two

'Doctor Baxter? Doctor Baxter?'

The voice pulled him up from the laptop, although he kept his eyes on the screen, waiting for the download to finish. 'Phinn,' he said wearily for what felt like the fiftieth time that day. 'Please.'

Through the crowded studio his assistant, Annie, was rushing towards him, her iPad held out like a jousting lance. He idly wondered if she was mounted on a camera dolly, but no, he could hear those perpetual heels she wore clattering against the hard lino of the floor

'Did they get the message to you? About next season – we're greenlit for next year, isn't that great?'

He eyed her warily. Since he'd left Yorkshire, Annie had been something of a perpetual fixture at his side, rushing him from studio to interview to photo shoot, from hotel to dubbing session with the efficiency of a very well-trained sheepdog working to an inaudible whistle; she had something of the same sharp sense of purpose and single-minded determination to get him through the gate. Phinn thought he had something of the same attitude towards her as he would have to a real dog, wary friendliness.

'That's great,' he echoed. 'Yeah. Wonderful.' He shut the laptop screen, not wanting her to see the picture of Howe End.

'Research?' Her eyes were bright, fierce. She liked him, he realised, was just trying to be pleasant, it wasn't her fault he was so unsociable. That gave him a little tremor of memory of Molly and her gentleness, which he brushed away with a sudden twitch of an elbow.

'Just filling in some time. Checking up on the estate agent's progress,' he added.

'Oh, okay, cool.' She rested a hand on his shoulder in an attitude of possession. He wished she wouldn't do that either, but his attempts to move away from her touch led to her hand following him almost as much as her eyes did. 'Well ... that's it you're pretty much done here.'

Phinn felt the weight of being rootless settle on him again and the image of Molly's eyes rose like a ballcock of guilt. 'Great. I'll get my stuff and ...' *And what, Phinn? Where is left for you to go?*

'Would you like to come to my place?' Her voice, answering his unspoken question, made him frown.

'No, really, I should ... I mean, now that I'm selling the place in Yorkshire, I should go round some London estate agents, look for somewhere here.'

He could feel the drag at his heart even at the thought of it. Howe End passing out of his family for the first time in generations, the horrible relentlessness of London living; being at the beck and call of the BBC with only the Bristol flat to escape to, no high purple hills between him and the horizon. *But what else is there? Go back and watch her living a life you can never be a part of? Sitting at a distance cursing yourself for your cowardice and your weakness?*

Annie laughed. 'Oh, nothing like that! God, no, if I wanted *that* we'd have to go to a hotel!' She stepped a little closer, the palm of her hand scraping his shoulder through his shirt. 'No. My son, you see ... he's seven, and he'd very much like to meet you. I told him I'd ask you, but he wasn't to get too excited because you're very busy. But ... I just thought ...'

The first touch of vulnerability Phinn could remember her ever showing crept into her voice. 'He's seen some of the recordings of the series ... not meant to, of course, but I had some childcare issues and he came into the studio with me when we were showing some rough-cuts to advertisers, and ...' She cleared her throat, lost the fast, breathless, self-justification. 'He thinks you're really great,' she said.

'Oh.' *Oh? I stand in front of a green screen, or in a hole somewhere, and talk about physics. That doesn't make me 'great', it makes me 'employed'.*

'Plus, you keep going on about how horrible hotel tea is. I can at least make you a cup of something you'll drink. You know, you're getting dangerously diva about tea.'

'Well.' Phinn did a whistle-stop mental check of the alternatives. Yorkshire? Nothing there to hurry back for, except some ritual humiliation and the thought of having to dash to the shop after dark so as not to risk running into Molly. And Link's awful barrage of questions that would force him into weak excuses and another step down into self-hatred ... or another hotel room. Another night with the TV turned up too loud, staring at tablets he was too afraid to swallow down.

'What's his name, your son?'

'Lucas.'

'Then tell Lucas we're on our way.' *It'll be nice to meet someone who thinks I'm great and hasn't had a chance to experience the many and varied ways in which I am a total failure of genetic material. Plus, she's trying to be friendly, to extend something to me that no one else can be bothered to. They all see me as a commodity. At least Annie sees me as a person. And she's right, hotel tea is awful.*

My mother's flat was beautiful. Pale grey walls and white woodwork were the perfect counterpoint to an arrangement of pink carnations which splayed from a white vase like a controlled explosion. The furniture was soft and toning and immaculate. I sat on an upright chair and tucked my feet in, legs crossed at the ankles – it was the kind of room that brought out the Finishing School even in someone whose idea of being Finished was brushing her hair.

Across the table sat my mother. Thin wisps of newly greying hair showed underneath the scarf she wore, tastefully wound around her head, her face looked softer somehow, for the adornment.

'Well,' she said. It was practically the first thing she'd said at all, since I'd turned up at the door. 'I suppose Tim told you, then.'

'Should I make some tea?' I stood up, nearly crippling myself because the deep pile carpet hadn't allowed the chair to slide back far enough to clear the table, and I caught both thighs on its Louis Quinze underside.

My mother did something surprising then. She smiled. 'No. I think we should have a talk, don't you?' There was still a teacherly tone to her voice, one that made the word 'detention' flash in front of my eyes, and made me want to apologise for whatever it was that I'd done, but I stopped myself. *This is just how she is. She's as lost in the situation as you are, it's nothing personal.*

'Yes. I think we should.' And my answer obviously surprised her. Maybe she'd been expecting tantrums, although having a vase of flowers nearby wouldn't have been the smartest move if I *had* lost my temper. Maybe, given the way I'd behaved whilst growing up, I'd given her cause to expect overreaction. 'Properly. I'm sorry, Mum.'

And she was surprised again. 'I should have thought it was I who must apologise. We never meant to hurt you, Molly, it was ...' A head shake, momentary doubt in a woman who'd never shown a second's hesitation in my entire life. 'It was wrong. And yet.' She smiled a smile that showed me the woman that she must have been all along. Underneath. 'Some things are just meant to be.'

And then we talked.

There was no breaking down in tears on either side, neither of us was ready for that. But there *were* explanations, of a sort.

'I never wanted children,' my mother said. 'But that didn't mean that I never wanted *you*.' And that pretty well summed up her side of the conversation, she didn't try to excuse my upbringing but she did make me understand how it was to find yourself living a life you'd never asked for and trying to make the best of it.

And, in return, I tried ... I *really* tried, to tell her that I understood. Neither of us really had the words or the experience to say what we *truly* felt, but I no longer blamed her for my older-man fixations, my teenage rebellions, or tried to pin a deprived childhood on her. I'd had *riding lessons* for God's sake, how had I ever thought I'd been deprived? I'd never gone hungry, never had to wear outgrown shoes ... and if she'd been distant and always working, well, now I was starting to realise, that's what she'd had to do to keep us both. She'd really had little more understanding of the situation than I had, barely more than a child herself when I'd arrived and thrown her life plan out of the window.

I left when Tim came home. We might have reached a stage of tentative forgiveness but *that* was going to take a while to get over. My mother and I weren't exactly falling into one another's arms, but I no longer felt as though she resented me and, hopefully, she now knew that my off the rails behaviour was over. Done with. She'd even managed to mutter, albeit between slightly gritted teeth, that she'd read the book that won the Anderson Award, and appreciated my part in it.

I looked back when I got to the car. Up at the window of the flat that Tim had bought her. She'd retired from teaching when the cancer had returned, and was now doing a little exam marking and tutoring from home. *Her* home, all tasteful and soft and very much Tim's style. The key rattled in the Micra as I started the engine, on petrol I'd had to borrow the money from Caro for, and it was my turn to grit my teeth. And yet … even the chilly cavernousness that was Howe End felt more welcoming than all those squishy cushions and colour-coordinated furniture. Maybe she deserved it, maybe she and Tim deserved each other?

I looked up again. The lights were just coming on in this carefully middle-class south London suburb, evening settling around everything like a blanket, everyone all tucked up and cosy in their certainties and their lifestyles. None of it belonged to me. Perhaps it was the place my mother had fought for, this comfortable existence in a colour-coded environment with a man who obviously cared about her. Maybe this was what she'd wanted all those years, just someone to love her and a life where she didn't have to get up at six to get me to the childminder before the first teacher's meeting.

And me? What did I want?

I sat in the Micra, which smelled more of chickens than any car should do, and leaned my head back against the seat. *London isn't mine any more. I've got used to the countryside, to shops where they know you, a pub that has your 'usual' on the bar even before you get there. Lovely, velvet-muzzled Stan trying to eat my head … and I want Phinn. As he is, all ridiculously over-dramatic and emotional, not as some micromanaging bossy alpha male. But he's never going to let me tell him so, because he thinks that's what he should be, even when he knows he can't.*

My head was heavy and my eyes were tired, it had been a long drive down from Yorkshire. And now I was driving up to North London to stay with Mike and his wired family – oh, I'm sure my mother would have offered me the spare bedroom, all maroon and cream, very tasteful if you liked the feeling that you were sleeping in someone's lower intestine. If I'd asked. But truthfully, I didn't think I could bear being that close to her and Tim, they'd cheated on me after all, however understandable it might have been, however much I thought I knew how their relationship felt, they'd still cheated, and I didn't think good manners and tea would get me through an entire night without wanting to throw something. And Mike had offered his sofa bed and a chat about my future with *Miles to Go* magazine. So. I let my head fall onto the steering wheel, then lifted it slowly, raising my eyes again for one last look at the life I no longer wanted.

And there they were. Hazy, as though reflected on the cloud from a distance, almost like a projection; dancing their carefree fandango on that boundary where the night was shifting in to ease out the daylight. *The lights.* There for a moment, a ghost of a dream, and then gone on a gust, like the party candles of an impatient child.

I didn't even wonder this time. I knew now where I had to go. *Home.*

'Lucas, this is Doctor Baxter.'

Annie ushered Phinn through into a surprisingly cluttered living space. He'd imagined that her home would have been as sparsely fashionable as her appearance, as organised and consciously stylish as she was. But it was a turmoil of Lego and clothing, an ironing board set up near the window and boxes of toys overflowing as though a tsunami of plastic had just passed. 'Mum! I'm back.'

An older woman emerged, wiping her hands on a tea towel, but Phinn barely had time to register her presence before his hand was grasped surprisingly firmly, and shaken, by a small blond boy wearing a green velvet jacket and huge glasses. 'I am very pleased to meet you, Doctor Baxter.'

Phinn blinked for a moment. Was this really a child, or had a professor of restricted growth somehow just introduced himself. 'Er, hello ... Lucas?' he said, tentatively. *At least he's small. And I'm cleverer than him.* He took in the velvet jacket and glasses. *Probably. I'm better dressed, anyway.*

'Would you like a cup of tea?' the vision asked him, solemnly. 'I'm not allowed to boil the kettle, but Grandma can do it for me.' This was followed by a huge, face-splitting grin that turned the miniature don into a proper boy again. 'I can't really believe that *the* Doctor Baxter is in my living room! Can you make a Lego Death Star?'

And so, Phinn Baxter, PhD, Lecturer in Astrophysics and BBC4's 'Great Hope' in the viewings war, found himself on his knees in a cluttered living room in Chiswick, piecing together Lego bricks with a list of his greatest achievements chattering into his ear.

This is some kind of brainwashing attempt, got to be. He slotted another set of bricks together, whilst hearing about how 'excellent' he'd been at making a joke about plasma. *But fun though, actually. Why did I never get to make Lego Death Stars when I was seven? Oh yes, too busy getting my A* GCSEs in Physics and Maths.* He glanced around the room quickly. The two women were sitting on the newspaper strewn sofa, chatting quietly while in front of him a little boy dressed as though he was auditioning to be the next Doctor Who gave a precis of the bits he'd seen of the new show. *Is this what I missed? Mum and Grandma making tea, the smell of old toast and seven Christmases worth of plastic toys?*

Yes. His heart gave an uncomfortable double-beat. *This is what should have been. How I should have been. Why did they never let me be a child? Why have I always had to be so fucking grown up? It's not fair!*

He only realised he said the last bit aloud when Annie and her mother glanced up at him, their chattering temporarily interrupted. Lucas reached over and patted him gently on the shoulder. 'I know,' he said, gravely. 'But life's not fair, Doctor Baxter. We just have to do what we can with what we've got.' A nod towards the Lego and a confidentially lowered voice. 'I really wanted a Diagon Alley set, but ... this was what I got.'

Phinn looked down at the growing model in his hands. *And I wanted Molly. But I've settled for not having her, because ... why? Because I let being clever dictate who I am? Because I'm afraid I'm not ... Death Star enough for her?*

A sudden flicker outside the window caught his attention and snagged it away from the plastic model. It drew him over to the washed-grey of the net curtains across the glass, which he tugged aside to reveal the thin strip of sky visible between the brick gables and satellite dishes, with his heart pounding his chest like an internal Tarzan. There, dimpling the darkening sky, pricking at the night as though to incite it to action, were the lights. His lights. His and Molly's.

'Doctor Baxter?' Lucas was standing beside him.

He reached out a hand. After a moment's hesitation, Lucas put his hand in Phinn's.

'Is there a good toyshop near here?' Phinn found himself asking.

'There's a Toymaster just down the road, near the Italian Deli,' Annie said, frowning.

'Good.' Phinn headed towards the door, Lucas trotting along with him. 'Because we need a Diagon Alley, and we need one right *now*!'

Chapter Twenty-Three

I'd seen the 'For Sale' sign up outside Howe End as I drove into the village, a local estate agency that specialised in selling large houses to the London set, who'd buy them as weekend places, come down in summer and for Christmas and complain that the local shop didn't sell Kohlrabi. Still, it would be nice to see Howe End done up a bit rather than allowed to crumble. I supposed Phinn would be living in London now, part of the social whirl of agents and *Radio Times* photo shoots. *I wonder if he hates the place as much as I do? He's not really the social whirl kind, he's more one for the big skies and huge, open spaces.*

'Molly? That had better be you because, if it's not, I'm warning you that Stan eats people. Well, bits of them.' Caro's voice drifted in to me where I stood in Stan's loose-box, resting my head against his neck.

For a horse with such a high background level of misogyny he was being very accepting of me leaning against him. Occasionally he'd nuzzle me with a nose that felt like straw-stuffed velvet, if I'd had any kind of anthropomorphic tendencies I'd have said he was concerned about me.

'All the bits he can reach, actually, and he's not above crouching ... Oh good, it is you.' Caro loomed into view, jacket obviously draped hastily across her shoulders, and her boots on the wrong feet.

'It's me. I got back from London and I wanted ... thought I might take Stan out. Why are you dressed like you just got out of bed?'

She didn't answer, just unbolted the door and came in, bending to run her hand down Stan's leg. 'Better do it later. I had him out yesterday and I'm giving him the morning off. You know, because he didn't kill me or anything.' She straightened and pulled the jacket closer around herself. 'So, how did it go?'

She's wearing a camisole, my brain told me, but I couldn't process that right now. 'We talked.'

'Right. And?'

'I think I understand a bit better now. I mean, it wasn't easy for either of us, but she was only doing what she could, like most mothers. Doing her best. It wasn't her fault that I was a bitch queen from hell.'

Caro stared at me. 'Who?'

'My mother. Why, who did you think I'd gone to see?'

'Well, Doctor sexy-pants, of course! I thought you'd gone to talk to him about why he took off on you. I mean, for God's sake Molly, I've known racehorses that were less highly-strung than that. What does he think he's playing at?'

'Since I *didn't* go to see him, I have absolutely no idea.'

'But he really *likes* you! God, I don't know what's the matter with the pair of you.' Caro gave me one of her patented 'hard stares'. 'All "I like you but I'm not worthy …" Hell's teeth, makes me want to bang your heads together! Sometimes you just have to take it when it's offered and forget everything else.'

I shook my head and shrugged my shoulders, trying to ignore the fact that Stan was slowly chewing his way into my pocket. 'I couldn't make him stay,' I said, sadly. 'If I tried, I'd only be doing what his wife did and manipulating him.'

Caro shivered. She really wasn't wearing a lot under that hacking jacket, my brain told me.

'Look,' she said carefully. 'I … have a feeling that this is the kind of thing he might do a lot, feeling bad about himself. I mean, look at his background, parents who are such high achievers they are practically giving God a run for his money! He was pretty much programmed to feel worthless from conception onwards, and if you want to talk about rubbish parenting, well, *his* he only got to see once a year! At least your mum was there for birthdays and Christmas and prize-givings, wasn't she?'

'How do ...?' Then the penny dropped with an almost audible clang. 'Caroline Edwards! You've got Link in there, haven't you? What, in your bedroom?'

Caro cast her eyes down, but they were sparkling. 'Might have,' she muttered.

'But he—'

Now she looked up sharply. 'Yes, I know, he's a sexist idiot who writes greetings card verse and he'd probably sleep with *steak* if it was rare enough, but his parents have horses, so he *understands* and,' now her gaze was diamond-hard, 'he's pretty damaged too. Your Doctor Delicious doesn't have the monopoly on having had a rough time growing up. Plus,' and the grin was back, 'he's got a huge willy and a trust fund, and that makes up for quite a lot.'

I was dumbstruck and couldn't do much more than open and close my mouth, hoping something suitable to say would present itself, but all that came out was, 'Huge?'

'Oh, yes. Really quite enormous.' Caro gathered the jacket back over her bust. 'So I'm going to go back to bed before it evaporates or something. I haven't had anything quite that glorious in my bedroom since I put up that print of William Fox-Pitt riding Idalgo over the dressing table.'

'Or quite as well hung, apparently.' I went to follow her out of the box. 'I'll just go back to the cottage then.'

Caro gave me an insouciant wave as she crossed the yard. 'I'll see you ... in the morning. Yes, probably in the morning. But I don't think I'm going to be riding out ...' were her parting words, before she slammed the side door quite emphatically and left me to walk across the track to my house, still in a stunned state.

Caro? And Link? Well, no, it didn't surprise me that he would ... well, that he would do anything really, but Caro? All right, she was probably lonely, and everyone's entitled to some R&R but ... seriously, Link? The man who put the ass in harassment?

Still shaking my head, I pushed open the cottage door, and picked up *Folktales of Riverdale*.

Welcome back to real life. You've still got an article to write, money to earn and a life to live, lights or no lights. I flopped down in the chair and opened the book to the last point I'd read. *Phinn or no Phinn.*

There was a huge emptiness in that thought and I tried not to remember that night, that one, crazy night when he'd been all fire and ice like a deep-space explosion. *His fingers, so gentle and knowing, his joy in my pleasure. The sweet taste of him, the wildness that didn't seem faked or drug-induced but more like an extension of who he really was, who he could be if he'd only stop being so afraid. I miss him. Ridiculous really, but I miss his sudden, frenetic pronouncements, his self-containment and his smile, I even miss his random anxieties. He's a cross between Brian Cox and Woody Allen and I'll never get to tell him that.*

The book wobbled in my hands. *If only he could see that he doesn't have to live up to some macho ideal; that maybe gentleness and understanding are worth more than a sports car and ambition. That what we had felt like something real. The lights ...*

I shook my head. Why the hell was I worrying about the lights? He'd gone. Made his decision and left, and here was I, thinking about ...

The lights.

I read the words that were leaping up from the page to

meet my eyes. Then I read them again and my mouth fell open. *Folktales. Only folktales. Just a story to make sense of an environment so harsh that people wear hats for ten months of the year* ... But I was swallowing hard as I went over each word again. *Is there ... could there be anything in it? I mean, really? No, of course not.*

Of course not.

Phinn jerked awake to the pounding of his pulse, sat suddenly upright in the bed and tried to snatch away the sense that he was suffocating. 'Molly!'

'What about her? Thought you'd be dreaming about all those London sci-fi fans.' The laconic voice of Link drawled into his panic, accompanied by the reassuring sound of a mug being put down beside him. 'And your daily time check – it's twelve fifteen, p.m. Saw you were back last night, and, believe me, I have had to sacrifice quite a lot to come over; warm bed, hot food, basic hygiene.'

Footsteps creaked across the boards. 'Still, horses are horses and it's all early mornings and healthy exercise when they come into the picture.' Link's face suddenly lurched into approximate focus. 'You came back then. What's this, a flying visit? One last look over the old roots before you leg it for the joys of fame and fortune?'

The face backed away and blurred. Phinn screwed up his eyes but without his glasses Link's expression was just a pale smudge.

'Are we okay?'

The sudden change in conversational tone, coupled with his abrupt awakening, made Phinn feel dislocated, a bit *Alice Through the Looking Glass*, and then he had to berate himself for waking up in a camp metaphor. *What's wrong with a* Matrix *comparison?* He ran hands through his hair and searched almost subconsciously for his glasses. 'Okay? What?'

Link kept his face turned away. Phinn could see the dark smear that was the back of his head outlined against the window. 'I hoped I'd never have to say any of this, that none of it would come out.' His voice was low and the words were barely audible. 'But I guess, if you're off hitting the dizzy heights, this might be our last chance to have this shit out and settle stuff. I should have realised – I wasn't keeping quiet to protect you, I was doing it to keep myself in the clear.'

'I know.' Although his heart felt as though it had turned sideways, Phinn managed to keep his voice low.

'You know? What do you know, man? That I was screwing around with your wife? Yeah, thought you'd have figured that one by now. Or you know that I spent so long lying to you that I can't even remember what the truth is? I can't remember who started it, or even much about how it ended, only that it did, that she went back to you. Even then, even in the end I lost out to you, man.'

Phinn dragged himself up out of the bed, feeling the strain and pull on muscles that had been stiff with misery for so long. He unfolded himself and tried to judge how far away Link was standing. Without his glasses his depth perception was gone and his friend was a smudged shadow in front of the bright daylight.

He raised a hand and tried for a shoulder-slap. 'Suze ... I think we both got taken in. She didn't want me, not really, with, you know, the terrible eyesight and the obsession with the skies; she wanted the illusion of me that she had in her head. And when I couldn't be that man, she moved on to the next illusory male she could find, one with the money and the family connections to really *be* someone.' His hand dropped through empty air. 'She never really wanted either of us. She wanted what she thought we were.'

'But she knew I was never going to follow my father into

all that landowning crap. Soon as he goes I'm selling all that rubbish. All those acres and acres of mud and sheep and toffee-nosed gimps with guns, all "haw haw" and spaniels. That's not me, Bax, that never was.'

'But it might have been, and that's what Suze saw. She had problems, I know we don't want to admit it, we want to keep her memory all pure and make her the victim in all of this, but she used both of us, plain and simple. She was a player.' He shuffled another step closer and this time his raised hand made contact. 'We got played. Let it go.'

Link's head dropped forward. 'She was going to have my baby.'

Phinn felt the air sting his throat. Pain settled like a rock in his belly. 'It could have been *anyone's* baby. Mine, yours, some other random guy that she thought was offering more than he could ever fulfil. Suze was lost, looking for something none of us could ever give her. I thought I could make her happy, but ...' A deep indraught of breath. 'The only thing that can make someone happy is themselves. Suze was doing what I did, trying to find happiness through other people, and it's only now ...' Phinn felt the steel thing that lay deep within him, coiled and ragged, '... I'm realising what she never got the chance to. We have to make ourselves happy. We have to find out who we really are, not pretend, not try to lay all that on another person. She never found that, never could. She never knew how.'

'I wish you'd told me this before.'

'I didn't know you and she were involved until ... recently. Didn't think it would matter to you.'

'Oh, man.' Phinn heard the effort in Link's breathing, the unshed longing and pain pulling at his words. 'Bax.'

'She made me think I was worthless, y'know? Over and over, all I heard was how crap I was in bed, how I should beef up, work some weights, get out there and lay myself on the line to get noticed. Be somebody. She left me feeling that the only way I'd get a woman again would be to drug her and lock her up, that every other woman would look straight into me and see what she saw, this pathetic, transparent jelly of a guy.'

Link made a noise somewhere between a snort and a sob. 'She told me I was a sexist pig with all the sexual technique of Cro-Magnon man and being in bed with me was like sleeping with a rutting boar. Of course, she could have meant B.O.R.E but, you know, I never asked her to spell it, so jury's out on that one.'

A silence fell. Phinn stayed where he was, arm halfway across Link's shoulders, wishing he could see the expression on his face. The shoulders under his arm were trembling, either unshed tears or ones being shed very carefully, designed not to be seen. Phinn decided to pretend he hadn't noticed.

'So, you've been using your charms on Molly's friend, eh? That where all the "horsey" stuff is coming from? Could be well in there. She owns a bloody farm, so not exactly after you for your money, is she?'

The inward breath was so deep it made his arm brush Link's ear. 'Can see you weren't brought up with horses, man. They're like Lamborghinis. Expensive, uncomfortable and unreliable.'

'Yep.' Phinn kept his voice light. 'Anyone who thinks differently never met Stan.'

'But now you've got the telly deal you can get out there and Armani yourself up the wazoo, and, let's face it, if you're a "Personality", no bugger cares if you've got the upper body strength of a flatworm, you'll have the chicks rolling over and begging for you, and it won't just be the science-groupies any more, you'll get your pick!'

For the first time since they were about fourteen Link

gave him what they'd called at school a 'noogie', rubbing his knuckles over the top of Phinn's head. Phinn had never liked to tell him that it hurt like hell, and now was certainly not the time.

'I don't want groupies.'

The noogieing stopped and was replaced with another slap. 'So, why did you come back then? Caro says ... I mean, you and Molly?'

'I want it to be. I thought I'd got it straight in my head, but now I'm here I'm having second thoughts ... I'm worried maybe she might expect me to be something I'm not, after that night when I ... I took those pills, Link.'

Link's face was, as they say, a picture. But it was the *Laughing Cavalier*. '*Seriously?*'

'Yeah. And they made me – they made me someone else. The kind of person that I think she deserves. She said she loved every second of it, but, false pretences, you know?'

'Man. Oh, man, you are such an idiot.' Link was laughing out loud now and the laughter had an undertone of relief. 'How long? How long have you known me? Come on!' Another, harder slap, this time around the back of the head. 'Seriously?' The laughter threatened to block out the words. 'You think I'd waste good gear on a four-eyed twat like you?'

Phinn stared at him. 'You are making even less sense than usual, and for you, that's really going some.'

'The stuff I gave you.' Link wiped his eyes with the back of his hand, tears of laughter seemed to have wiped out the previous ones. 'Aw, come on, man! They were just headache tablets I got from the chemist! You looked so down, so head-up-your-own-arse, I just thought I'd make the gesture, y'know? You mean you ...? And you seriously thought ...?'

It was me. The sudden realisation rocked Phinn back on his heels. *I thought it was the drugs making me all macho and take-charge, and all the time ... it was me. All me. Everything before, sabotaging relationships, the wimpishness, it's all been me trying to hide. Trying to be all things to all men. Women. But one stupid trick and I let myself be the me I knew I could.*

Oh my God.

'I think, maybe, I do need to see Molly.' His hand hurt and things began to slide into place.

'Reckon?'

Phinn slowly opened his hand to reveal the small plastic square that had been embossing itself on his palm for the last twenty-four hours. 'This. This is what it's all about.'

'*Lego?*' Link spun away, laughing. 'This is it, you're officially a nutjob. You're going to build yourself a woman?'

Phinn shook his head. He could feel the smile spreading across his face, unstoppable now, driven by the kind of certainty he couldn't remember ever having felt before. 'Not Lego. Molly.'

'Okay then. You get Molly and *I* get the groupies, deal?'

Phinn half turned. Link's face was so close that, even with his trial-and-error eyesight, he could see the expression in his friend's eyes. A wariness that said he still wasn't sure that things were okay between them, a tight withdrawal behind those pale lids. *He's as screwed up by his childhood as I am. Looking for something in all the wrong places.*

'Groupies are all yours, Link,' he said, and saw the guardedness drop away into relief.

'Always have been, my man, always have been.' And Link patted his groin. 'Now, put some of your TV clothes on, because we are going visiting Moll and her mate and, as my wingman, you owe it to me to reel 'em in so that I can *pounce.*'

Phinn sighed. 'Sexual revolution really passed you by, didn't it?' But he felt lighter, as though that clockwork coil that had kept him running for the last year had finally reached a limit and unwound. As though he was managing himself now.

'*Vive la revolution!*' Link shouted, and Phinn shook his head. Life might change, his whole outlook on the future might change, but Link … Link would remain Link until the day he died.

Chapter Twenty-Four

It was one of those still, crisply warm days that spring occasionally throws our way to reassure us that summer will, eventually, come and we shouldn't give up and move to Rio or wherever. Stan and I had pottered up onto the hill, where I'd scanned the skies but seen nothing more than flocks of starlings wheeling over the field boundaries, the peat had smelled like coffee and the ground squidged under his hooves. The world was as empty as the sky, just a blanket of unfurling bracken and winter-grey heather and my heart flopped about in my chest like a deadweight.

Sod it. When I get back I'm going to ring all those people I knew through Tim, get myself some proper writing gigs. I've had enough of martyring myself to the cause of some stupid illusion. My grip on the reins must have tightened, because Stan peeled through the mud to a standstill and I had to nudge him forward quite hard, turning his head so that we went down the trackway to the village.

The river was running in full spate, I could see and hear it before I even came down onto the bridge. The flat area alongside the banks was waterlogged and the green where the children would be dancing around the maypole in a couple of weeks' time, was under six inches of murk. I halted Stan on the bridge and looked down. Tree branches were sweeping underneath us like drowning arms, jamming briefly against the underside of the bridge before the force of the water ripped them clear and bore them downstream in a roar of meltwater. I shuddered.

'Molly!'

I thought I'd imagined the call, that the water was making me hallucinate, but Stan's head came up and, when

I looked, I could see Phinn running towards us, taking no notice of the fact that he was splashing through liquid mud. He was wearing what I thought of as his 'astrophysicist' clothes, normal black jeans and his old jacket, not his TV stuff, so I knew he must have been back at Howe End.

'Phinn? What are you doing here?'

He puffed up, stopping just before he got within eating distance of Stan, and eyed him warily. 'I came … to see you. To tell you stuff. Things.'

I didn't know whether those things were good or bad, but couldn't stop myself from smiling at the sight of him. 'You—'

'This,' he said. 'It was this.' He uncurled his fingers. 'Look.'

I leaned forward in my stirrups to see. On the centre of his palm sat something square and white that looked like a sugar lump. Clearly Stan thought so too, because he leaped forward to intercept the snack, his hooves slithered on the wet road and his shoulder dropped as he tried to keep his feet underneath him. I grabbed for his mane, but the chopped nature of it meant there was nothing to get hold of. I lost my balance completely and fell, scraping myself on the bridge parapet before I plunged down into the racing water below.

Phinn and the horse stared at one another for a second. 'Shit,' was all Phinn could think of to say. '*Shit!*' His mouth was too dry for anything else.

He leaned over the stone bridge, catching a glimpse of her hair, an arm – and then Molly was gone, swept along with the flotsam of a moorland winter, in the nightmare black water. In his hand the edges of the plastic brick cut into his palm and made his fingers ache. For a second he stood there in the middle of that bridge, balanced between one bank and another, one *life* and another.

'Okay, okay.' He whirled on the spot a couple of times. 'Nobody about. Houses too far to go to. No phone signal.' Another quick look down into the stained waters cascading beneath his feet. 'Fuck.'

And then he looked at Stan. Stan looked back at him. There was an air of quiet panic about the horse, Phinn thought, although he couldn't say how he knew, and Stan stepped towards him, reins flopping along one side of his neck.

'Okay,' Phinn said again, his heart loud in his ears even over the sound of the water. 'Death Star time.' And he grabbed the saddle, hauled himself on board and, using a combination of yanking and kicking, Phinn forced the horse into a shuffling run.

The breath clanged out of me, squeezed by the shock of the fall, and I sank. Currents and eddies pulled at my clothes, my boots came off and I felt my feet trail against rock, slam into boulders and then trawl briefly along a sandy bottom before I broke surface again. Couldn't call out, the water was too cold to allow me to draw breath, too fast to fight, dragging me, forcing me scarily fast downstream.

I caught one quick glimpse of Phinn's face, shocked white, before I was pulled back under the surface again, turned around and hustled past the bridge supports, the water in my ears and over my head banging and clattering and muffling until I didn't know which way was up and took one brief lungful of what turned out to be liquid mud.

Couldn't cough. Not enough air. The world stung and spun, my head surfaced again and I saw the blurry image of the village, vanishing, pulled away from me by the speed of the water. The weight of my clothes pulled me under but the force of the current kept shoving me to the surface again, I could hear my riding hat clonking and banging against objects in the water with me, but I was travelling so quickly that I couldn't grab anything to help me to float. All I could manage to do was to flap my arms, almost insurmountably heavy in their sleeves, and breathe whenever my head broke water.

Couldn't call. Now too cold even to move. My back slammed into something hard and I found myself wedged in a tree trunk that had itself jammed in the centre of the river, a whole heap of detritus caught where its dead branches dipped the waters. And there I hung, unable to fight the current to move towards the shore, no air to shout with; just another piece of flotsam waiting for a small alteration in the flow patterns to be knocked free and carried further on downstream to where the river widened and deepened and the farmers fetched the bodies of the cows out with hooks on poles every winter.

I'm going to die.

Mud filled my eyes. I couldn't feel anything below my waist and what I could feel above it didn't feel healthy. My lungs ached as though a huge fist had closed around them and there was an equally tight band around the top of my skull where my hat had gone sideways and wet hair flailed around my face.

So this was it. I was going to die, a stupid, careless death. Why had I got so close to the water, when I knew the river was dangerous? Why had I lost concentration, let Stan take me unawares? *Stupid, stupid ...* but too late. I was going to drown, or die of exposure or hypothermia or some obscure river-borne disease and my body would be washed up on some strange riverbank, embedded in the mud with half my clothes missing, torn off by rocks. By the time Phinn had run to one of the houses, found someone to help, phoned the Emergency Services, it would all be over.

I'd resigned myself now. A curious warmth was beginning to slide over me, as though mild currents were travelling down the river, it made me feel sluggish and I was glad. Through numb lips I muttered 'just let it be soon'.

And then there was a thundering noise above me where the banks of the river rose high and vole-pocked, a pounding sound that was familiar and yet strange, echoing down this stretch of river like a drummer accompanying the apocalypse. If I stretched my head back I could see the edge of the bank and a shape, stretched and strained through the mud in my eyes. A long shape, bunched and uneven in the middle, a shape that wheeled away almost as soon as I'd seen it, disappearing out of my vision. I closed my eyes. Hallucinations. A volley of water struck me in the chest and swept me from my perch to whirl me around once more rootless and then pitched me back into the tree's embrace, this time pegged on a series of branches which impaled my shirt. So cold now that I'd stopped being cold.

And then another sound, this time coming closer. An evil, blowing sound, a bit like someone trying to start a recalcitrant chainsaw, a regular chuffing, deep and threatening. I opened my eyes again.

A dragon?

No, but something coming for me, nostrils first. A curled back lip over yellow teeth, coming closer, a wet-black neck suspending a Loch Ness head above the water in an attitude of strain. And behind it … no, *on top of it …*

'*Phinn?*'

And then I saw what I was seeing. Stan swimming towards me through the sweeping waters, snorting and puffing to keep the river out of his nose. Phinn astride, one arm wrapped around Stan's neck to keep him from being swept off, eyes wide, glasses gone.

'Molly.' His voice was quiet but carried to me over the noise of the rushing water and the horse's constant snorting. 'If you can hear me, lift your hand.'

Feebly I tried, but my limbs weren't working well. One wrist broke the surface amid the twig and plastic nest that was accumulating around me. It was the best I could do.

Stan swung round to face upstream, coming at me now around the wedged tree, hooves thrashing at the water like a paddle steamer from hell. One leg clouted me from below and then Phinn was reaching down, disentangling me from the branches and hauling me across the broad back, looping his arms around my waist to keep me on board as Stan huffed and spun gently around to face the way he'd come, head extended above the water as far as it would go, all the veins on his neck standing out with the effort of swimming against the current.

'Phinn.' I could barely speak.

'It's okay, I've got you.'

With some signal to the horse that I couldn't detect he steered us down to where he must have entered the water, a shallow stretch of bank where cattle came down to drink and the water level was parallel to the ground. With one mighty heave Stan dragged himself up out of the river, cantered three strides into the field and then floundered to a halt, sides dragging in and out, head down and gasping.

Phinn slithered to the ground and pulled me down along with him, wrapping his body around me until he could feel my heart beating.

'Oh my God,' he was saying. 'Oh my God,' over and over again with each breath, with each thud of my heart. 'Oh my God.'

Beside us Stan shook himself like a dog, looked around for a second then began to graze.

'Phinn, you …' I started to cough and carried on, coughing until I retched up some black water, then felt better. My lungs still felt as if they were on fire and my ankles ached, but feeling was coming back to everywhere else in slow dribs and drabs. 'You came for me.'

Phinn leaned forward, hands on thighs and started to laugh. One more round of 'Oh my God,' and then he couldn't speak, just laughed and laughed so hard that I thought he'd fall over. Laughter that was the wrong side of fear. I reached out and touched his hand and he turned to look at me out of eyes that were full of tears.

'Molly.' And the laughing turned to crying and he was sobbing, holding on to me while his whole body shook. 'Molly.'

And then I was crying too, with his arms tight around me and his chest hauling and dragging at the air and we wept ourselves to a standstill while my horse steamed himself quietly dry and ate thoughtful dandelions around us.

Eventually we moved, letting reluctant fingers disentangle. He tipped my chin to see my face. 'We need to get back. You'll need a doctor.' He began reeling Stan in by his reins. 'You can ride, I'll walk. I think both of us might be a bit much for him at the moment.'

'But you can't. Ride. Couldn't ride. You fell off. How did you …?'

Phinn paused, halfway to helping me to my feet. 'Well, I decided that riding a horse shouldn't be *that* difficult for someone who knows what the Large Hadron Collider is actually *for*, so I just put my mind to it. It might not have been pretty or accurate, but it got the job done.'

'And you're afraid of rivers.'

Gosh his eyes were dark. 'No. I'm afraid of what rivers can *do*. I wasn't going to lose you, Molly, not to the water. And then I couldn't see you, you'd been carried too far away and …' He stopped talking. Fumbled where his glasses ought to have been and then appeared to notice their loss with some surprise.

'What? How did you find me? I was moving so fast.'

'You'll think I'm mad.'

'Bit late to worry about that now.'

'The lights. They were hanging in the sky above where you'd washed up. Just hanging there, Molly, like they were pointing right at you.'

'That's mad.'

He shook his head, wet ropes of hair coiling around his neck. 'That's what happened. Otherwise ...' He stopped again. Coughed. Ran the back of his hand over his eyes and then went on in a voice that choked. 'Otherwise I wouldn't have had a clue. I'd have had to follow the river all the way and there are fences and gates and I wouldn't have been able to ... I wouldn't have found you.'

As though overcome with fellow feeling, Stan nudged gently at his shoulder and then bit his jacket in an exploratory way.

I felt incredibly tired all of a sudden. 'I want to go home.'

'You're in shock. Here.' Phinn legged me up onto Stan, where I collapsed thankfully, resting my face on his mane as Phinn began to lead us back to the village. The river had taken me further than I'd thought, it had only seemed as though I'd been in the water for a matter of moments and yet we had to trudge for nearly half an hour to get back to the outskirts of the village. His jacket was lengthening with every stride, the leather stretching until he had to keep shoving it up his arms to keep his hands free to manage Stan, but he didn't seem to notice.

'Here.' He helped me slide down onto my garden wall. 'Sit there a second. Okay?'

I could only nod.

Caro and Link came dashing across the road, hand in hand but arms flailing. 'Molly! Link said ... he saw you fall!'

'He saved me,' I said quietly. 'Saved my life.'

Phinn leaned against Stan, who carefully ate his lapel.

'Which he are we talking about?' Caro looked at the pair of them and I could see her chest rising and falling with the emotion that was coming out as anger. 'Because I am going to slowly kill the other one.'

'And I am going to kill the one that's left, just in case.' Link's face was grey with shock.

'Both of them.' I now felt so tired that the wall under me was spongey. 'Phinn and Stan. What a pair,' and then I collapsed, falling slowly backwards over my own garden wall, unconscious before I even landed on the gnomes.

Chapter Twenty-Five

When I woke up I was in my own bedroom. There were three duvets piled up on the bed, so it was a little like being buried alive, but otherwise everything seemed normal. My chest hurt a bit and cautious examination told me that I had scrapes and scratches all over me. I groaned and tried to turn over under the immense weight of wadding.

'Oh, hello.' Almost shyly, Phinn came through the narrow door. 'How are you? I mean, you're obviously better because you're not, you know, unconscious or anything.'

He looked amazing. Okay, he was wearing a weird amalgamation of what looked like Link and Caro's clothes, and his hair had dried into a combination of dreadlocks and quiffs, like Bob Marley doing an Elvis impression, but his smile was the most beautiful thing I'd ever seen.

'You saved my life,' I said, almost wonderingly. 'You rode my *horse* into the *water* and saved my life.'

Another grin. 'I hear that if I can overcome another phobia within the next twenty-four hours I get some kind of medal,' he said and came over and sat on the side of the bed. 'Duke of Edinburgh or something.'

I rubbed the back of my hand over my eyes. 'Probably not that one.' I coughed. My chest hurt and my brain felt as though I was thinking through treacle. 'Why are you here?'

He looked wild. Gorgeous, but wild, as if he'd been up for days, unshaven and the collar of what looked like one of Link's rugby shirts was sticking out from under an old hunting jacket on one side. 'Reasons,' he said.

We stared at one another for a moment or two.

'I missed you,' I said quietly, at last.

He inclined his head slowly.

'You never really gave me a chance to say anything. Before you went.' I spoke very fast, as though the words had been dammed up behind my heart for too long and were now falling over one another to get out. 'And you'd just made love to me like no one has ever done before, like I've never given anyone the *chance* to before, and I'd just found out about my mother being ill and then you *left* me, Phinn. You *left me*.'

'I know. And I came back to talk to you, because I wanted to make it right. I had an idea that I could try. But I still thought I was a fake, that night, I thought it was fake, and that I was jealous of Tim because he was more of a man than I could be. But really ...' He took half a step back and slowly uncurled a hand that I saw he had clenched. And if the bluey-grey colour of his knuckles was anything to go by, it had been clenched a long, long time. 'I came back,' he said carefully, 'because of this.'

At first all I could see were the indentations in his palm, but then my eyes focused on a small, white piece of plastic sitting astride his lifeline. The thing he'd tried to show me on the bridge.

'Lego? You came back because of *Lego*?'

'Lego and lights and your mad horse, and Link ... is there any word for "horse" that begins with L? Seems a shame to ruin alliterative moments on that monster. Love.'

Love. The word hung.

'I thought you'd gone for good this time.'

'*I* thought I had. But then there was this.' He juggled the Lego brick from hand to hand. 'A little boy telling me I was his hero like he meant it, and I realised that I didn't have to be a Death Star when I really wanted to be Diagon Alley. Not any more.' He caught hold of my hand and stood, all in one fluid movement. 'I didn't think I deserved you, Molly. I didn't think I deserved *anything*.'

271

He bent down, put his face close to mine. 'Suze and my parents and everything … I've worked all my life to be good enough for other people.' So close now I could feel the heat of his skin. 'But yesterday I realised I don't have to be good enough for other people.' A gentle, almost trembling hand pushed my hair away from my face, while those brilliant, dark eyes held me, deeper than space. His lips touched mine for a second, then he was away again. 'And then Link told me … well, something that showed me I could be whatever I wanted. If I let myself. And I realised I'd really just been making excuses all this time, that I didn't have to conform to whatever I thought I had to be, I just need to be good enough for myself … Oh, and you, obviously, I need to be good enough for you. Am I, Molly? Can I *ever* be good enough for you?'

I looked at him before I spoke. A pat, quick-returned reply would sound insincere, but also I really just wanted to look at him. Lean and dark, those sharp eyes softened by glasses but their quick gaze still as bright, still as full of that fierce intelligence. And I didn't see a soft man, a man who should have been more manly. I didn't see someone so far down the alphabet that he couldn't touch alpha with a pole. I saw a man who overcame his fears, for me. *A man I loved.*

'You don't have to be good, Phinn.' Now it was my turn to lean in, to move my lips to his cheek and whisper in his ear. 'You only have to be *you*.'

He kicked his feet up and lay on the bed next to me, shoving several hundredweight of duvet out of the way so that we could touch. We kissed, a long, deep kiss and I closed my eyes to appreciate the taste of him, the salty smell of his skin and the feel of his body's angles and planes resting against me. Eventually he moved, rocking his weight away from me although I stayed with my head nestled into the collar of his shirt and his hand still raked into my hair.

'While you were gone, I read something,' I said slowly. I didn't know whether this was the right place to introduce it or not. 'In the folklore book. About the lights.'

'What the Alice lights?' Phinn looked down at me. His whole face was relaxed, his eyes huge, sparkling with lights of their own. He'd got his boots up on the bed, but I didn't have the heart to reprimand him, not when he looked like he was modelling for a soft furnishing warehouse.

'Yep. This is Yorkshire,' I said.

'Um, yes.' He held up a hand. 'Been here a while now, think I'd have spotted it being Cornwall.'

'Alice, Phinn.' I coughed again. 'We've been hearing it as A.L.I.C.E, because we're not from round here. But it's not.'

His eyes flickered, he was doing that thing he did, where he slotted ideas in, made connections. Link was right, it was phenomenal to watch him. 'Allus,' he said, after a moment. 'They're called the Allus Lights. As in …?'

'As in "always", Phinn. Dialect.'

A serious look. 'Always is a long time, Molly,' he said, quietly. 'I've been promised "always" before.'

'But never backed up by UAPs, though.' I reached out a hand from under the covers and touched his face. 'And I'm pretty sure the universe knows what it's talking about.'

The Allus Lights of Riverdale
– by Molly Gilchrist and Dr Phinn Baxter

Riverdale is a fairly typical North Yorkshire village, farmworkers' cottages, farmhouses, medieval bridge … and mysterious lights in the sky. Not only are the lights mysterious, but, in the words of Jack Edwards, in his *Tales from an Ageless Village*, 'they can only be seen by two people at any one time'. Two people who, so the story goes, are destined to be together 'allus' in Yorkshire dialect, always.

The lights have been seen and documented since the eighteenth century, the first recorded sighting being in 1769 when a local farmer, writing to a friend in London, told of 'a circlet of lights, as if the lamps of God shone forth, witnessed by myself and Ellen, who was in the yard at that time'. Whether he and Ellen got together after the event is unrecorded but, given the number of subsequent sightings followed by the wedding of the observers, it has to be a possibility!

Jack Edwards goes on to list several couples of his own acquaintance who have come together either during a sighting or as a result of separately seeing the Allus Lights and – at the end of his book he lets the reader in on a little secret – that he and his own wife, Betty, saw the lights together one Christmas Eve, after they'd attended Midnight Mass in the local church. 'No one else even looked up,' he says, 'it was like the Star of Bethlehem and all its attendants danced there beneath the clouds for our eyes only.' Jack and Betty were married the following Christmas, having seen the lights several more times during their courtship, 'to make sure we knew', as Jack says.

Molly Gilchrist is a regular contributor to the magazine and her new book, *Riding for the Weak and Feeble* is released in March.

Phinn Baxter is another regular contributor, a lecturer in astrophysics and presenter of BBC Four's *The Science behind the Fiction*.

They live in what they call 'a shambling farmhouse' in Riverdale, North Yorkshire and are expecting their first baby very soon. They really hope the story of the Allus Lights is true, because their two best friends have just seen 'something' in the sky.

About the Author

Jane was born in Devon and now lives in Yorkshire. She has five children, four cats and two dogs. She works in a local school and also teaches creative writing. Jane is a member of the Romantic Novelists' Association and has a first-class honours degree in creative writing.

Jane writes comedies which are often described as 'quirky'. *How I Wonder What You Are* is Jane's sixth Choc Lit novel. Her UK debut, *Please don't stop the music*, won the 2012 Romantic Novel of the Year and the Romantic Comedy Novel of the Year Awards from the Romantic Novelists' Association.

Jane's Choc Lit novels are: *Please don't stop the music, Star Struck, Hubble Bubble, Vampire State of Mind, Falling Apart* and *How I Wonder What You Are*.

For more information on Jane visit
www.janelovering.co.uk
www.twitter.com/janelovering

More Choc Lit

From Jane Lovering

Please don't stop the music

Book 1 in the Yorkshire Romances

Winner of the 2012 Best Romantic Comedy Novel of the Year

Winner of the 2012 Romantic Novel of the Year

How much can you hide?

Jemima Hutton is determined to build a successful new life and keep her past a dark secret. Trouble is, her jewellery business looks set to fail – until enigmatic Ben Davies offers to stock her handmade belt buckles in his guitar shop and things start looking up, on all fronts.

But Ben has secrets too. When Jemima finds out he used to be the front man of hugely successful Indie rock band Willow Down, she wants to know more. Why did he desert the band on their US tour? Why is he now a semi-recluse?

And the curiosity is mutual – which means that her own secret is no longer safe ...

Visit www.choc-lit.com for more details including the first two chapters and reviews, or simply scan barcode using your mobile phone QR reader.

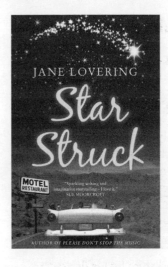

Star Struck

Book 2 in the Yorkshire Romances

Our memories define us – don't they?

And Skye Threppel lost most of hers in a car crash that stole the lives of her best friend and fiancé. It's left scars, inside and out, which have destroyed her career and her confidence.

Skye hopes a trip to the wide dusty landscapes of Nevada – and a TV convention offering the chance to meet the actor she idolises – will help her heal. But she bumps into mysterious sci-fi writer Jack Whitaker first. He's a handsome contradiction – cool and intense, with a wild past.

Jack has enough problems already. He isn't looking for a woman with self-esteem issues and a crush on one of his leading actors. Yet he's drawn to Skye.

An instant rapport soon becomes intense attraction, but Jack fears they can't have a future if Skye ever finds out about his past …

Will their memories tear them apart, or can they build new ones together?

Visit www.choc-lit.com for more details including the first two chapters and reviews, or simply scan barcode using your mobile phone QR reader.

Hubble Bubble

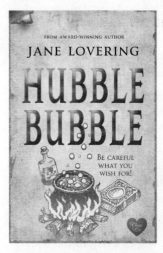

Book 3 in the Yorkshire Romances

Be careful what you wish for ...

Holly Grey only took up witchery to keep her friend out of trouble – and now she's knee-deep in hassle, in the form of apocalyptic weather, armed men, midwifery ... and a sarcastic Welsh journalist.

Kai has been drawn to darkest Yorkshire by his desire to find out who he really is. What he hadn't bargained on was getting caught up in amateur magic and dealing with a bunch of women who are trying *really hard* to make their dreams come true.

Together they realise that getting what you wish for is sometimes just a matter of knowing what it is you want ...

Visit www.choc-lit.com for more details including the first two chapters and reviews, or simply scan barcode using your mobile phone QR reader.

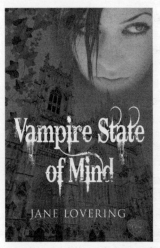

Vampire State of Mind

Book 1 in the Otherworlders

Jessica Grant knows vampires only too well. She runs the York Council tracker programme making sure that Otherworlders are all where they should be, keeps the filing in order and drinks far too much coffee.

To Jess, vampires are annoying and arrogant and far too sexy for their own good, particularly her ex-colleague, Sil, who's now in charge of Otherworld York. When a demon turns up and threatens not just Jess but the whole world order, she and Sil are forced to work together.

But then Jess turns out to be the key to saving the world, which puts a very different slant on their relationship.

The stakes are high. They are also very, very pointy and Jess isn't afraid to use them – even on the vampire she's rather afraid she's falling in love with …

Visit www.choc-lit.com for more details including the first two chapters and reviews, or simply scan barcode using your mobile phone QR reader.

Falling Apart

Book 2 in the Otherworlders

In the mean streets of York, the stakes just got higher – and even pointier.

Jessica Grant liaises with Otherworlders for York Council so she knows that falling in love with a vampire takes a leap of faith. But her lover Sil, the City Vampire in charge of Otherworld York, he wouldn't run out on her, would he? He wouldn't let his demon get the better of him. Or would he?

Sil knows there's a reason for his bad haircut, worse clothes and the trail of bleeding humans in his wake. If only he could remember exactly what he did before someone finds him and shoots him on sight.

With her loyalties already questioned for defending zombies, the Otherworlders no one cares about, Jess must choose which side she's on, either help her lover or turn him in. Human or Other? Whatever she decides, there's a high price to pay – and someone to lose.

Visit www.choc-lit.com for more details including the first two chapters and reviews, or simply scan barcode using your mobile phone QR reader.

Introducing Choc Lit

We're an independent publisher creating
a delicious selection of fiction.
Where heroes are like chocolate – irresistible!
Quality stories with a romance at the heart.

See our selection here:
www.choc-lit.com

We'd love to hear how you enjoyed *How I Wonder What You Are*. Please leave a review where you purchased the novel or visit: **www.choc-lit.com** and give your feedback.

Choc Lit novels are selected by genuine readers like yourself. We only publish stories our Choc Lit Tasting Panel want to see in print. Our reviews and awards speak for themselves.

Could you be a Star Selector and join our Tasting Panel?
Would you like to play a role in choosing which novels we decide to publish? Do you enjoy reading romance novels? Then you could be perfect for our Choc Lit Tasting Panel.

Visit here for more details…
www.choc-lit.com/join-the-choc-lit-tasting-panel

Keep in touch:
Sign up for our monthly newsletter Choc Lit Spread for all the latest news and offers: www.spread.choc-lit.com. Follow us on Twitter: @ChocLituk and Facebook: Choc Lit.

Or simply scan barcode using your mobile phone QR reader:

Choc Lit
Spread

Twitter

Facebook